To anyone who has ever dated someone who made you question your worth.
You are worthy of love. You are enough.

TOO HARD TO RESIST PLAYLIST

Still Bad – Lizzo
Cold – Maroon 5 ft. Future
Numb – Linkin Park
All by Myself – Celine Dion
Cruel Summer – Taylor Swift
Summertime – DJ Jazzy Jeff and the Fresh Prince
Holiday – Madonna
Running From Myself – Caity Baser
Growing on Me – Foxes
Sunshine In the Room – James Bay ft. Jon Batiste
3D Feelings – Alfie Templeman
Better – Khalid
Are You Even Real – Teddy Swims ft. Givēon
Diamonds and Gold – JP Cooper
Deserve to Be Loved – Zak Abel
Enough – Jess Glynne
I'm Too Sexy – Right Said Fred

1

SAMMIE

'So.' My date, Ronald, leaned in closer, before his gaze dropped to my chest. 'Have you ever thought about getting a boob job?'

My eyes popped and I almost choked on my white wine.

He did not just say that.

No. I must've misheard.

'What did you say?' I scanned the pub for the nearest exit.

'I said you should get a boob job.' He pointed at my breasts as he casually sipped his beer.

Un-bloody-believable.

He'd already asked me how many men I'd slept with and now he'd chosen another inappropriate first-date question.

'It's just that, y'know,' he ran a hand through his short blond hair, 'I prefer my women busty and you're a bit lacking in the boobies department.'

Boobies department?

How old was this guy? Eight years old?

I opened my mouth to speak, then snapped it shut again.

Anyone who knew me would tell you that I wasn't often lost for words, but right now I was struggling to understand how this muppet could think that it was okay to not only comment on my body, but also suggest that I got plastic surgery after knowing me for less than twenty minutes.

Ronald had more red flags than a carnival.

I shouldn't be surprised. In the two years since I'd broken up with my ex, I'd been on more bad dates than I'd had hot dinners. And considering how much I loved food, that was saying something.

There was the guy that invited me to a swanky bar in central London, ordered champagne, then, when it came to paying the bill, had conveniently 'lost' his wallet.

Then there was the man who brought his mum and sister to the date to 'get a second opinion' (no, I wasn't joking).

Oh, and I still remembered the dude who invited me back to his place, but conveniently forgot to tell me he was married.

Yep. Name a nightmare date and I'd bet that I could top it.

And when you added the unsolicited dick pics and the men I thought I'd had a good time with but conveniently ghosted me once we slept together to my list of crappy experiences, it was easy to see why my love life was a certified dumpster fire.

When I matched with Ronald on a dating app last night and he invited me out, I'd caved. He was attractive and I'd just finished reading a swoony romance novel that tugged on my heartstrings. It made me believe that love was possible and that I was destined to find *the one*. So I thought, *sod it*. I'll take one last roll of the dice.

Big mistake.

I should've just stayed at home and clipped my toenails or cleaned the toilet.

Anything would've been better than sitting in front of this wanker.

'No, I haven't considered getting my *boobies* done.' I folded my arms across my chest. 'Have you ever considered getting a personality transplant?'

Ronald's face contorted with confusion.

'Come again?' His frowned deepened. 'Why would I need to do that? The ladies love me,' he winked.

Ugh. If there was one thing I hated more than a twat it was an arrogant twat.

'Some women might be happy with a man that thinks it's acceptable to tell them to get a breast enlargement, but not me, sunshine. I'm done with this date.' I reached into my purse, pulled out a ten-pound note to cover the cost of my wine, dropped it on the table, then stood up. 'Me and my *boobies* are going home, *alone*. Have a nice life.'

I tossed my curly pink ombre hair over my shoulder and strutted out of the bar with my head held high.

Once I'd walked around the corner, I leant against the wall, my heart pounding against my chest, then blew out a heavy breath.

I'd never walked out of a date before. Normally I suffered through the awkwardness until the man decided it was time to call it a night. But I'd done the right thing.

As a memory of how the boys at school used to call me 'pan-cake' and 'tiny tits' popped into my head, my stomach clenched. It was like being teased in the playground all over again. I couldn't keep putting myself through this.

I was tired.

Tired of the swiping.

Tired of men judging my body and treating me like shit.

Tired of men thinking I was so desperate for their usually underwhelming dick that they could do or say whatever they wanted.

I slid out of my heels, pulled my trainers out of my bag then sank my feet inside. *That felt so much better.*

When I thought about the fact that I'd squeezed myself into a sparkly knee-length dress, push-up bra and a pair of horrendously painful stilettos for this date, when I could've been chilling at home in a comfy onesie, anger bubbled in my chest. But that was life.

Every day, millions of women like me probably went on one disappointing date after another in the hope that maybe *this* time they'd find *the one*.

We believed that as long as we kissed enough frogs, we'd find our prince.

Perseverance was the name of the game, right?

I'd tried everything: apps, speed-dating events, being set up by well-meaning family members. I'd even paid a thousand-pound deposit to sign up for the Love Hotel: a fancy resort that promised to find my Mr Right.

My best friend Stella went there and ended up being matched with her ex. Sounds wild, but it was true. Now they were crazy in love.

Even her Love Empress, Jasmine (a silly job title they gave to the people at the hotel who helped bring couples together) found her dream man there.

And they weren't the only ones. I'd lost count of the number of success stories I'd read about people who went to the hotel single and came back besotted.

That was what I wanted, but with every day that passed, it was looking like I had more chance of winning the lottery.

When I saw Jasmine at Stella's fortieth birthday party, she thought I might have a chance of getting a place at the hotel. But that was months ago and I still hadn't heard anything from the matchmaking team.

Maybe it was for the best.

Being single wasn't so bad. I could do whatever I wanted, whenever I wanted, I didn't have to keep putting the toilet seat down or clean up piss stains because a grown man didn't know how to aim his dick properly in the toilet bowl.

I didn't have to hold in my farts or smell his.

And I didn't have to be left hanging on a string for years whilst I waited for my crappy boyfriend to finally commit.

Or feel like I was never enough.

Yeah. I was totally fine just how I was. I'd rather fly solo than be shacked up with a twat like Ronald. I'd had a lucky escape.

After pulling out my phone, I deleted every single crappy app, then exhaled.

There.

I was officially done with dating.

Filled with renewed confidence, I strutted towards the Tube station like the busy, wet London pavement was my catwalk.

Once I got home, I took a shower, put on my comfiest pyjamas, prepared an epic tray of snacks then fired up Netflix.

I was about to opt for bingeing *Emily in Paris* for the hundredth time, but then decided that one of the steamy *365 Days* films was the perfect choice.

That date had made me tense, but a good orgasm would cure that frustration and swooning over that Italian hottie actor, Michele Morrone, was guaranteed to get me off.

I sprinted into my pink-and-white-decorated bedroom, opened the top drawer and pulled out my Waterfall Turbo 3,000. At least my vibrator wouldn't comment on the size of my boobs.

Up yours, Ronald.

Just as I was about to return to the living room for my virtual date with the hot Italian stallion, my phone rang. I glanced at the screen and saw it was Stella.

'Hey!' I said, instantly feeling happier.

'Hey, you!' Stella said. 'Just a quick one as I'm out having dinner with Max, but Jasmine called to say an important email was sent yesterday and you haven't replied.'

'Wait, *what*?' My heart thundered against my chest as I raced back to the living room and jumped on my bubble-gum-pink sofa. 'Do you think I got *the* email?'

If Jasmine said there was a message, that could mean there was news on my application to the Love Hotel.

'She wouldn't say. But there's only one way to find out!'

'Oh my God!' I said, my fingers trembling with excitement as I logged into my email account.

Despite scrolling through my overflowing inbox twice, I still couldn't see anything from the Love Hotel and my heart sank.

Then I checked my junk. Once I'd sifted through dozens of boring emails about car insurance and flash sales, I spotted a message that made my eyes pop.

'No fucking way!' I shouted. 'It's from the Love Hotel!'

'Amazing!' Stella squealed. 'Come on then! What does it say?'

My pulse raced as I scanned the beginning of the message.

Congratulations!

You are cordially invited to join us at the Love Hotel in Italy.

We've found your Mr Right!

'Shut the front door!' I screamed. 'I'm in! I'm going to the Italian Love Hotel!'

'Congrats, bestie! I'm so happy for you!'

'I can't bloody believe it!'

A couple of hours ago, I was cursing the hotel for not getting back to me and was firmly sworn off dating. Now, I'd just got the green light to go there.

I'd heard of coincidences and was open to the idea of putting stuff out to the universe, but it never really worked that quickly, did it?

Then again, I'd been asking the powers that be to send my Mr Right for years, not hours. And now it looked like they'd finally delivered.

'Well, you'd better believe it! Make sure you confirm and pay the rest of the money ASAP, okay? I'll call you tomorrow to chat properly. Congrats again!'

'Thanks, hon. Enjoy your dinner and say hi to Max.'

As I hung up, excitement fizzed in my stomach. Places at the hotel were like gold dust so this was a once-in-a-lifetime opportunity. This was something I'd dreamed about ever since Stella went and told me how amazing the Love Hotel was.

If only I'd seen the email sooner, I wouldn't have wasted time going on that crappy date with Ronald.

Anyway, it didn't matter now. I was going to meet an amazing man.

I knew I'd said that I was done with dating, but this email changed *everything*.

After all the heartache and frustration, the search for my Mr Right was over.

No more dating apps.

No more dick pics (unless I asked for them, of course).

No more frogs.

No more fuckboys.

I wouldn't have to put up with any more crap from Rude Ronalds.

My perfect match had been found.

And I was off to sunny Italy to meet him!

2

ROMEO

'Oh, my God! Are you that actor from those sexy films?' Cindy, one of the new hotel guests, called out as she rushed over to where I was standing by the hotel's main swimming pool.

She had arrived later than scheduled last night and one of my colleagues had checked her in, so this was the first time we had met in person.

'No.' I plastered on a smile. It did not matter that she could not remember his name. I already knew who she was referring to. 'I am your Love Alchemist, Romeo. I will explain everything when the official welcome briefing begins in ten minutes.'

'But you look just like him!' She wound a strand of her long dark hair around her fingers. 'You're tall, dark and so *sexy*.'

She licked her lips then rested her hand on my bicep.

Merda.

I quickly stepped back, causing her hand to drop. And when I scanned the daybeds on the opposite side of the pool I saw her partner, Giles, glaring at me.

This was not good. Naturally, Giles was not happy to see her flirting with me and the management would not be either.

This was not the first time someone had said that I looked like the actor Michele Morrone. I was flattered. Although I had not seen his films, he was a handsome guy, so it was a compliment. But all I wanted was to do my job and help the couples that had been matched to fall in love. And when the guests started to become *overfamiliar*, it usually led to trouble.

But it was important to keep our guests happy, so I had to find a way to communicate that I was not interested, without upsetting Cindy, which I knew from experience would not be easy.

'*Grazie.*' I widened my fake smile. 'Would you and Giles like to dine inside or outside of the restaurant this evening?' I said, hoping the swift subject change would help.

'I dunno. So, is he like related to you, or something?' she said, not taking the hint. 'I swear he could be your twin. You've got the same jet-black short wavy hair, gorgeous olive skin, beautiful beard and *your body...*' She bit her lip. 'Your muscles, arms and chest are like... *wow.*'

'I am very sure that we are not related. Is there anything else that you and Giles would like to make your stay here at the Love Hotel more comfortable? I can check if we have availability in the spa for a couples massage?'

'Will *you* be doing the massage?' She tilted her head flirtatiously.

'No, it is a lesson, for you to learn how to give a massage to your partner and vice versa.'

'What if I'd prefer *you* to do it?' She touched my arm and I stepped back again. I had hoped that changing the subject and moving away would communicate that touching me was not okay, without offending her, but it looked like the subtle approach was not working.

'Cindy, I am flattered by your compliments, but like I said, I am your Love Alchemist. My job is to bring matches like you and *Giles* together. I do not get involved with guests. Those are the rules.'

'Rules are boring. I'm sure you can make an exception...' She winked.

'No,' I said firmly. 'So if there's nothing else that I can do to help you and Giles to bond as a couple, then I must finish preparing for the induction.'

Her face turned to thunder. I knew she was not happy that I had turned her down, but I was not about to jeopardise my job for a guest.

Especially when I was already treading on thin ice.

* * *

After the induction was finished, I walked down to the beach. Sinking my feet in the soft white sand and watching the crystal-clear waters always calmed me. If I had time later, I would love to go for a swim in the sea. It was one of my favourite things to do.

Just as I was about to continue further down the shore, my phone buzzed. It was a message from my boss, Victoria. She wanted to see me.

Something told me this would not be good.

I knocked on the door.

'Come in. Sit,' Victoria said, pushing her black-rimmed glasses further up the bridge of her nose and running a hand through her short dark hair.

'You wanted to see me?' I asked.

'Yes. We've had a complaint.'

'From who?'

'Giles Ashcroft. Said you've been flirting with his match, Cindy.'

I squeezed my eyes shut with frustration. I knew this would happen.

'That is not true.' I shook my head. '*She* was flirting with *me*. She touched my arm. *Twice*. I told her that I was not interested and my job was to bring her and Giles together.'

Victoria rested her finger on her chin and paused, considering her response.

'I want to believe you, Romeo, but it isn't the first time we've had a complaint like this. Last month that guest Rochelle's partner also said you were being flirtatious. And then there was the incident with Harriet...'

'You know what happened with that.' I ground my jaw. 'That was not my fault.'

'All I'm saying is that this puts me in a difficult position. I want to support you. You are an excellent Love Alchemist.'

'*Grazie.*'

'But ensuring our guests' satisfaction is paramount. I can't exactly call Giles a liar or tell him that his match is a shameless flirt. Honestly, who gets matched with their Mr Right and then starts trying it on with someone else?'

'It is frustrating,' I said diplomatically.

'Management have relaxed the rules about single employees dating, but the rules about getting involved with guests are still very clear. It's an absolute no-go. It doesn't look good if guests pay to come to the hotel to be set up with their match and then one of the staff steals them away. This kind of thing causes guests to start ranting online, demanding refunds, and slagging off the hotel. We have to make it clear that our only focus is our guests' happiness. They need to know that this isn't a pick-up joint for our Romance Rockstars.'

Romance Rockstars was the hotel's name for its staff. Everyone who worked here had unconventional job titles. Victoria was a 'Love Empress' who was the person in charge of all of the Love Alchemists like me, who were basically guest relations managers who helped to bring the couples together.

'I take my job very seriously. I would never get involved with a guest. If they become overfamiliar, I always try to be polite, but firm. Giles saw her flirting and misunderstood.'

'Okay. I'll speak to them. And if she makes you uncomfortable again, let me know. Your safety is also important. You don't come to work to get harassed. But please be careful. I defended you before, but if you have another incident like that, I can't promise your job will be safe. Are we clear?'

'Understood.' I blew out a frustrated breath.

I knew she was in a difficult position and like Victoria, I did not understand why guests would invest time and money coming here to find their perfect match then risk it all by flirting with me.

What did they expect? That I would jeopardise my job at one of the most prestigious hotels in Italy for a quick fuck? It was not worth it.

I enjoyed playing a role in the guests' happiness, but flings or relationships were not for me. Especially not right now.

In less than two months, the management would start accepting applications for Romance Rockstars who wanted to apply to work at their new resort in California.

From what I had heard, it was going to be the biggest and most luxurious Love Hotel created. Successful applicants from their existing resorts would have their flights and accommodation paid for and the company would arrange our working visas and all of the paperwork.

It was a once-in-a-lifetime opportunity.

For years I had wanted to travel to the US. And my dream almost became a reality, but then my whole world came crashing down.

Now that I had been given a second chance, I would not allow anything or anyone to stand in the way of my goal again.

And I definitely would not risk it all for a one-night stand with a guest.

As I thought about Cindy, I shook my head. I never understood why women who had a good man were willing to throw it all away just to have some 'fun'.

My chest tightened as memories of that day came flooding back...

No. I could not think about that. It was too painful.

'Was that everything?' I stood up.

'For now,' Victoria said. 'But remember what I said. Be careful.'

I nodded, then left her office.

I just had to find a way to be firmer. Perhaps wearing a T-shirt with 'My Name Is Not Michele' might help.

Victoria was right. I could not afford any more trouble.

If a guest tried flirting again, I would make my position clear.

My liaisons with guests would always be strictly professional.

Zero exceptions.

3

SAMMIE

This was mad.

Even though it'd been weeks since I'd received the email from the Love Hotel offering me a place at their resort in Puglia, which was a region in southern Italy, it still hadn't sunk in that I was actually going.

Like Stella had recommended, I'd replied to the email and paid the balance straightaway. I'd spent the weekend ordering loads of clothes online and chatting with her about what to expect. Then on the Monday morning I'd begged my boss to give me the time off and thankfully she'd agreed.

I was currently sitting on the back seat of the swanky Mercedes the hotel had sent to collect me from Bari airport and according to my chauffeur (look at me!), I was now less than fifteen minutes away from arriving at the resort.

And most importantly, minutes away from meeting the love of my life.

Honestly, I didn't think I'd been so excited in my whole life.

I wondered what he'd be like.

The questionnaire I'd completed when I applied was really

detailed and as well as answering a gazillion questions about myself, my hobbies, personality and relationship history, I'd also told them about the kind of man I was looking for.

That part was easy. One advantage of dating a lot was that you got to find out all the things that you didn't want in a partner.

I was self-aware enough to realise that I always went for the same type of guy: good-looking, charming and emotionally unavailable.

Somehow I was drawn to the players and pretty boys with the banter and sweet talk, who were around the same age as me or sometimes younger, who couldn't or wouldn't commit.

Shamefully, my type was the guys who knew they had options and weren't ready to settle down. The men who inevitably stopped messaging me whenever someone prettier or better came along.

Before I applied, I'd done a lot of reflecting and realised that I couldn't keep going after the same type of man and expect a different result.

What I needed was a man that was older than me. I was thirty-two, so ideally someone in their late thirties or early forties. At that age they would've had time to screw around and would be ready to settle down.

I needed a man that was okay-looking. Dating the super-hot guys always ended in tears. The last thing I needed was a bloke who attracted attention and had women queuing up around the block to date him.

And I needed a man who was a decent human being, had a good job (he didn't have to be rich, just able to pay his own way) and someone who was easy to talk to, who I had a lot in common with.

Although that wisdom lasted long enough for me to fill out

the questionnaire, unfortunately, by the time I'd given up hope of getting the place at the hotel and logged back on to the dating apps, it'd evaporated and I'd ended up falling back into the same habits. Hence my last disastrous date with Rude Ronald. But I didn't have to worry about that any more.

The Love Hotel matchmakers had chosen my soulmate for me so there'd be no more bad decisions.

My stomach bubbled with a mixture of excitement and nerves.

The sound of my phone vibrating came from my bag. When I tapped the screen, I saw it was a message from Stella asking if I'd arrived yet. Instead of replying, I hit the call button. Speaking to her would help calm my nerves.

'Hi!' She answered on the first ring. 'You there yet?'

'Almost. The driver, sorry, my chauffeur,' I added in a posh voice, 'said we should be there soon, so naturally I'm shitting bricks.'

'It's normal to be nervous, but don't worry. These people are the matchmaking experts. I bet they have someone amazing lined up for you.'

'Does Jasmine know who I've been matched with?'

'No. If you were going to the Spanish resort, then yeah, she would, but she doesn't get to see matches in their other locations.'

'Don't they have some kind of centralised database she can hack into or something to give me a heads up? Not that I want her to risk her job or anything, but the suspense is killing me. I just want to meet him already!'

'Sammie, you've waited most of your whole adult life to find your soulmate, so waiting another hour or whenever you two will be introduced today isn't going to make a difference.'

'You're right.' I blew out a breath.

'I know it's easier said than done, but try to relax. You're in good hands.'

'Okay. I'll let you know how it goes.'

'Good luck.'

Just as Stella ended the call, the chauffeur turned into the resort's driveway.

Wowsers.

My jaw dropped.

I'd looked up the Italian Love Hotel online hundreds of times, but as slick as the website was, it didn't compare to being here in person.

The large white stone building was surrounded by lush manicured gardens, plus a pretty mixture of olive, palm and fruit trees. I even spotted a glimpse of the sea in the distance.

As the chauffeur opened the door and I stepped outside, I noticed the shift in temperature straightaway. The car was beautifully air conditioned, but now I felt the warm Italian sunshine heating my skin.

The scent of lemon trees mixed with the salty sea air surrounded me and I inhaled deeply. This definitely beat the eau de pollution and car fumes stench I was used to smelling in London.

And, blimey, look at the sky! It was so blue anyone would think it was painted.

Just as I was taking in the breathtaking views my eyes popped. And this time it wasn't because I was still in awe of the hotel's amazing exterior.

It was because of the tall, dark and ridiculously handsome god that was walking towards me.

'Samantha?' he asked, stretching out his hand for me to shake. '*Benvenuta*. Welcome to the Love Hotel, Italia.'

I blinked, then blinked again.

Holy macaroni.

Standing in front of me was the fittest guy I'd ever seen. He was about six foot three, with short, slightly wavy black hair, deep olive skin, a neatly trimmed beard, light brown eyes, framed by long lashes, gorgeous thick eyebrows, full lips and a body that looked like it'd been carved by angels.

He was the spitting image of that actor Michele Morrone in those steamy *365 Days* films.

As I thought about how many times I'd got myself off whilst watching those films, my cheeks flamed.

'Samantha?' Mr Smokeshow repeated and I almost melted into a puddle as I listened to how he pronounced my name in his divine Italian accent.

It was only then that I remembered that he'd said something.

'Shit. Sorry. I was miles away. I'm Samantha,' I replied, my eyes still transfixed on the Italian stallion in front of me. Then I realised that he already knew my name because he'd said it. Twice. 'Doh! You just said that! Bloody jet lag.'

Jeez Louise.

What the hell was wrong with me? The flight to Bari was less than three hours and Italy was a miniscule one hour ahead, so I was hardly suffering from sodding jet lag.

'Jet lag?' Mr McHottie Hot Stuff laughed. 'You came from London, no? The flight time is normally around two hours and fifty minutes.'

Okay, smart arse.

I knew what I'd said was dumb, but he didn't have to point it out.

'Yeah, obviously it wasn't the jet lag.' I rolled my eyes. 'It was probably all the wine I had on the plane.'

All the wine?

Nice, one Sammie.

'I just had one bottle,' I said, attempting to clarify what I meant. 'Not a whole proper big bottle, obvs. I'm not an alcoholic. Not that I'm judging alcoholics. I know it's a disease. I just meant that I'm not one. Because I only had one teeny weeny bottle of wine. Actually, it was more like half a bottle because to be honest, it tasted like vinegar. Not that I'm insulting Italian wine. I'm not even sure if it was Italian. It probably wasn't. Then again it was a flight to Italy so maybe it was, but it could've been out of date or something.'

Oh. Dear. God.

I should've just called it quits with the stupid jet lag comment. Now not only would he think I was one of those stereotypical Brits who got pissed on planes, he'd also think I was insulting his country.

'I see. So you like to drink...' He raised a judgemental eyebrow. 'But not Italian wine, because it tastes like vinegar.'

'No, I didn't say that! I said *that* particular wine tasted like vinegar, not *all* Italian wine.'

What was his problem? I even said I wasn't even sure if it was Italian wine, so why was he trying to make out like I was dissing his country?

What was it with these good-looking guys? Why did they always have to be such dicks?

He was supposed to be welcoming me to the hotel, not judging me. Okay, yeah, I admit that everything that'd come out of my mouth so far was a pile of crap, but still.

'Has anyone told you that you look like—'

'*Sì*,' he jumped in quickly, then rolled his eyes and sighed like I was the millionth person to mention it.

I was going to tell him that he looked like that hot actor to lighten the mood and try to steer this conversation out of the disaster zone, but now I'd changed my mind...

'Oh,' I said casually, 'so I'm not the only one who thinks you look like Mr Bean?' The corner of my mouth twitched.

'Mr Bean?' His face dropped, creased with confusion, then contorted in a million different directions.

Gotcha.

That'll teach you to mess with me, you arrogant little fucker.

I barely knew him, but it was obvious who he looked like. Instead of taking the compliment graciously and saying thank you, he got all arsey and acted like it was a hardship to look so hot.

Poor thing. Must be so difficult resembling an Italian god.

Boo-fucking-hoo.

He thought it was okay to laugh at me, so I was going to have fun messing with him.

'Yeah! Mr Bean's a character from a really famous old British comedy show. You've got the same dark hair and thick eyebrows. The resemblance is uncanny. You two could pass as brothers!' I smirked. 'Don't tell me no one's mentioned it before?'

'N-no,' he stuttered. 'No one has ever said that.'

'Oh!' I brought my hand to my chest, pretending that I was shocked. 'That's a surprise. I thought from the way that you jumped in and rolled your eyes before I'd even had a chance to finish my sentence, you heard it all the time.'

'No.' He narrowed his eyes. 'Usually people say I look like someone else.'

'Really?' I put on my best bimbo voice. 'Who?'

'An actor.' He paused as if he was weighing up whether or not to say his name.

'You sure it's not Rowan Atkinson? He's the guy who plays Mr Bean. Honestly, you look like twins!'

'No.' He ground his jaw. 'I know who Mr Bean is and it is not him.'

'Wait! I've got it. I bet people say that you look like the guy who plays Sheldon in *The Big Bang Theory*, right? Yes! I can see it now.'

Mr I Love Myself's eyes were now the size of saucers and I resisted the temptation to burst out laughing.

Personally, I thought that actor was kind of cute, but I could tell that this guy was insulted.

Yes, I was being petty and it probably wasn't a good idea to make enemies with the staff when I'd just arrived, but I was tired of people taking the piss out of me.

'No,' he huffed, crossing his arms. 'They say I look like the actor Michele Morrone.'

'Michele who?' I put on my best fake frown. 'Never heard of him.'

His face dropped and I flashed him a cheeky smile.

I wasn't sure if he knew that I was joking, but at least next time someone said he looked like him, he wouldn't act so put out.

If he wasn't so ridiculously good-looking, I wouldn't have wound him up like this, but I was pretty sure he knew I wasn't being serious because obviously he looked nothing like Mr Bean.

The truth was, he looked nothing like the rest of the guys on the planet.

I wasn't kidding when I said this man was a god.

Stella's boyfriend Max was handsome and so was Jasmine's partner, Alejandro, but this guy?

He was so hot I was surprised someone hadn't called the fire brigade.

WTF?

No, no, no.

What was I doing?

First up, I was objectifying him. I mean, let's get real, we all did it, but, still, didn't mean it was right.

Secondly, based on the smart navy shorts (did I mention how bronze and muscular his legs were?) and the crisp white branded shirt he was wearing, he clearly worked here. Which meant he was not my match. So I had no business ogling him. Which was why I was going to nip that shameless behaviour in the bud, right now.

'I am sorry to disappoint you but I am not related to Mr Bean or Sheldon. I am Romeo. Your Love Alchemist.'

'What?' My jaw dropped. Although I knew he worked here, I hadn't considered that he was my Love Alchemist. From what Stella had mentioned, most of them were women.

Yep. Now that I knew he was the person who'd be responsible for helping me and my match fall in love, I was definitely regretting my decision to wind him up.

No. It was fine. He knew it was just banter, right?

'You were not expecting a male Love Alchemist?' he asked.

'No,' I blurted out. And definitely not one who looked like a freaking supermodel. 'But it's all good. So, Mr Romeo, are we gonna continue this chit chat, or you gonna show me around this fancy joint and take me to meet my match?' I grinned.

Romeo's eyebrows hit his hairline.

Some people found me a little direct sometimes, but I couldn't help it. That was just the way I was.

'Our Suitcase Superintendent will take your bags to your room, but yes, if you follow me, I will check you in and show you around *this joint*.'

'Great!' I smiled again and followed him to reception.

The large open space had white stone walls, tall columns

and plush cream sofas with metallic-blue cushions. The posh glass coffee tables had expensive-looking white bowls filled with fresh lemons which were still attached to the vine.

This place was so cool.

'Here.' Romeo handed me a flute of prosecco. '*Benvenuta*.'

'Thanks. I'm parched.' I took a gulp. 'Bloody hell!' I shouted. 'This is delicious!'

'So, not like vinegar?' He cocked an eyebrow and I swore I saw a glimmer of a smile tug at his unfairly full lips.

I wasn't perving, honest. It was just that ever since I'd arrived he'd been a bit serious. I thought my Love Alchemist would be all full of smiles and sunshine like Jasmine was, but so far this Romeo was a bit of a grump.

'Not even close! It's much better than the one I usually get for a fiver from the corner shop too. Who made this? Angels?'

'This is the finest Italian prosecco. You will find that all of the wine at the Love Hotel is delicious.'

'Can't wait to try it all!'

Foot in mouth incident number 1,001.

I was about to attempt to clarify yet again that I didn't have a drinking problem, then decided I couldn't be bothered. It didn't matter what Romeo thought of me. It was my match that I needed to impress.

'So,' Romeo sighed, clearly not willing to justify my comment with a response, 'your match has already arrived and you will be introduced at dinner. Your reservation is at nine.'

'Can't wait!' I punched the air like a plonker. I'd never been the coolest person, but ever since I'd started talking to this guy, the cringe moments just kept on coming.

Although I was gagging to find out who my match was, Stella said they normally did the introductions at dinner, so a couple of hours wasn't long to wait.

Once we'd gone through the normal check-in procedures, Romeo gave me a tour of the hotel including the spa, which looked like it was straight out of a luxury wellness brochure, the immaculate restaurant that had uninterrupted sea views and the enormous pool, which was flanked by the most ginormous, comfiest-looking daybeds I'd ever seen.

This place was paradise.

'And this is your room.' Romeo stopped in front of a white door. 'If there is something you need before dinner, press the love heart button on the phone in your room and one of our Romance Rockstars will help.'

'Cheers, I mean, *grazie*. Laters, Romeo.'

He nodded in acknowledgement.

As he walked away, my eyes dropped to his arse and I mentally slapped myself.

Romeo was my arrogant, surly Love Alchemist. I shouldn't be checking out his butt, no matter how good it looked.

I didn't spend my savings coming all the way to Italy to ogle another fuckboy. I could've done that in London by swiping on the apps for free.

I was here to fall in love.

A flutter of excitement rippled in my stomach.

In less than an hour and a half I'd be meeting my perfect match and he was going to blow Romeo and all the wastemen I'd had the misfortune of dating out of the water.

Yep.

This date was going to be epic.

4

ROMEO

Mr Bean?

As I stormed into my office and replayed my conversation with the new guest, Samantha, I ground my jaw.

I looked nothing like Mr Bean.

He was old enough to be my father. Maybe even my grandfather.

And Sheldon?

I did not mean any offence to either of those actors, because I knew both were very successful and popular, but the only resemblance we shared was that we were men.

Her comments were ridiculous.

I should not be surprised considering she had admitted that she had too much to drink on the plane.

Anyway, I had more important things to worry about than what a guest with a smart mouth thought about me.

Sì, it was a pretty mouth, but what came out of it was nonsense.

When I first saw her get out of the car, I admit that I thought she was attractive.

She had light brown skin, striking hair which was dark brown at the roots and pink at the ends and a beautiful, curvaceous figure.

But I was attracted to strong, intelligent women and someone who believes they could have jet lag after a short flight with a one-hour time difference did not fall into that category.

Perhaps I was being too harsh.

I pulled out the chair and sat at my desk. Some people may feel affected when flying even a short distance. Or maybe she was just nervous.

Ordinarily, I would have agreed that she was right about the wine on planes often being terrible, but she had caught me at a bad time. I had received some upsetting news just before she arrived, so I was not as friendly as I would normally be.

I blew out a breath then picked up my phone.

'*Ciao*, Mamma. Sorry I took so long to call back. I had to check in one of the new guests. How is Biscotti?'

Earlier our family dog, a beautiful chocolate Labrador called Biscotti was rushed to the vet and just before Mamma called, she told me that they were not sure whether she would make it.

'She's in surgery now. As soon as I have some news, I will let you know.'

I swallowed the lump in my throat. Biscotti was part of the family and Mamma was particularly close to her.

Ever since me, my brother and sister had left home, she spent all day with Biscotti. She was her best friend. Her companion. I was sure she preferred spending time with Biscotti to being with my father, so I knew this affected her the most.

'If you want, I will ask my boss for some time off. I cannot promise, because the new guests arrived today, but maybe I can leave earlier and—'

'No,' she jumped in. 'It is better if you keep busy. It will take your mind off things. And you need to be careful after what happened before. You can't give them any other reasons to get upset with you. I'll be fine.'

'You are sure?'

'Certain. And thank you for the scarf. It arrived today.'

'*Prego.*'

When I took last week's guests on an excursion, I saw an orange scarf in a shop window and knew that Mamma would love it. Orange was her favourite colour.

'You will wear it the next time I take you out, *sì*?'

'Yes. I promise. It's beautiful.'

'I am glad that you love it. I will come and see you soon, okay?'

'Okay. I'll keep you updated. Try not to worry. I love you.'

'*Ti voglio bene*, Mamma. *Ciao.*'

'Bye, son.'

As I hung up, I dropped my head in my hands. I hoped that Biscotti would be okay. She was strong. She was a fighter. And Mamma needed her. I wished I could be there at the vet with them now, but like Mamma said, I had to work.

After an unfortunate incident with a guest last month, the bosses were watching every move I made, so I needed to be the perfect employee.

Which meant that even though I did not feel like working and smiling, I had to do it anyway.

As the English liked to say: the show must go on.

* * *

'Romeo. *Edoardo è arrivato.* Romeo?'

I snapped out of my thoughts. Thankfully, the operation had gone well but Biscotti was not out of danger yet.

I was at the hotel's restaurant and Tommaso, the Dining Director, had just told me that Edward, Samantha's match, had arrived at the restaurant.

Samantha.

The guest who thought I looked like Mr Bean.

I shook my head, thinking how ridiculous her comments were and a small smile touched my lips.

'Edward, *benvenuto*.' I stretched out my hand.

We had met briefly when he arrived, but he said he needed to get to his room, so we had not had time to talk properly.

'Hi, Ronaldo.' He gave me a weak handshake.

'It is Romeo.'

'Oh, sorry, mate. She here yet?' He rubbed his hands together.

'No. Would you like a drink at the bar whilst you wait?'

'Yeah. Nice one.'

I escorted him over to the bar and pulled out a stool.

'How are you settling in? Is the room to your satisfaction?'

'All good, yep.'

'*È arrivata Samanta*,' Tommaso announced and I looked towards the door.

As I took in the sight of Samantha, I swallowed hard.

She was wearing a short white and gold dress which clung to her beautiful curves and had a deep V neckline which was incredibly sexy.

I was speaking objectively of course, not because I was attracted to her, because for the reasons I explained earlier, I was not. But I was certain that anyone would agree that she was a beautiful woman. Edward was sure to be delighted with his match.

'*Grazie*.' I nodded to Tommaso.

'Is that my date?' Edward wrinkled his nose.

'*Sì.*'

'Oh.' His face fell. 'She's got pink hair. She's a little on the large size too. There's not much going on in the chest department either.'

I ground my jaw.

Was the man blind, stupid or both?

Samantha was stunning.

He thought she was large? Did the man not see the beautiful curve of her hips in that dress and how the fabric clung to them like it had been custom-made for her?

Her hair was very cool and not that I had spent too much time studying her because that was unprofessional, but from what I had briefly seen, there was nothing wrong with her breasts.

Naturally, different men found different things attractive, so he was entitled to his opinion. But real men knew that small breasts could be just as sexy and feminine as large ones. In any case it was the woman that the breasts were attached to that was important, not the size.

Samantha could be his soulmate, but he had judged her on her appearance before he had even greeted or spoken to her.

This was not a great start, but once they had dinner and got to know each other better, things would improve.

'Let me introduce you to your beautiful match,' I said, then regretted using the word beautiful. Even though it was true and Edward clearly needed a reminder, I had promised Victoria that I would tread carefully with our guests, so I did not want Edward to get the wrong impression and think that I was interested in his match.

'Hi!' Samantha's face lit up as we approached her.

'*Buonasera,* Samantha.' This time I made an effort to smile. I knew it probably did not look genuine, but it was all I could manage right now. 'Allow me to introduce you to your soulmate: Edward.'

'Nice to meet you.' She stretched out her hand.

'Pleasure.' He shook it limply.

Although my mother was English and I had been to visit her family several times in London and Kent, it always surprised me how formal the British could be.

Edward was here on a first date with a beautiful woman and instead of greeting her with a cheek kiss or taking her outstretched hand to kiss it, he shook it like they were at a business meeting.

With his derogatory comments about Samantha's appearance and lacklustre welcome, this match had not got off to a good start.

But the night was young and my opinion was not important.

Although I had not warmed to Edward yet, it was what Samantha thought of him that mattered.

And judging by the smile on her face, she was happy with her match, which would make my job much easier.

5

SAMMIE

'Let me show you to your table,' Romeo said as I followed behind him and Edward.

At least Romeo was more polite than he was earlier. The smile he just gave was totally half-arsed, but whatever. I wasn't here for him, I was here for Edward.

So, Edward was my Mr Right.

If I was being totally honest, I wasn't instantly attracted to him. Don't get me wrong, he was fairly good-looking. He had short brown hair, clean-shaven white skin, brown eyes and was dressed in an expensive-looking dark suit.

Edward didn't inspire the same *phwoar* reaction that I'd got when I first saw Romeo. But that was a good thing because that was *exactly* what I'd said I wanted. A decent-looking guy who wasn't going to attract women like flies to shit.

Romeo was the kind of guy I swooned over on the dating apps and it always ended in tears.

I was here to break that toxic cycle. *Edward* was my perfect match. And just because there wasn't that initial spark of attraction, it didn't mean we wouldn't hit it off.

I'd had more sparks than a fireworks display with loads of guys and they'd all fizzled out faster than the flick of a switch.

Yeah, Edward's handshake was limper than a lettuce leaf and his palms were sweaty, but he was probably nervous like me.

Like Stella said, the Love Hotel peeps were matchmaking experts. They knew what they were doing when they set us up.

It was time to push myself out of my comfort zone and try a different type of man.

'Here we are.' Romeo gestured to a table by the window with sea views. This place really was stunning.

Like the rest of the hotel, the restaurant had a clean, mini-malist décor. White stone walls, tables with crisp white table-cloths with a single red rose in a vase in the centre.

'Thanks, mate.' Edward sat down straightaway and Romeo frowned.

'Please.' Romeo pulled out my chair and I sat down.

'Thanks,' I said, surprised at the gesture.

Even though I was capable of pulling out my own chair, I kind of liked that chivalry stuff. Not that I'd experienced it often.

Romeo was probably trained to do this kind of thing as part of his job. It would've been nice if Edward had done that, but it was fine.

'*Prego*,' Romeo replied, which I guessed meant: you're welcome. 'Take a look at the menus and one of our Cuisine Champions will be here shortly to take your order. Enjoy your meal together.'

Cuisine Champions! Stella was right. The job titles in this place were hilarious.

As Romeo left, I picked up the menu and fixed my gaze on it, not knowing whether I should speak first or let Edward do the honours.

I'd imagined this moment a million times. Thought about

what I might say and as cringey as it sounded, I'd even rehearsed it in front of the mirror a couple of times. Okay. Maybe a couple of *dozen* times was more accurate. But now Edward was in front of me, I couldn't remember a single word from those conversation starters.

'So.' Edward broke the silence. 'The weather's pretty nice here. Much better than England.'

The weather?

Seriously?

Come on, bruv, you can do better than the freaking weather.

Then again, at least he'd tried to make conversation, which was more than I had.

'Yeah! But that's not hard,' I laughed. 'Where are you from?'

'London,' he replied.

'Me too!' Relief washed over me. At least we lived in the same city. I'd tried the whole long-distance relationship stuff twice before and it never worked out. 'I'm from South London, I live in Tooting.'

'I grew up in Dulwich.'

'No way!' I shrieked. What were the chances? I came all the way to Italy and ended up meeting a man who grew up not far from where I did. This was brilliant.

'Yeah. I live in Shoreditch now.'

'Very cool.' Shoreditch was in East London and was known for having loads of trendy bars and restaurants.

'I like it. And it's close to work. I'm a Finance Director for a computer software company.'

'Oh, wow. A finance guy,' I grinned. According to social media, dating a *finance bro* was the Holy Grail. This was another good sign.

'How about you?' Edward asked.

'I work as a receptionist for a pharmaceutical company.'

'Oh, right. What kind of pharmaceuticals?'

'Our bestselling products are haemorrhoids cream and diarrhoea relief tablets.'

'Gross!' he grimaced and my stomach twisted.

It wasn't the world's most exciting job, but it was honest work and it paid the bills. Plus, although I was a receptionist now, if I played my cards right, in a couple of months, once I'd been there for five years, there was a strong possibility that I'd get promoted to head receptionist, which would open up a new level of opportunities.

And yeah, our bestsellers weren't exactly glam, but most people had diarrhoea at least once in their lives and haemorrhoids could be painful, so it was important to have stuff to treat it.

I was about to tell him that, but then remembered I was supposed to be making a good impression and in hindsight talking about getting the runs and lumps in and around your arse weren't exactly top-tier first-date conversation material. In my defence, I was just answering his question.

'Shall we order?' I asked. Maybe the date would improve after a glass of that amazing prosecco.

'Yeah.'

Once we'd scanned the menu, we placed our order and the waiter, or should I say, *Cuisine Champion*, lol, brought over a bottle of prosecco.

'This prosecco is *so* good!' I said.

'It's not bad,' Edward replied.

Not bad? I didn't know what Edward usually drank, but this was like heaven in a glass.

'What kind of things do you like to do in your spare time?' I asked.

'The usual stuff. Rugby, going out with friends. I also enjoy swimming.'

'Me too!' I instantly brightened. *Another big green tick.*

'I go to the pool most mornings before work. I like to stay in shape.'

'Impressive. I usually just go at the weekends, but I wish I could go more.'

As Edward talked about how he'd loved swimming since he was a boy, I began to relax.

I was starting to see why we'd been matched. He'd already ticked several of my boxes: decent-looking, good job, lived in London and we shared a similar hobby. High-five to the match-making experts.

Soon after, our food arrived and I swear the fresh ear-shaped pasta, which apparently was called *orecchiette* and was typical for this region, was the best pasta I'd ever tasted.

'How long have you been single?' I asked.

I hoped it would come up naturally but it hadn't and I didn't want to pussyfoot around. I wanted to know more about his dating history.

'About a year and a half.'

'If you don't mind me asking, what happened with your ex?'

'Chardonnay was a brilliant girl: super attractive, fun, we got on like a house on fire and the sex... our chemistry was amazing. But we just wanted different things.'

'How so?' I didn't want this to sound like an interview, but I'd wasted so much time on dating the wrong men, that I'd rather know sooner rather than later whether we were on the same page.

'I'm thirty-eight, so I wanted to settle down and have a family whilst I'm still fit enough to play with the kids. She was in her twenties so she wasn't ready for that.'

OMG.

He was thirty-eight. I'd said I wanted a man that was older than me because he'd be more likely to be ready to settle down.

And he wanted kids. *Plural.*

Tick and double tick.

The Love Hotel experts had delivered exactly what I'd asked for.

'A similar thing happened to me. I was dating a guy for three years but he could never make up his mind about what he wanted. I was keen to settle down but he always said it was too soon. In the end, we broke up.'

I didn't need to go into the fact that he'd dumped me because he'd fallen for someone else who he very quickly committed to. I was supposed to be selling myself, not advertising the fact that my long-term boyfriend traded me in for a younger model once I'd outlived my usefulness.

'That's a shame.' His eyes dropped to his plate and he popped the last forkful of chicken salad in his mouth. 'Shall we go?'

'Don't you want dessert?' I asked.

'It's too late for that and you must be full after all that pasta.'

'A bit, but everyone knows it's a separate stomach for dessert, right?' I laughed. Edward frowned like I was a lunatic and my smile dropped. 'Not a dessert fan, then?'

'Not really.'

'Maybe you could get a cheeseboard instead?'

'Too many calories. Let's go,' Edward repeated.

Too many calories? We were on holiday, FFS.

'Okay,' I agreed reluctantly. We were here for two weeks, so I supposed I could get dessert another day.

Edward got up and I followed him, excited about the next part of the evening.

When Romeo gave me the tour he said that there was a cock-tail bar open until midnight, so we could get a drink there and chat.

Or once our food had settled, I'd definitely be up for skinny-dipping. Could be a fun way to help break the ice.

It wasn't every day that I got to spend time in a five-star, all-inclusive hotel in Italy with a beach and the sea right here to enjoy, so I wanted to make the most of it.

'You are leaving?' the maître d', whose name and crazy job title I couldn't remember, asked as we reached the door.

'You do not want dessert?' Romeo added, his face crumpled, but still annoyingly handsome.

I was gagging for dessert. I spotted the couple on the table opposite ours sharing a panna cotta and was dying to see if it tasted as good as it looked, but spending time with my match was more important.

'No,' Edward answered for me. 'The salad was sufficient and Samantha ate enough pasta to sink the *Titanic*, so it's better if we don't.'

Wait, what? I didn't eat *that* much pasta. Just a standard portion.

I opened my mouth to tell him so, then clamped it shut. It wasn't worth messing up our first date by debating how much I ate.

'If you are sure?' Romeo's eyes flicked to mine and I looked away before he saw from my expression that I absolutely was *not* sure.

'Certain.' Edward jumped in before I had a chance to reply. 'Night, Ricardo.'

'Thanks, *Romeo*,' I added, emphasising his correct name.

'*Prego*,' he replied. He looked like he was about to say something else, but Edward opened the door and stepped outside before I followed.

It was still warm and the stars lit up the sky so beautifully. This was the perfect time for an evening stroll.

'I'm that way.' Edward pointed. 'Sleep well.'

As he walked off, my jaw dropped.

So we weren't going for a beach walk or for cocktails.

I didn't get it.

One minute we were chatting about the stuff we had in common.

Then the next he suggested we leave (without dessert) and instead of going on to do something else, he'd decided to go to his room.

What the hell?

6

SAMMIE

'Already?' I groaned as my alarm sounded. This king-sized bed was so comfortable, I'd be happy to stay here all day.

I'd slept like a baby. Everything from the perfect pillows to the crisp white bed linen and the mattress which must've been made by the sleep angels was heavenly.

My whole bedroom was next level. It had stone whitewashed walls decorated with colourful art, vaulted ceilings and a large balcony with direct sea views. This was a world away from my flat in London. I felt like I was living like a celebrity.

I didn't get to sleep straightaway because I was trying to work out why Edward ended the evening so abruptly. In the end I'd reasoned that he was just tired. I was too. Coming here knowing you'd been set up with your perfect match was intense.

Plus, we'd only known each other a couple of hours, which was nowhere near enough time to draw any conclusions one way or the other.

After breakfast we'd have a briefing and take part in our first couples task which would help us to bond faster. Right now, as comfy as this bed was, I needed to get my arse out of it, in the shower then down to breakfast. I was in gorgeous Italy and I wanted to make the most of this trip.

Forty minutes later I was heading to the restaurant. I didn't know if Edward was already there yet. If he wasn't, I'd wait until he arrived so we could have breakfast together, or call him from reception.

As soon as I stepped through the large glass doors, I saw the maître d' from last night standing next to Romeo.

Fuck, he was fit.

But he was also a dick.

Okay, he was a smaller dick last night than when we first met, but that was only because I didn't have to spend more than a minute talking to him. Anyway, why was I even thinking about him? I was here to see Edward.

'*Buongiorno*, Samantha,' Romeo nodded in acknowledgement.

'Morning,' I said flatly.

'Edward is already here. Come. I will take you.' He gestured at me to follow.

As he walked ahead, I attempted not to look at his arse and failed miserably yet again. He might be an arrogant fucker but his arse looked damn good in those shorts.

I was sure that Edward's arse looked good in shorts too. Edward, y'know, the guy who was my match.

Now that I thought about it, I didn't even look at his arse yesterday and I walked behind him twice. But that was good. My match wasn't here to be ogled. Romeo wasn't either. Which was why I was going to stop perving and focus on falling in love with my match.

When we got to the table, Edward was pushing his knife and fork together on his empty plate.

'Morning!' I smiled.

'A Cuisine Champion will arrive shortly,' Romeo said, before leaving.

'Hi.' Edward looked up and gave me a tight smile.

'I see you've finished, or was that just the first round?' I laughed.

'*First round*?' Edward frowned. 'No. That's the trouble with these all-inclusive places. They encourage overeating. Food is for fuel. We only need a certain amount of calories to function, the more we eat, the harder we have to work to burn off the excess. It's completely inefficient.'

'Haha!' I laughed, thinking he was joking, then clamped my jaw shut when I realised he was being serious.

Hmmm. This was tricky because I disagreed with almost everything he'd said.

'Course we need food to survive, obvs, but food's also for enjoyment, right? Everyone knows it's important not to binge on junk every day, but what's the point of life if you can't treat your-self to a bit of cake once in a while?' I said.

And, *hello*? We were in Italy. The land of pasta and pizza. Pretty sure it was illegal to come here and not indulge in those dishes.

If I told Stella that I hadn't taken full advantage, she'd disown me.

'A "bit of cake" turns into two, then before you know it, you're overweight. It's a slippery slope.'

'We're talking about cake, not cocaine, right?' I laughed again, thinking he couldn't be serious. His face turned to stone. Okay, so we didn't agree on cake, but it didn't matter. In the grand scheme of things, it wasn't a big deal. 'Anyway, there's a gym here and the sea, so there's no shortage of ways to exercise.'

'I was at the gym at six. What did you do this morning?'

'Er...' My face crumpled. 'I went for a walk on the beach.'

Why the hell did I lie?

I was tucked up in bed, probably snoring. That was what people did on holiday. I thought I did pretty well waking up at eight considering our briefing wasn't until ten.

'It's some form of cardio, I suppose,' he huffed. 'After the pasta you ate, you'll need to do *much* more than that. If you like, I can put together a workout regime and some tips on the food and portion sizes you should be eating.'

Wait, what? Was he seriously suggesting I follow a diet on holiday?

No chance.

'I'm good. I've been choosing my own food for a while now and it's worked out fine,' I shot back.

'Sorry to interrupt.' A waitress stood by our table. 'May I take your order?'

'Yes, thank you. I'll have some OJ and an omelette. Do you have any pastries?'

'There is a selection of pastries, fresh fruit and cold meats in the buffet over there.' She pointed. 'If you tell me what you like I could bring some to you?'

'I can go myself, *grazie.*'

'*Prego,*' she said before leaving.

'You're getting an omelette *and* pastries?' Edward asked. 'That's a *lot* of food.'

Jesus. This guy was obsessed. 'I'll leave you to it.' Edward pushed his chair back then stood up.

'You're *leaving*?' My eyebrows shot up.

'There's not much time before the briefing, so I should get ready.'

There was over an hour until it started. Seeing as we'd been matched and were in the restaurant at the same time I thought he'd at least sit with me and talk.

'I guess I'll see you there then,' I replied.

'Yes,' he said, not meeting my gaze. 'See you later.'

7

SAMMIE

Considering Edward had made such a big song and dance about leaving so he could get to the briefing early, it was strange that he wasn't here yet.

I was currently lounging in one of the fancy outdoor chairs by the pool admiring the surroundings whilst I waited, which wasn't a hardship because, like everywhere in this hotel, it screamed luxury.

The enormous, pristine swimming pool was surrounded by luxury sun loungers, large comfy-looking white daybeds, complete with extra cushions, all shaded by a mixture of palm and olive trees. And holy macaroni. The sea was so close. In just a few strides, I could be sinking my feet into the powdery white sand and swimming in the gorgeous clear turquoise sea.

There were nine other couples here and they seemed to be chatting happily amongst themselves, whilst I was trying not to look at the tempting view in front of me.

And when I say the *view*, I was referring to a certain Italian Love Alchemist.

Directly in my line of sight was Romeo, who'd just finished

setting up a table with a whiteboard beside it. He'd been trying to do it for the past ten minutes, but kept getting stopped by guests who wanted to talk to him.

Most of them were female and as exaggerated as it might sound, I was pretty sure that *all* of them fancied him.

I was no Enola Holmes, but the way they'd twirled their hair around their fingers, cocked their heads flirtatiously and giggled at whatever he was saying was a dead giveaway.

Oh, and the fact that, as I established yesterday, he was bloody gorgeous might also have something to do with my assumptions.

And from the way he was smirking, it was clear he loved the attention.

Yep. Romeo might be Italian, but he seemed just as arrogant as all of the other good-looking guys back home.

'Good. It hasn't started yet.' Edward finally appeared beside me, snapping me out of my thoughts.

'Not yet. There's been some... interruptions. Everything okay?' I said, which was my polite way of asking where he'd been. I didn't get why he'd rushed off, leaving me to eat breakfast on my own, only to turn up here late.

'Yes,' he said quickly. 'I wonder what the first activity will be.'

'My best friend went to the resort in Spain and she said they did a pool activity.'

'If it's swimming related, I'll enjoy that. How did your friend get on? Was she happy with her match?'

'No. At first she was furious because they matched her with her ex!'

'Oh...' Edward's voice trailed off and his face fell.

'Crazy, right?' People were always shocked whenever they heard the story. 'Now they're inseparable.'

'Initially, it must've been a big surprise for them to see each other again. But sounds like it all worked out in the end. Clearly they were meant to be.'

'Definitely. I give it a year before they're either engaged, married or expecting. Maybe all three!' I cackled. It was true. Stella and Max were at it like rabbits and I knew they both wanted kids.

'Looks like the briefing's about to start,' Edward said bluntly, gesturing towards Romeo.

'Oh, right, okay,' I said, surprised that he'd cut me off. Maybe he was just excited to find out what the activity would be.

'*Buongiorno!*' Romeo said.

'*Buongiorno!*' everyone replied.

'Welcome once again to the Love Hotel. As you may already know, my name is Romeo and I am your Love Alchemist, which means that I plan to do everything I can to help create that magical chemistry between you and your match.'

'Yay!' a woman at the front cheered.

'Every day during the first week you will do an activity with your match in a group setting. Then during the second week you will choose your own activities to do just as a couple. You'll create a daily playlist with at least five songs that remind you of the time spent with your match and we'd also like you to take photos together for your "memory book" photo album.'

I remembered this stuff from when Stella stayed here.

At the moment, zero songs were springing to mind for the playlist, well, apart from 'All by Myself' by Celine Dion, because Edward had left me to eat breakfast alone. But he must've had a good reason. Maybe he had a bad stomach and didn't want to tell me. I should've offered him some of my company's diarrhoea relief tablets.

I was trying to approach relationships differently, so I

couldn't write him off yet. The day was still young. Hopefully once we started the activity we'd connect more.

'Sound good?' Romeo asked and everyone replied with a collective '*sì!*' '*Perfetto.* The first couples activity will start in half an hour and will be in the pool. If you are not already in your swimwear, please return to your room and change.'

'I better go.' Edward jumped up.

'I've already got my bikini on under this.' I gestured to my kaftan. It'd said to wear swimwear in the welcome pack on the iPads in our room, so I'd come prepared.

'Back in ten,' he said, without even bothering to look at me.

Did he even find me attractive? He hadn't commented on my dress last night, so I genuinely had no idea.

Some of the other guests headed off to change and others started chatting.

Just as I started to think about how to kill time, Romeo strode over.

'Samantha, *come stai*?'

Fuck. His accent was so hot.

As his rich woody scent surrounded me, I swallowed hard.

Get it together, girl. He's nothing special. Just another fuckboy.

'You asked me how I am, so I say *bene*, right?'

His eyes widened with surprise.

'*Sì.*'

'What?' I took off my sunglasses, folded my arms and raised an eyebrow. 'Surprised that the British girl knows some Italian?'

'Honestly?' he asked.

'Yeah.'

'A little,' he smiled and I was tempted to roll my eyes at how ridiculously perfect his teeth were.

'Rude! So, what – you think us Brits can't speak other languages?'

'No. You asked me if I was surprised that *you* knew some Italian and I am, so I just told the truth.'

'The *audacity*!' I mock gasped. 'For your information, I know ten whole words of Italian. And I studied hard to learn every single one of them!'

'Ten whole words?' His eyes widened. '*Wow*. You are right. That really *is* impressive.' He smiled again. 'Well, do not let them go to waste, Samantha. Share them with me. Tell me what you know.'

'Challenge accepted!' I stretched out my arms and flexed my neck from side to side like I was preparing for a workout, then exhaled deeply. 'Okay, so number one: *Ciao*, two: *grazie*, three: *bene*, er...' I paused, racking my brain.

'Three words. Like I said, that is impressive. I see your Italian is as good as your maths.' A small smile touched his lips.

'I hadn't finished!' I protested. 'Four: prosecco, five: pizza...'

'Are you serious?' Laughter rumbled in his chest.

'Still not finished! Six: pasta, seven: vino, eight: *sì*, nine: gelato and ten: mozzarella. Boom!' I pumped my fist in the air triumphantly.

'*Brava*.' He slow clapped. 'I clearly underestimated you. I had no idea you'd be able to successfully list ten of the most popular Italian food-related words, which are also common in the English language.'

'Hey!' I slapped his arm playfully. Jesus, his bicep was even firmer than it looked. 'They weren't *all* food-related!'

'You are right. I apologise. Your Italian is exceptional. I did not realise the extent of your talents before, but now that I am aware, if any of our guests need a translator, I will make sure that you are at the top of our list.'

'*Finally*, he gives me the respect I deserve!' I laughed and our eyes locked.

Fuck. How were his eyes so damn pretty? They were light brown and sparkly and of course he had to have those long lashes. What a waste.

And I liked that today he actually cracked a smile and even laughed. Yesterday he was so serious and grumpy.

Some people would've been offended about him taking the piss out of my Italian, but I liked a bit of good-hearted banter and let's face it, my Italian was shit. I knew it and he knew it, so why not have a laugh about it?

'So,' Romeo broke the silence and I looked away, 'how is everything with you and Edward? You like him, *si?*'

'Yeah!' My voice squeaked. 'He's… everything I asked for: decent-looking, good job, lives in London, we share some hobbies and both want the same things in the near future. Y'know, to settle down and stuff. All good!'

My stomach churned. Maybe Edward was right and I shouldn't have had an omelette and pastries. But I'd finished eating over an hour ago and I felt fine before. Weird.

Anyway, everything I'd just said was true. Edward ticked *loads* of boxes.

Okay, his obsession with calorie counting didn't seem healthy, but that was his personal choice and no one was perfect, right? Compared to the red flags a lot of the guys I'd dated had, that was minor.

Everything was fine.

'Excellent,' Romeo nodded. 'The matchmakers have done well.'

'Yep,' I said, popping the 'p' for extra emphasis.

'I must check on the other guests, but call if you need something.'

'Okey dokey.' I did a cringey thumbs-up gesture, then winced internally. One day I'd have an entire conversation with a man without doing or saying something stupid.

Minutes after Romeo left, I saw Edward striding towards the pool, in a pair of brown and orange striped speedos.

A shiver ran down my spine.

And not in a good way.

With all his gym workouts and healthy eating, I wasn't surprised that Edward was in decent shape. His body was a million times more toned than mine, so I wasn't judging. But as I looked at him, I wasn't overcome with desire. Instead, I was over-come with a major case of the ick.

Maybe it was the speedos or the brown and orange print, which I noticed when he turned around had an unfortunate brown stripe running down his bum-crease which made it look like he'd had an 'accident'.

I didn't know what it was, but all I knew was that Edward wasn't doing it for me.

At all.

Shame washed over me.

A long-lasting relationship was about more than just lust and attraction. I couldn't dismiss an opportunity to build a future with the love of my life just because he chose to wear a pair of speedos which looked like he'd shat his pants. That was his choice.

Just because I preferred men in swimming trunks, that wasn't the basis for questioning our compatibility. That was shallow.

I was better than that.

'Did I miss anything?' Edward said as he sat on the sun lounger beside me.

'No.'

'I think everyone is here,' Romeo said. 'So, your first activity will be pool volleyball.'

That was what Stella said she did first too. Should be fun.

And with any luck, pairing up with Edward and working as a team should help us come closer together.

At least I hoped so, anyway...

8

ROMEO

As I watched Samantha and Edward in the pool, I knew there was a problem.

I first suspected it last night in the restaurant, then again at breakfast this morning. And now my gut told me the same thing: they were not bonding well.

Admittedly, I had only done this job for about eight months, so I was not the most experienced Love Alchemist, but during that time I had worked with hundreds of couples and I knew the signs.

Not all matches hit it off immediately. Some needed more time. But even though Samantha and Edward had barely been here for twenty-four hours, I had noticed a lot from their interactions.

It was not just the fact that Edward was not very complimentary when he first met Samantha or that he did not even pull the chair out for her at dinner that raised alarm bells. It was also the way that he commented on the amount of pasta she ate.

Plus, I got the feeling that Samantha wanted to stay for

dessert last night, but because Edward did not, he selfishly insisted they both left.

When he arrived for breakfast this morning and I asked whether Samantha would be joining him, his reaction suggested that he had not even given her a second thought. Those were not the actions of a person who was serious about finding love.

And what kind of man left his match to eat breakfast alone?

'How could you miss that shot?' Edward barked at Samantha, snapping me out of my thoughts.

'It was on *your* side of the pool!' Samantha spat back, narrowing her eyes.

'We still would've had a chance of winning if you got that!' Edward's nostrils flared whilst Samantha's gaze dropped to the pool and her shoulders slumped.

This was exactly what I was talking about. I did not like that he had just scolded Samantha for not hitting the ball which caused the other team to win the match.

Seeing her wounded expression made my chest tighten.

My first impression of Samantha may not have been the best, but speaking to her earlier was not as bad as I had feared. Her attempt to list her *extensive* Italian vocabulary was amusing.

Anyway, it did not matter what I thought of her. The important thing was that she enjoyed her time at the hotel.

This game was supposed to be a fun way to bring the couples together, but Edward was taking it too seriously and upsetting his match in the process which I did not like.

Especially because Samantha told me earlier that Edward ticked many of her boxes. This did not surprise me. The Love Hotel matchmaking team had an exceptional track record of bringing the right people together.

But nothing was perfect. And it did not matter how detailed and rigorous the selection process was, sometimes, there were things that no amount of questionnaires, research and analysis behind the scenes could uncover.

Sometimes, the only way to know whether a match worked and whether or not two people had chemistry was when they interacted together in person.

But I could be wrong.

Perhaps I had misjudged Edward.

This was only the first activity and maybe Edward's competitive nature had affected his behaviour.

Tomorrow was the first external excursion.

The couples would spend the time together visiting the *trulli* houses in Alberobello and usually visiting beautiful places like this helped our matches to bond.

If this fairytale town could not work its romantic magic on Samantha and Edward, I did not know what would...

9

SAMMIE

I flopped on the bed and blew out a frustrated breath.

The pool volleyball was a total bust.

Me and Edward just weren't in sync.

We should've worked together as a team to get the ball over the net, but instead he tried to hit it all the time, so it was like I wasn't even there. And then when *he* missed the shot that caused us to lose the game, he blamed *me*.

We were supposed to stay until the end to see the winners crowned, but Edward stormed off early because he said he had to make an 'important call'.

Talk about a bad loser.

I still had no idea how Edward felt about me and to be honest, right now he wasn't at the top of my Christmas card list.

Don't get me wrong, I wasn't thinking about throwing in the towel. Like I'd said to Romeo, Edward had a lot of the qualities I'd asked for. But some of the things he did cheesed me off.

My mind was more tangled than a bunch of computer cables. I needed a second opinion.

After picking up my phone, I dialled Stella's number. Luckily, she answered on the third ring.

'Hey!' she chirped. 'I've been waiting to hear from you! How's it going? How's your match?'

'He's...' I paused as I tried to search for the right words, 'fine.'

'*Fine* as in, *girl, he is fine*,' Stella put on a terrible American accent, 'or *fine* as in, *yeah, whatever?*'

'As crappy as it sounds to say it out loud, it's more like he's *fine* as in, *meh.*'

'Thanks for that extremely detailed explanation.'

'I know that *meh* isn't the most descriptive word in the dictionary, but it's how I feel. I'm kind of indifferent. It's strange because he's decent-looking, has a good job, lives in London, wants to settle down and he likes swimming.'

'That all sounds great! So what's the problem?'

'I'm just not *drawn* to him. I don't feel that attraction. There's no spark.'

'Not all romances are insta love. Some are slow burns. It's only been twenty-four hours. There's loads of time for those feelings to grow. Look at me and Max. I hated him on the first day. It was a week until we really connected.'

'When you say *connected,* you mean, *shagged!*' I cackled.

'Oh, sweet memories...' Her voice turned wistful. 'Anyway, it wasn't until our first excursion outside of the hotel that things started to change, so you never know, maybe that's when it'll click for you too. When's your first outing?'

'Tomorrow. According to one of the other guests I was chatting to, we're going to Alberobello.'

Apparently the Love Alchemists didn't usually tell us where we were going in advance as they preferred the locations to be a surprise, but this woman overhead Romeo talking about it to another staff member.

'That place rings a bell. I think it's the town with those cute cone houses. That'll be the perfect place to help you connect. You'll see.'

'I really hope so. After everything you and Jasmine told me about the Love Hotel, I was *so* excited about coming here. Then when I arrived and saw how hot Romeo was, I was even more excited because I thought if I could feel a spark with someone like *him* then the whole place must be powered by some kind of magical romantic electricity and that when I met my match, the connection would be ten times stronger and...'

'Wait, hold up, rewind.' Stella raised her voice. 'Who the hell is *Romeo*?'

'Shit,' I muttered under my breath. I shouldn't have mentioned him. Now she'd get the wrong idea. 'He's just my Love Alchemist. My very arrogant and judgemental Love Alchemist.'

'You have a *male* Love Alchemist?' Stella replied, completely ignoring my descriptions of his personality.

I mean, he wasn't so judgy today. Bantering with him was kind of fun, but still, he was ridiculously good-looking and I'd dated enough of those kind of guys to know how self-absorbed they were.

'Yeah.'

'And what, you felt sparks with *him*?'

'No...' I lied. 'I just thought he was hot, that's all. But then he opened his mouth and I realised he was a dick. Didn't matter anyway because all I was interested in was meeting my match. It's just that I thought when I met my Mr Right, I'd feel *something*. Y'know?'

'I hear you, but it's still early days. Like I said, everything could change tomorrow. In the meantime, try and focus on all the great things about Edward, like the things you have in common and why he's the right man for you. Did they give you your Love Tasks?'

'Yep. And I'm already struggling. I'm supposed to do a playlist with at least five songs that convey how I feel about him, but my mind's more jumbled than a bowl of spaghetti soup. I can't think of a single song.'

'I *loved* doing the playlists! At first when they told us about them, I thought it'd be a nightmare, but then I really got into it. I'm sure that whatever you choose won't be as bad as the songs I chose for Max during those first few days!' She laughed.

That was true. At the beginning, she still hated Max because of the way things ended between them so I remember her choosing songs like 'Dickhead' by Kate Nash and 'We Are Never Ever Getting Back Together' by Taylor Swift. But despite those angry early playlists, they fell in love again, so it all worked out in the end.

'At least he sparked some kind of emotions from you – even if it was hatred. I don't even have that. I don't feel *anything*. At the moment, the only song that comes to mind is "Numb" by Linkin Park.'

'Wow, okay...'

'No, wait. I've thought of a second song.'

'What is it?' Stella replied excitedly.

'"Don't Blame Me" by Taylor Swift, because it wasn't my fault we lost the volleyball game like he accused me of!' My cheeks heated with anger as I remembered how much I hated how he glared at me in the pool. 'Oh and I just remembered that earlier I thought that "All by Myself" by Celine Dion would be a great choice too.'

'Why's that?'

'Because he left me to eat breakfast *alone* this morning.'

I explained to Stella what happened and, like me, she thought it sounded strange and rude.

'And he seems kind of obsessed with calories, which is fine if that's what *he* wants to do, but I didn't like his comment about the amount of pasta I ate. He made it sound like I was a greedy pig. He even asked if I wanted him to create a diet plan for me.'

'What the hell?' Stella gasped.

'Exactly.'

'That's a definite red flag.'

'I know, right?'

'Hmmm, well, I'm not liking the way that he left you for breakfast, blamed you for missing a volleyball shot and his food-shaming vibe, but because it's the first day and we trust the matchmakers, let's give him the benefit of the doubt. See how things go tomorrow and if you've still got concerns, then speak to your Casanova guy.'

'*Romeo*,' I corrected. 'Although the ladies do seem to love him and he didn't seem to mind them fawning over him, so Casanova is an accurate description.'

'Oh!' she said, sounding like she'd just had a brainwave. 'Was *Casanova* taking photos of everyone during the pool volleyball match?'

'Yeah.'

'Great. So when I was at the Spanish Love Hotel and I went to collect the photos of our pool volleyball match, I was convinced they'd be terrible and all be shots of me and Max scowling at each other. But when I saw them, they were all surprisingly gorgeous. I was looking at Max like he was walking on water and he was looking at me like I was freaking Beyoncé, but neither of us had realised. I reckon that also helped us to see that there was something brewing between us, so it could be the same for you and Edward too. When you see the memory book pics that'll definitely help you to bond. Don't worry, I'm sure it'll all work out.'

'I hope so.'

'Anyway, hon, I better get back to work, but good luck with the playlist, stay positive and let me know how the excursion goes tomorrow.'

'Will do.'

As I hung up, another song came to mind.

'Cold' by Maroon 5.

So based on my song ideas so far, when I thought of my ideal match I felt wrongly accused, cold, numb and lonely.

Obviously, I wouldn't include any of those tracks on my playlist because I didn't want to be rude, but I was worried.

You didn't need to be Einstein to work out that feeling that way about a guy who was supposed to be my perfect match wasn't good.

But like Stella said, tomorrow was a new day and my feelings could change.

And after I'd spent time and every penny of my savings coming all the way here to find love, I really hoped she was right...

10

ROMEO

As I scrolled through the photos that I had taken of the pool volleyball tournament earlier today I blew out a frustrated breath.

This was the fifth time I'd looked at the photos of Samantha and Edward on my computer screen and I still could not find enough pictures of them looking happy together to consider printing for their memory book shortlist.

I had taken at least twice as many photos of them compared to the other couples, but I struggled to find more than two that were barely okay. And normally we aimed to provide at least six or seven amazing choices.

Samantha looked sad and frustrated, and in the photos where Edward was looking at Samantha, he was either scowling or had his lip curled in disgust. And I could not understand why.

When Samantha removed her kaftan to reveal a bold orange and white bikini, I am not proud to admit that my eyes roamed over her body for longer than they should have. But as soon as I realised I was staring, I quickly tore my gaze away.

I had no interest in dating right now and even if I did, like I had reassured my boss, I would never get involved with a guest. That would be stupid.

My point was, Samantha was an attractive woman. And based on our conversation earlier, she seemed to have a good sense of humour too, so I did not know why Edward was not making more of an effort.

I knew he was a guest, but I did not like him.

My phone rang and I was glad of the distraction.

'*Ciao*, Mamma,' I smiled.

'Hi, darling. Sorry I missed your call earlier.'

'I was just calling to check on you and Biscotti.'

'She's much better!'

'*Fantastico!*' My shoulders instantly loosened.

'It's such a relief. The vet said she should be fine now. She just needs to rest. Will you be coming for dinner this week?'

'Ah, I do not think that I can, I am sorry, Mamma. I have a new group of guests. Next week will be easier though because they will organise their own activities.'

'Oh, right. Okay.'

My chest tightened. I could tell that she was lonely. My mother was English and although she had moved here many years ago to be with my father I knew she still felt isolated.

With my sister away studying in Rome, my brother living in London and me busy working at the hotel, she missed us. Even though I did not live far from her, because of the long hours at the hotel, it was difficult for me to see her and my father was rarely home. He was always off doing his own thing.

'Are you sure you will be okay? I can speak to my boss and see if...'

'No, no. I'm fine. Don't worry. I just miss you, that's all.'

'I know, Mamma. I miss you too. Have you thought any more about going to London, to see your family?'

'I can't...' Her voice trailed off. 'I need to be here for your father. He needs me.'

'He can take care of himself.' I ground my jaw.

'He'll... It's better if I stay here.'

I hated that she felt she could not go away. All because of what happened the last time she did. I hated him for doing that to her. But I did not want to get into that again with her now. It would only upset her.

'I promise to visit on Sunday. And maybe next week we can go to the beach together.'

'I'd love that!' Her voice instantly brightened.

'And I will bring a surprise for you.'

'I can't wait!'

'I must get back to work now. Give Biscotti a kiss from me. *Ti voglio bene, Mamma. Ciao.*'

'I love you too, son. Have a good day.'

After I hung up, sadness washed over me.

My mother was a broken woman, all because of my father. She would be better off without him.

If she had left him years ago, she would have had the chance to start a new life.

I knew this for sure because I had experienced the same betrayal and hurt.

It took a long time to get my life back on track, but now I was doing well. As long as I continued to stay focused, soon I would have the opportunity to follow my dream again, like I had tried to do years ago before my plans were derailed.

I wished that Mamma would realise soon that it was not too late to change her fortunes. But because my father controlled the finances, she was worried that she would not be able to survive without him.

That was why I had set up a secret bank account and every

month I had put every cent that I could into it, so that when she did finally decide to leave my father, Mamma would have money for a fresh start.

If I kept working hard at the hotel, in just a few months, there would be enough for her to move back to England and pay for at least three months' rent.

This was important to me because if I got the opportunity to work in the US, I would not feel comfortable leaving Mamma in Italy with my father. But if she moved to England she would have her family, friends and my brother nearby which would put my mind at ease.

I dragged my gaze back to my computer.

After going through the photos for a sixth time, I admitted defeat. A batch of better photos were not going to magically appear if I kept staring at my screen.

But if I could only submit two photos, I needed to cover myself with management. I could not afford any more complaints. My future and Mamma's happiness were at stake.

I picked up the phone and dialled Victoria's number.

'Victoria, sorry to disturb you, but I have an issue with one of the couples.'

I explained my concerns about their initial interactions and the photos dilemma.

'I appreciate you bringing this to my attention, but it's still early. See how they get on over the next few days and if by the end of the week you're still worried, let me know. As for the photos, submit the two you have and on the trip tomorrow, make a note to take some extra photos. Maybe ask them for some posed shots too and prompt them to smile or look into each other's eyes. That way you know you'll get some decent shots and hopefully when they see how good they look together, they'll start showing more affection.'

'*Va bene*,' I agreed.

'And check the screen straight after taking them to see how they've come out.'

'I will.'

I had done that earlier, but they were in the middle of playing volleyball games so I could not ask them to stop and pose. Tomorrow would be easier though.

'Good luck.'

'*Grazie*,' I said, sensing that I was going to need it.

11

SAMMIE

I stepped out of my room and smiled.

It was another gorgeous sunny day and as the heat warmed my skin, I thought about how lucky I was to be here.

I'd lived in London all my life, so I was used to waking up and seeing grey, cloudy skies. But here, the scenery was like a postcard. The sky was a beautiful clear blue shade and the surroundings were lush and colourful. This was only my third day here and I was already wishing I could stay longer.

After having another blissful sleep, I was feeling more positive. I'd thought about it and I'd come to the conclusion that the reason why I wasn't into Edward was because I'd set my expectations too high.

Having seen how happy Stella and Jasmine were, I'd assumed that I'd come here and instantly fall head over heels. And because their boyfriends were the total package, I'd expected my match would be another Mr Perfect. But that wasn't realistic.

If I'd met someone like Edward in London, I would've been

content. He was an improvement on pretty much every guy I'd dated in the last two years, so I shouldn't grumble.

Yeah, I hadn't clicked with him as much as some of the other guys I'd dated, but that was the point of coming here, right? To push myself out of my comfort zone and try going out with a *different* type of man.

The Love Hotel experts knew what they were doing. They'd matched hundreds of couples: including Stella. They'd put me with Edward for a reason. I had to trust their choice and roll with it.

Although Edward didn't light my fire right now, like Stella said, I barely knew him, so I had to give him time to warm up. If I included today, I still had twelve full days left for the romance to grow. I just had to be patient.

I set off down the path that led to reception to collect yesterday's photos. Although the pool volleyball wasn't as fun as I'd hoped, I was looking forward to seeing our highlights in print. Then in just over an hour, we'd head off on the excursion which would help us bond even more. It was gonna be a great day.

Once I picked up the envelope, I went to the restaurant. I'd deliberately arrived extra early to have breakfast with Edward.

Yesterday, after I'd finished speaking to Stella, I'd had a shower, then went for a long walk on the beach which was amazing.

When I got back, I did my playlist and told myself I'd have a little cat nap, but then I ended up waking up after ten and I didn't have the energy to go the restaurant, so I'd ordered room service. That meant I hadn't seen Edward for dinner, so I wanted to make the effort to start the day with him today.

'*Buongiorno!*' I said to the maître d', Tommaso, and Romeo as I stepped into the restaurant.

'*Buongiorno*, Samantha.' Romeo gave me a small smile and

for some dumb reason my stomach fluttered. I must be hungrier than I thought. 'I see you have been studying.'

'Eh?' I frowned.

'You said *buongiorno*. Now we have another word to add to your extensive list of Italian vocabulary.' The corner of his mouth twitched.

'Ha!' I grinned. 'By tomorrow, I'll practically be bilingual!' I laughed.

'Anything is possible.' He cocked an eyebrow. '*Come stai?*'

'*Bene,*' I replied.

Romeo gave me a nod of approval and my stomach flipped again. I really needed to get some food ASAP.

'Let me take you to your table.'

'*Grazie,*' I said, feeling proud that I'd said three whole words of proper Italian. 'Is Edward still here?' I followed Romeo through the restaurant.

'I have not seen him this morning.'

'Oh.' My face crumpled. 'I thought he was an early bird?'

'Perhaps he will come later.'

Romeo stopped at a table and pulled out the chair for me. This time my heart fluttered which meant it couldn't be because of my hunger pangs.

When I realised that it was fluttering because it liked Romeo's romantic gesture, I sent it a strong warning to calm the fuck down.

Yes, pulling out a chair was chivalrous and sweet, but Romeo was just doing his job. This wasn't the time to start getting stupid ideas about my Love Alchemist. Especially as today was the day that me and Edward were going to hit it off.

'*Grazie.*'

The Cuisine Champion (yay, I remembered the crazy job title!), took my order and Romeo left.

Maybe Edward was still at the gym or doing a hundred pre-breakfast laps in the pool. I thought about waiting to go through the photos, but I was too excited so decided it wouldn't hurt to have a quick peek whilst I waited.

I fished the envelope out of my bag, then opened it faster than a kid unwrapping a birthday gift. But when I did, I noticed there were only two pictures. Given how much I'd seen Romeo snapping away whilst we were playing volleyball, I'd expected a lot more.

Anyway, it was *quality* not *quantity* that counted. I'd prefer to have two awesome photos than a hundred rubbish ones.

I slid them out of the envelope and as I glanced at the first one, my face fell.

It was a photo of Edward holding the ball over his head, like it was a trophy.

I was smiling, but he wasn't even looking at me. I think that was taken when we won a point. There wasn't much else to the photo. Yeah, he was shirtless, but as I studied him, I felt nothing and when my eyes landed on those speedos, I cringed.

Okay, so the first photo was disappointing, but there was still one more.

I flicked to the next shot and it was of me. I was standing at the net and was smiling and punching the air.

See. That was good.

But then I remembered, that was when I'd hit a winning shot in the first round. Edward was in the background, but for some reason his face seemed a little blurry.

So that was it? Those were the only pictures we had for our memory book? I wasn't seeing that 'hidden bond' that Stella had spoken about, but I wouldn't let it affect me.

I checked my phone to see if there had been any messages from Edward. We'd exchanged numbers during a break at the volleyball match. At that point we were in the lead so he was in a good mood.

There was nothing from him so far. I hadn't received a link to download his playlist yet either.

In the end I'd chosen generic holiday songs, like 'Summertime' by DJ Jazzy Jeff and The Fresh Prince, 'Holiday' by Madonna and 'Cruel Summer' by Taylor Swift.

After breakfast, I returned to my room, got my stuff, then headed back to the reception where they said the coach would be waiting to take us to Alberobello.

Wow, I said to myself as I took in the sight of the coach. The Love Hotel never did anything by halves.

This 'coach' had a sleek, glossy black exterior and looked like one of those luxury tour buses the celebs travelled on.

As I climbed the immaculate steps and saw the interior, my eyes popped. It had tinted windows, wooden flooring and plush grey and white reclining leather seats which looked like they had loads of legroom. At five foot six, it was wasted on me though.

At the back of the coach there was even a kitchen with a coffee machine, fridge and microwave, plus loads of drinks and snacks.

I could definitely get used to travelling like this.

Edward wasn't here yet, so I found two empty seats then sat down.

Five minutes later he still hadn't arrived, which was strange seeing as he was worried about being on time for yesterday's briefing. I took out my phone.

ME

> Hi Edward, it's Samantha. The coach is leaving soon. Everything okay?

A few minutes later, I saw that he was typing a message and exhaled. Phew! He was probably just running late.

Finally, his message popped up, but when I read it, my heart sank.

EDWARD

Not feeling well. Not coming today.

ME

Oh no! What's wrong?

EDWARD

Stomach bug.

ME

Can I bring you anything?

EDWARD

No. I'll be fine. Have fun.

Shit. My stomach tightened. I should've checked on him earlier.

I jumped up and headed for the coach door. I didn't know Edward's room number, but if I went to reception, given the circumstances, hopefully they'd tell me. Being sick in a foreign country was the worst, so I needed to make sure he was okay.

Although I'd been looking forward to this trip, it wouldn't be right for me to swan off and enjoy myself whilst he was in his room feeling like shit.

Just as I was about to get off the coach, Romeo got on.

'Samantha?' He frowned. 'Is everything okay?'

'Edward's not well. He's too ill to come today, so I'm gonna check on him and stay behind in case he needs something.'

Romeo's face tightened and he ground his jaw.

Seriously?

Just when I was starting to think this guy wasn't a total dick, he had to prove me wrong. How could he be angry that Edward was ill? It wasn't his bloody fault.

'You stay here,' he said. 'I will go.'

'But...'

'I will tell Edward you wanted to check on him, so he knows that you were concerned. But if he is sick, he will not want you to see him at his worst so soon.'

'Okay. Tell him I said get better soon and I'll stay if he thinks it'll help.'

Poor Edward.

So far today hadn't gone to plan, but I was still optimistic.

Once Edward was back on his feet, things would be better.

I was sure of it.

12

ROMEO

As I stormed towards Edward's room, anger bubbled in my chest.

Call me cynical, but something told me that Edward was not sick. Or if he was, it was because he had drunk too much last night.

When he arrived at the restaurant for dinner, I had asked if he was going to call Samantha to invite her to join him, but he said he preferred to eat alone.

It took all of my strength to stay calm. Why had he signed up to come to the hotel if he was not even going to make an effort with his match?

That was why I asked him what he thought of Samantha – just as I had done with Samantha earlier that morning. But when he replied, I wished that I had not.

'Nice enough girl,' he'd said. 'I'd asked for someone who lived in London, was in their early thirties, who was pretty and wanted to settle down and yeah, she fits that criteria. She's not as pretty as my ex, especially with her silly pink hair. But I also asked for someone who liked to keep fit and Samantha doesn't.'

'But Samantha enjoys swimming, no?' I added, annoyance rippling under my skin. I remembered that was listed as her favourite hobby on the profile the hotel provided.

'She says she does, but look at her. I thought she would've at least made an effort to lose some weight before coming here.'

That was the point that I wanted to knock Edward out. I was disgusted by what he had said. Then I reminded myself that I was on thin ice with the management. I told myself repeatedly that it would be best to keep my mouth shut, but I could not.

'Many men would appreciate a curvaceous woman.' Although I had no romantic interest in Samantha, it did not mean I could not see that she had a beautiful body.

'Don't get me wrong, mate,' he'd said. 'I appreciate curves, but in the right places, y'know what I'm saying?' Edward had laughed. I did not. 'I'm a sucker for a great pair of knockers. My ex had huge tits and I fucking loved them. She set the standard. I came here looking for someone at *least* as good as her, if not better. The women in all the articles and ads I saw for this hotel were super hot.'

Of course he was entitled to his opinion, but he was wrong. But if I told him that I thought he was an ignorant sexist pig who did not deserve to be at this hotel or for any woman, including Samantha, to even spit on him, I would lose my job.

'Love is about more than just physical appearance,' I had said diplomatically, thinking I deserved an award for my restraint. 'It is still very early. Tomorrow we have a great excursion where you will be able to connect on a deeper level.'

Even saying those words had made me feel sick. Although Samantha appeared to be a strong and confident woman, I felt like I was leading her straight to heartbreak.

'Yeah, I dunno, mate. I've...' At that point, his phone had

rung. 'Oooh, hello! Speak of the devil.' He'd grinned, glancing at his phone.

'Is it Samantha?'

'No, mate.' He'd jumped up from the table. 'It's my ex.'

That was when Edward had left the restaurant and I had messaged Victoria.

I had already expressed my concerns to her about the photos, but now I was even more concerned about his behaviour.

Victoria repeated that it was still very early in the process and suggested we met to discuss it this morning, but earlier she had messaged to say she would not be at work until lunchtime.

She told me to monitor how Edward interacted with Samantha during today's trip, promised we would meet once I returned then could decide what action to take.

When Edward did not come for breakfast, I feared the worst. That was why I insisted that I go to his room. The last thing I wanted was for Samantha to realise he was not sick, but just did not appreciate her.

I knocked on his door. There was no reply, so I knocked again.

'Edward, this is Romeo. I have come to see if everything is okay.'

After hearing footsteps, the door finally opened.

'All right, mate,' he said. Edward did not look ill. Perhaps tired or hungover, but not too unwell to come on the trip.

'I am here to see if you will be joining us on the excursion today.' I looked past him and spotted an empty bottle of what looked like brandy.

'Nah.'

'Samantha is looking forward to going,' I said. Edward shrugged and I clenched my fist behind my back.

'I've got other stuff to deal with and my head's pounding.'

'I am sorry to hear that,' I said as politely as I could. Drinking a whole bottle of alcohol the night before an excursion was selfish. He must have known that Samantha would be upset.

Most likely he just did not care.

'Is there anything I can get for you to make you feel better?'

'Nah, room service is bringing paracetamol. Anyway, I've got shit to sort out, so if you don't mind...'

As Edward closed the door in my face, I clenched my fist.

Stronzo.

The guy was an arsehole.

Now I had to tell Samantha that Edward really was not coming on the trip and that she'd have to go on a romantic excursion alone.

Merda.

13

SAMMIE

It'd been ten minutes since Romeo had left. Although I didn't know Edward well, I still hated the idea of him being laid up in bed, feeling like crap. I wished I could do something to help. I pulled out my phone and messaged Stella.

ME

Edward's got a stomach bug so he's not coming on the trip.

He's told me to go anyway, but I feel crap for leaving him on his own.

Luckily, Stella came online straightaway.

STELLA

Oh no! Poor thing.

There's probably not much you can do if he's got a stomach bug. The hotel staff will get him whatever he needs so he's right. Go and have fun by yourself.

When I read Stella's words, the reality suddenly hit me.

I'd been so focused on worrying about Edward that I'd completely forgotten to think about what him not coming meant for *me*.

I was about to go on a romantic couples excursion: *alone*.

Shit.

Everyone was here to bond with their match, so I couldn't exactly start hanging out with them. *Three's a crowd* and all that.

ME

Not sure how much fun I'll be able to have on my own...

STELLA

You'll be fine!

ME

We'll see... Meant to ask earlier, how many photos did you get to choose from every day for your memory book?

STELLA

Usually six or seven. Sometimes more. Depended on how many we took and what activity we did that day.

ME

I only got two.

STELLA

That's not a lot to choose from! Ask your Love Alchemist guy for more.

'Samantha,' a deep Italian voice called out.

My head snapped up and I saw Romeo on the coach steps.

'How's Edward?' I asked.

'Could I speak with you a moment?'

Stell, I've gotta go. Will message later.

I jumped out of my seat then followed Romeo outside.

'What's up? Is Edward okay?' I said, concern dripping from my voice. Romeo's stone-faced expression and the fact that he'd called me off the coach worried me.

'I have just seen Edward. He has a bad headache, so he cannot make it today.'

'Headache?' I frowned. 'He said he had a stomach bug.'

Romeo's eyes widened for a second.

'Perhaps... he must have both... Hopefully he will feel better soon. In the meantime, you are of course still encouraged to attend today's trip.'

'Yeah...' My voice trailed off. 'About that. I don't want to start third-wheeling, so I'm just gonna stay here.'

'That would not be fair,' he protested. Considering I probably wasn't Romeo's favourite guest, I would've thought he'd be relieved. 'There is no reason for you to miss it because your match is... unable to come. If you are worried about being alone, I suppose I can...' He paused. 'I will stay with you.'

I could tell from the pained expression written all over his face that he'd rather have a root canal without anaesthetic than spend time babysitting me.

'Thanks, but I'm no one's charity case, so it's fine. I'll stay here.'

'No,' he growled. 'You want to come on the trip. My job is to make sure every guest is looked after and that includes you.'

'Hmmm.' I narrowed my eyes and studied him. 'Ah, I get it. If I don't come, you'll get in trouble with your boss.' *That and because he wanted me to give him and the hotel a glowing review.* 'So, I'm basically doing you a favour, right?'

'Absolutely.' He flashed a small smile.

'Personally, I'd rather eat my toenails than walk around with you, but I've heard a rumour about where we're going and it sounds cute. Plus, if I get you in trouble with your boss, that'd be bad karma, which I definitely don't need.'

'Exactly.'

'Because you're basically *begging* me, I'll go,' I said, resisting the urge to laugh.

Despite my first impression of him, we'd had a few funny interactions since yesterday, so I reckoned he could take a bit of banter.

'*Grazie*, Samantha.' He put his hands together like he was praying. 'I am *so* grateful that you are such a selfless angel that you would suffer through visiting one of the most beautiful places in Italy, just for me.' He smirked. 'Now, if you do not have any other charitable acts to perform, please could you get back on the coach, so we can leave? We are already running late.'

'Yes, sir!' I did a mock salute and he rolled his eyes. I wished I could say he had evil peepers, but of course they were pretty, just like the rest of him.

Ugh.

I wasn't supposed to notice that he was hot. But yet I had...

My mind should be filled with thoughts of Edward. Especially given how ill he was.

As I returned to my seat, I questioned my decision. If I couldn't talk to Romeo for a few minutes without thinking about how fit he was, how the hell could I cope with talking to him on a romantic excursion for *hours*?

Fuck.

14

ROMEO

We had just arrived at Alberobello and although we had not even started the tour, something told me that I had made a big mistake.

It was not a good idea for me to spend so much one-to-one time with a guest. But what was I supposed to do? I could not leave Samantha alone.

I felt bad for her. She was so concerned about Edward, yet he did not care about hurting her. As a guest it was my job to keep Samantha happy. And if that meant spending a few awkward hours with her, that was what I had to do.

If my gut feeling was right, she already had disappointment coming her way. I had to make sure that she at least enjoyed this excursion so her holiday would not be completely ruined.

'*Benvenuti!*' I said as the guests stepped off the coach. 'This is Alberobello, an ancient town and one of UNESCO's World Heritage Sites.'

'Who's UNESCO?' one of the guests, Phillipa, asked.

'UNESCO stands for the United Nations Educational, Scientific and Cultural Organization. They have a list of World

Heritage Sites which are special, natural or cultural places that are important to preserve for future generations.'

'So, like, pretty old places?' she asked.

'More or less. In the United Kingdom, cities like Bath and landmarks like the Tower of London are World Heritage Sites. In Italy we have many places including Rome. We will also visit another special site this week, but today, we are here to see the *trulli*, which are limestone huts constructed around the fourteenth century. As you can see, the roofs are shaped like cones.' I gestured towards the houses in the distance.

'They're so pretty,' Samantha said as she appeared beside me.

Her fruity scent filled the air. It smelt citrusy, but was sweet at the same time. Like lemon sherbet. Or a shot of delicious limoncello.

What was I just saying to the guests? I had completely lost my train of thought.

'So...' I attempted to focus again. 'Alberobello is a small but very beautiful and romantic town that I am sure you will enjoy discovering as a couple. We will meet back here in two hours which will give you plenty of time to explore the houses, shops, bars and restaurants within these beautiful buildings. Remember to take lots of photos together for your memory book.'

'Will do!' one of the guys, Casper, replied.

'And as you may have noticed, unfortunately Samantha's partner, Edward, is unwell and has not been able to join us. So that she is not on her own, I will walk with her. But if there is anything you need, please call. You all have my number, *si*?'

'*Si*!' everyone replied.

'*Perfetto*! Enjoy exploring this beautiful place together. See you in two hours.'

As the guests dispersed, I turned to face Samantha.

She was wearing a pretty knee-length yellow sundress and her vibrant hair hung loosely around her toned shoulders. Her skin looked very soft.

I shook my head. I should not be looking at her shoulders. I was just here to keep her company.

'Thanks again for being my escort. Oops!' She laughed. 'Bad word choice. I didn't mean it like *that*. I know you're helping me out, but I promise I'm not expecting any sexual favours in return!'

I flashed her a half smile to communicate that I understood she was joking. I was starting to realise that Samantha often spoke before she thought, so her words did not come out as she had intended.

'My boss will be relieved to hear that,' I said, thinking how true that was.

'What I meant was, I hope I'm not cramping your style by making you babysit me. You've probably visited this place a million times before and usually just sneak off to get a pint. So, if you want to do that, I promise I won't tell your boss.'

'Do not worry. I already had four pints on the coach, so I am fine,' I joked.

I was going to add that of course I would not drink whilst I was working, but then realised I did not need to. I was learning that Samantha enjoyed banter, so she would know I was not being serious.

'Phew! You could've at least offered me a sip!' She smiled and I noticed how it lit up her whole face. 'And I'm glad you understood my English sayings too, y'know, like *cramping my style*. Your English is so good. Not as good as my Italian *obviously*, but y'know.' She burst out laughing and a warm feeling filled my chest.

I was glad that she had not let Edward's absence stop her from smiling.

'*Obviously!*' I laughed. 'Your Italian is flawless.'

'I know, right?' She giggled. 'But seriously, how come your English is so good?'

'My mother is English,' I replied.

'No way!' Her eyes widened. 'Must be cool to be bilingual.'

'You should know,' I grinned.

'Of course I do. I was just being polite!' She laughed again.

'Speaking English is helpful. Especially for this job. But growing up, we did not speak it much at home. My father preferred us to speak Italian. Mamma still tried her best to teach us, but if I am honest, when I was younger, I was not interested. It was only when I was a teenager and started to understand the benefits of travel that I began to pay more attention.'

'Yeah, us Brits are lucky that so many people speak English around the world. But it makes us kind of lazy. Like we don't have to bother making an effort because everyone will understand us anyway.'

'But *you* have tried to make an effort,' I added.

We had joked a lot about her language skills, but it was true. I liked how Samantha always tried to use some Italian. Even though they were small, simple words, they still mattered.

'*Grazie!* I'd love to learn more Italian.'

'Perhaps I can teach you,' I said, before instantly regretting it. I was just her chaperone for a couple of hours. Teaching her Italian was not part of the deal.

'Yeah?' Her face lit up. 'I'd love to learn some swear words!'

'Wait.' I stopped in my tracks. 'So, you are here at a beautiful World Heritage Site at one of the most ancient and prettiest towns in Italy,' I gestured at the *trulli*, 'and instead of asking me to tell you more about the history or language related to the houses, you want me to teach you curse words?'

'Yep!' she replied without hesitation and I laughed.

'*Va bene*. What words would you like to learn?'

'Whatever you want to teach me.' She tilted her head, and wrapped a strand of hair around her finger.

'I am sure there are many things I could teach you, so you need to be more specific...'

A jolt of electricity shot straight to my dick.

'*Cazzo*!' I said quickly, chastising myself.

When Samantha said she wanted me to *teach* her, she was referring to Italian, not something sex-related. And anyway, I was sure a confident woman like her had no trouble knowing what to do in the bedroom.

'Ooh, what does that mean?' She grinned and I dragged my mind out of the gutter.

'*Cazzo* literally means dick, but we use it to say fuck.'

'What like, having sex?'

My dick twitched again. What was wrong with me? I had thought about sex more in the past two minutes speaking with Samantha than I had in weeks.

'No. *Fuck* as in, *damn, shit,* that kind of thing. *To fuck* in a sexual way is... anyway.' I stopped.

Samantha bit her lip and the sight made my pulse race.

This conversation was wandering into dangerous territory and I did not like the thoughts that were now flooding my mind.

'That is your Italian lesson for today. Come, I want to show you Trullo Sovrano. It is the only two-storey *trullo* in the town. It was built by a rich priest's family and it is like a museum and it has a shop to buy souvenirs. I am sure you will like it.'

'Okay!'

As I led Samantha further along the street, I exhaled.

That was close.

I had almost crossed a boundary, but pulled back just in time.

Now I needed to stay professional for another hour and forty-five minutes.

I would be fine.

I had to be.

My job and future depended on it.

15

SAMMIE

It was official.

I was a terrible person.

I was in a beautiful town in Italy and instead of focusing on the gorgeous traditional whitewashed conical-roofed houses, my mind was firmly in the gutter.

As we wandered down the pretty little streets, although I was thinking about how cute everything was, most of my thoughts were dominated by how great Romeo smelt and how amazing his muscular arms looked in his branded dark-blue T-shirt.

And when he mentioned that the word he'd said in Italian meant 'fuck', the first thing that sprang to mind was how it would feel to do that with him.

Jesus.

My poor match was laid up in bed suffering and I was fantasising about screwing another man. I was officially going to hell.

Thankfully, Romeo wisely changed the subject and now we were wandering around a *trullo* house that had been converted into a little museum.

It had cute rounded rooms including a kitchen and even a little bakery.

I held up my phone and took another round of photos.

'Should I take one of you?' Romeo offered.

'Yes, please!' I handed him my phone and he snapped away.

'Later we should take some of you outside with the houses in the background.'

'Great thinking. Actually, I've been meaning to ask you something.' I turned to face him and reminded myself for the hundredth time not to look into his awesome eyes for more than two seconds. 'I picked up the photos earlier and there were only two. Do you know what happened to the others? Pretty sure I saw you taking more.'

'The photos?' Romeo's gaze dropped to the ground then shifted to the opposite side of the room. '*Sì*, I... I did take more but... I... they did not come out very well, so those were the best ones. *Scusa*. I will do better next time.'

'Could I see them anyway?'

'No,' he answered quickly. 'They... I have already deleted them. Would you like to buy some souvenirs?' Romeo asked.

'Yeah,' I said, wondering why he'd changed the subject so abruptly. Maybe I looked shit in them and he was trying not to hurt my feelings by letting me see how bad they were. 'I should get something for my bestie, Stella. She came to the Love Hotel too.'

'Really?' His eyes widened as he led me to the souvenirs. 'Which resort?'

'The Spanish one. They matched her with her ex.'

'*Cazzo!*'

'*Fuck*, right?' I smiled.

'You are a fast learner.' He smirked. 'I am thinking it was a mistake to teach you that word. And an even bigger one to repeat it just now.'

'Don't worry. I won't use it often. And only in the right context...' I grinned.

'*Va bene.*' He smiled and right on cue, the butterflies erupted in my stomach.

When I got that fluttery feeling at breakfast, I put it down to being hungry, but now I'd realised that it seemed to happen whenever Romeo smiled, laughed or said something funny, which was surprisingly often.

Happy Romeo was definitely much more fun to be around than *Grumpy Romeo* I'd met on the first day. The problem was that Happy Romeo was making my body react in a way that it absolutely shouldn't.

'So, they matched your friend with her ex? What happened?' Romeo said as I sifted through some keyrings to avoid looking at him.

'Yeah, but it all worked out well in the end. They're madly in love now.'

'*Fantastico!*'

'And I also know someone who works at the Love Hotel, Jasmine Palmer.'

'Jasmine is the Love Empress in Spain, correct?'

'That's the one.'

'I have not met her, but I have heard great things.'

'Yeah, she's amazing. And *she* fell in love with her colleague, Alejandro.'

'*Sì,* I read the article and it was discussed in our meetings. They have relaxed the rules about staff dating since then. But dating guests is forbidden.'

Romeo's gaze met mine and his eyes darkened. I swallowed

hard, wondering if somehow he'd noticed me perving over his muscles or staring at him for too long and was trying to remind me that nothing was ever gonna happen.

I mean, *doh*. Of course it wasn't.

I was with Edward. And even though me and Romeo seemed to be getting on better, I was sure that he still thought I was a stereotypical Brit who got pissed on planes and suffered from frequent bouts of verbal diarrhoea. So there was no way he'd be interested in me.

His warning message was received loud and clear though. I'd make sure that I stopped staring, but first I needed to reassure him that he didn't have to worry about me getting the wrong idea.

'I can imagine,' I said quickly. 'I mean, we come here to fall in love with our perfect match. Guests can't go around fancying their Love Alchemists. That'd be *crazy*!' My voice shot up several octaves, which definitely sounded suspect.

'Exactly,' he replied.

My eyes locked with his again and we both fell silent.

So much for not bloody staring at him.

'Anyway,' I broke the silence, then picked up some fridge magnets, 'I should definitely get something for Stella and my parents and my nan. She loves a good fridge magnet. Which one do you think looks nice?'

'Um.' Romeo scanned the display. 'How about that one?'

'This one?' I pointed at a colourful one.

'No, the white one.'

'This?' I went to pick up the magnet on the left of the display, before realising that wasn't the one he meant.

'Let me...'

Romeo reached for the other magnet at the same time I did and our fingers brushed against each other's, sending a jolt of electricity shooting through my veins.

He quickly jerked his hand back.

'Sorry, I...' I stuttered as I attempted to recover from the aftereffects. We'd only touched for a millisecond, but it might as well have been minutes. His skin was so soft and the brief sensation triggered some kind of reaction that caused every nerve ending in my body to spring to life.

'I... yeah.' I attempted to speak again even though my brain cells had turned to mush. 'I think that's nice. I'll get a few. I should get something for Edward too. Poor *Edward*.' I emphasised his name to remind my traitorous mind that he still existed. 'He's stuck at the hotel on his own, so the least I can do is bring him back a souvenir. And once I've bought this stuff, I should message him. See if he's feeling any better.'

A fresh wave of shame washed over me. We'd been here over an hour and I'd barely given Edward a second thought.

I wouldn't be surprised if when I checked my phone there was a text from the devil letting me know he'd reserved a special place in hell for me.

'That is a nice gesture. I hope Edward will appreciate it,' Romeo said, then ground his jaw. That was the second time he'd done that, which was strange. I still couldn't understand why he'd be angry at someone for being sick.

Edward, on the other hand, would definitely be pissed off with me if he knew I'd been having inappropriate thoughts about Romeo.

But it was fine. In just over half an hour, we'd meet up with the other guests so I wouldn't be alone with Romeo any more.

Then, after we'd had lunch, we'd head back to the hotel, I'd go and see Edward, who'd hopefully be feeling better and if he was, maybe we could go for a walk on the beach.

Yep. Good plan.

I might not have been proud of my thoughts since I'd arrived at this cute town, but from now on my mind would be purer than a bottle of holy water.

* * *

We'd just pulled up at reception. The rest of the time that we spent in Alberobello was great.

Once I'd bought my souvenirs, Romeo took some photos of me on my phone with the *trulli* houses as a backdrop and this time I checked they'd come out okay.

It was going to be weird to have a memory book with just photos of me on my own, but I still wanted to document the trip.

I'd thought about asking Romeo to join me in the photos, but the memory book was supposed to show the highlights with my match, not my Love Alchemist.

That'd reminded me to message Edward to check on him. He still hadn't replied, but he was probably resting.

After taking more photos, Romeo took me to visit a church. We bumped into some of the other guests there, so we'd hung out with them until it was time to meet the others, then we'd gone out for lunch.

Thankfully we were on a big table, so I was able to chat to other people instead of sitting at a table for two with Romeo which would've been awkward.

Once lunch was over we'd got back on the coach. During the journey I'd admired the views and replied to the messages Stella had sent asking for feedback on the designs she'd created so far for a romance library who'd recently hired her as their freelance graphic designer. Then, before I knew it, the driver was pulling into the hotel.

Everyone filed off the coach and as I stepped off, I saw

Romeo was chatting to the guests and checking that they'd had a good time.

Once he was alone, I went over.

'*Grazie* again for walking around with me today.'

'*Prego*. I know the day did not turn out as you hoped, but did you still enjoy it?'

'I had a great time, thanks to *you*,' I smiled. I was telling the truth. I'd smiled and laughed a lot today. Romeo wasn't as up himself as I'd first thought. He actually seemed like a decent guy.

'You know that I did not create the Alberobello or build the *trulli* houses, right?'

'No?' I clutched my chest in mock surprise. 'You mean you weren't born in the fourteenth century?'

'Surprisingly not,' he smirked.

'That's a shame, because I was going to ask you what anti-ageing cream you used to keep you looking so young and hot.'

Oh, fuck. I just called him hot.

'Sadly, I was only born in the *fifteenth* century,' he said, thankfully ignoring the fact that I'd just admitted that I thought he was fit. 'And you do not need anti-ageing cream. You look beautiful exactly how you are.'

My eyes popped and my brain froze.

Did he just call me beautiful?

'I, er... *grazie*,' I blushed. He was just being polite.

'Sorry,' he winced. 'I hope that did not make you uncomfortable. It is just... I have strong opinions about how society judges people just for getting older. People are beautiful and that beauty comes in many forms, not just the standardised image that is presented to us in the media. And now I am rambling,' he laughed. 'We were having a light-hearted conversation and I turned it into something heavy. Forget I said anything.' He waved his hand away dismissively. 'I am just glad you enjoyed the trip.'

'I ramble all the time.' I flashed him a reassuring smile. 'My superpower is that I always speak before I think. I'm surprised I can walk anywhere because my foot is permanently stuck in my mouth!' I cackled. 'I really enjoyed the trip, so thanks.'

We held each other's gaze again and I swear I felt a crackle of electricity pulsing between us. Must be the sunshine frying my brain.

The sound of a phone buzzing snapped us out of our trance.

'*Prego.*' Romeo pulled out his phone. 'I must get this.'

'Okay. I'm going to check on Edward.'

He nodded then waved, before walking off to take the call.

I headed to Edward's room. I'd asked Romeo earlier to give me his room number so that I could check on him without having to go to reception. For some reason he seemed reluctant, but I'd persisted and eventually, he'd given it to me.

When I got to the door I knocked, but there was no answer. I knocked again.

After trying a few more times, I phoned Edward, expecting to hear his ringtone through the door, but still no joy. Maybe he had it on silent so he could get some rest.

But what if something bad had happened? He could've passed out and be all alone.

I raced to reception. Someone must've spoken to him.

Just as I stepped into the main building, I saw Romeo walking towards me, his face looking harder than stone.

'Samantha,' he said and my stomach tightened. 'I was just coming to find you. It is about Edward.'

'I was heading to reception. I've been knocking on his door and calling for the last ten minutes but there's no answer.'

'That was what I was coming to tell you.' Romeo paused, like he was struggling to find the right words and my heartbeat rocketed.

'What's wrong?'

'He...' Romeo paused again. 'The reason Edward did not answer is because he has left.'

16

ROMEO

'What?' Samantha shouted and a sharp pain shot through my chest.

Clearly, she was just as shocked as I was.

When my phone rang during that conversation where I stupidly told Samantha I thought that she was beautiful (which was true, but an inappropriate thing to say about a guest), I was glad for the interruption.

But when I answered and heard the concern in Victoria's voice, I knew something was wrong.

Victoria told me that she had sent me several messages, but I had been so focused on the guests that I had not seen them. I went straight to see her and she told me the news.

'Come to Victoria's office and we will explain.'

'I... he's *gone*?' Samantha stuttered. 'Has he left for good? Was it something I said? Something I did?'

'No.' I shook my head quickly. 'You did nothing wrong. Here we are.' I knocked on Victoria's door.

'Come in,' she replied.

'Please.' I opened the door and gestured for her to go inside.

'Hello, Samantha.' Victoria got up from her desk and stretched out her hand. 'I'm Victoria, the Love Empress here. I'm sure Romeo has told you, unfortunately Edward's been called away.'

'*Called away*?' Samantha repeated.

'Yes. There's been a family emergency which meant he had to leave straightaway.'

'Oh, no! What happened? Is whoever it is okay?'

My heart squeezed. That one question said a lot about Samantha.

She immediately focused on the wellbeing of that person and not on what this meant for her and the rest of her holiday. She was a good person.

I had misjudged her when we first met. Samantha had a kind heart. I noticed how thoughtful she was earlier today in Alberobello when she took the time to carefully choose gifts for her friends and family.

'We don't know. He said it was a health-related issue, but didn't elaborate and it wasn't our place to push him on such a personal matter. He was probably upset and focused on getting back to London. We're hoping that once the situation has stabilised, he'll return and we'll assess the situation again then, but in the meantime, this obviously presents some challenges for *your* time here...' Her voice trailed off.

'But I've paid to have a match! I've spent all my savings coming here. And taken two weeks' holiday.'

'I completely understand. The Love Hotel takes both your financial and emotional investment very seriously, so we'll do everything we can to rectify the situation. And you will receive compensation for any inconvenience.'

Samantha was right to be upset. I was glad that at least she would get some money back.

'I know that you can't control if guests have personal issues.' Samantha softened her voice. 'It's just frustrating, that's all.'

'I agree.' Victoria nodded sympathetically. 'I appreciate that you'll need time to process this, but in order for me to consider the options available, I need to ask: would returning to London early be a possibility? Then perhaps you could return for the full two weeks again once Edward is able?'

My eyes bulged. I had not had the chance to tell Victoria about my earlier conversation with Edward. If she heard about the disgusting things he had said about Samantha she would not even consider inviting him back to the hotel.

'No,' Samantha sighed. 'I've already booked the time off. The company made arrangements to cover my holiday and I wouldn't get the time back. If I went home now, I'd just be sitting around doing nothing. I don't get much annual leave, so I can't afford to waste it. I definitely couldn't take another two weeks off anytime soon.'

'I see. I needed to ask.' Victoria took a deep breath.

My shoulders loosened. In my opinion, the only reason Edward should be allowed to return would be to apologise to Samantha face to face.

'This has never happened before, so forgive us for not having all the answers right now,' Victoria continued. 'For all we know, Edward could call to say everything's fine and be back here tomorrow. We just don't know. So perhaps in the meantime, you'd consider staying? We'll keep in contact with Edward to see if there's any developments we can share. What do you think?'

'So, if I stayed, I'd still go on the trips, but by myself?'

'Essentially, yes,' Victoria confirmed. 'But you'd still have the other guests around you because this week it's couples activities in a group setting and of course, Romeo will be there, so you wouldn't be completely alone.'

I smiled and nodded to help reassure her, but inside I was conflicted.

Of course, I was disappointed for Samantha. She had come here with such high expectations and her experience at the hotel so far had not been a good one.

I wanted to do whatever was needed to make it better, but I was concerned.

I had enjoyed spending time with Samantha, more than I should have. With Biscotti's health scare, I had not been feeling great these past few days. But today I had laughed a lot. More than I had with any woman in a long time. Which was probably why I slipped up earlier and called her beautiful.

Alberobello was a short and low-intimacy excursion, but the trips scheduled for the rest of the week would not be as straightforward.

This was a couples holiday and everything was carefully planned to stimulate romance. That was why spending so much time with a guest that I was starting to realise that I found attractive would not be ideal.

'Okay. It's not like I really have a choice,' Samantha huffed.

'I admit, the options right now are limited, but like I said, I'll be speaking to management and seeing what else we can do. Okay?'

'Yeah,' Samantha sighed, then stood up to leave.

'Thank you again for your patience and understanding. Romeo will let you know as soon as we hear from Edward.'

'Thanks.' Samantha gave us both a weak smile before leaving. 'See you later.'

A few moments after Samantha left, Victoria squeezed her eyes shut and shook her head with disappointment.

'I feel so bad for her. Samantha seems lovely and although I'm sorry that Edward has some family issues, he's put us in an impossible situation. If it got out that a guest spent the holiday without a match, it'd damage our reputation. People won't care that his absence wasn't our fault. They'll just see an opportunity to tear us down.'

I understood Victoria's concerns about the hotel's reputation, but I was more worried about Samantha.

Whatever was happening with Edward's family was of course terrible, but I still did not like the guy.

The way he spoke about her was disrespectful. And if he had to leave, he could have called or messaged Samantha in the taxi or airport to tell her personally.

He had not even attempted to contact me. The only reason Victoria found out that he was leaving was because the receptionist called to alert her that he had requested a car to take him to the airport and she knew it was not in the schedule.

Perhaps I was being harsh and unsympathetic, but I just did not trust him.

When I relayed my conversation with Edward this morning and told Victoria about his behaviour at dinner, her face fell.

'I agree that is unacceptable.' She blew out an exasperated breath. 'But if he had stuff on his mind about his family, perhaps that's why he was drinking heavily. We still need to give him the opportunity to explain himself and when he returns, we can have a serious conversation with him, and take it from there.'

'If it were up to me, I would tell him not to come back. He does not seem interested in Samantha.'

'I understand your concerns, but we have to do our due diligence. It's not unusual for a guest to believe their match is not their type, but as we've seen, when they spend more time together their perceptions can completely change. We have to persevere and show Samantha that the hotel has done everything possible to help.'

As much as I hated to admit it, Victoria was right.

'I believe that Samantha understands that it is not the hotel's fault. How we deal with the situation now though is important,' I said. 'We will have to work even harder to make sure she is happy.'

'Absolutely. Obviously, I'll need you to make an extra special effort with her during every trip so that she doesn't feel left out.'

'Of course.'

'Do you have any other suggestions?' Victoria asked.

'I know that she likes our prosecco, so perhaps we can send a special bottle to her room with some chocolates?'

'Good idea.'

'Actually, we can do better. I will call the spa to check their availability for a full-body massage and facial. A full pampering session will make her feel good, then when she returns, we will have the prosecco and chocolates waiting in her room. With a bouquet of flowers,' I added. 'And a handwritten card apologising for the inconvenience. It cannot compare to having her match here, but perhaps it will help.'

'Those are all excellent ideas!' Victoria beamed.

'I will make the arrangements straightaway.'

'Thank you, Romeo. You're a credit to the team.'

My chest filled with pride. One of the many things I liked about working at the Love Hotel was that initiative was appreciated by the management. I hoped that Victoria would remember this when I applied for the opportunity in California.

'*Prego.*'

'Please do everything you can to make Samantha happy. No expense spared. Do whatever it takes. I have no idea how things will go with Edward, particularly given everything you've told me about him. We can't control that, but we *can* ensure that Samantha is well looked after. We need to make sure she leaves here with a smile on her face and with nothing but praise for the hotel and our team. Understood?'

'*Si.*'

As I left Victoria's office, I swallowed hard, pushing away the illicit thoughts creeping into my mind about ways that I could make Samantha *happy*.

But like I had said to her earlier today, relationships with guests were forbidden.

I was Samantha's Love Alchemist and I could never be anything more.

Victoria, the hotel and the entire team were depending on me.

And I would not let them down.

17

SAMMIE

As I walked back to my room, I tried to fight back the tears.

I couldn't believe this was happening.

When Romeo initially said Edward had left, the first thing I thought was that it was because of me, so as awful as it sounded, it was a relief that it wasn't personal. But when I found out someone was ill, my heart went out to him and his loved ones.

It wasn't Edward's fault that he'd been called away. Although part of me thought he could've at least sent me a message, I supposed when something like that happened, his priority was obviously to get back home and be with his family.

But just because it wasn't my fault, it didn't stop me from feeling like shit.

Once I was in my room, I crashed on my bed and called Stella.

'Hey!' she answered. 'You back from the excursion? Thanks for your feedback earlier. I sent the designs over to the Romance Library and they loved them!'

'I knew they would,' I said, mustering up as much enthusiasm as I could.

'Wait, what's wrong? You don't sound like yourself.'

'Edward's left!' I blurted out.

'What the hell? What happened?'

After I'd finished explaining, Stella exhaled loudly.

'Shit. I'm so sorry. At least you'll get some money back and you'll get to stay.'

'I suppose. I'm not thrilled about spending the rest of the trip surrounded by a bunch of loved-up couples. But I was really looking forward to seeing more of Italy and this hotel is pretty amazing so I'm not ready to leave.'

'You're making the right decision to stay. There's still a chance he'll come back soon. Give him a few more days. How was it today by yourself?'

When I'd messaged Stella on the coach, apart from saying it was much better than I thought it would be, I didn't go into detail about my time in Alberobello. I'd just focused on giving her feedback on her designs instead.

'I didn't end up being alone in the end. Romeo offered to walk around with me.'

'The hot Love Alchemist?'

'My very off-limits Love Alchemist, yes. He was actually really sweet. Not as grumpy and arrogant as I thought.'

'That's good! I'm glad you weren't alone.'

'I was too, but I felt bad that he had to babysit me. Bet he's not happy about being lumbered with me again whilst Edward's away.'

'It's his job. I'm sure he doesn't mind.'

'I...' Just as I was about to tell Stella that I was worried about the sparks I'd felt, there was a knock at the door. It was for the best. I already felt bad about fancying Romeo, so I didn't want Stella to think I was a terrible person too. 'Hold on a sec.'

I jumped off the bed and headed to the door.

When I opened it and saw Romeo standing there, my eyes popped.

'*Ciao*, Samantha.' He flashed that hypnotic smile again and my stomach shamelessly flip-flopped like a dolphin on happy pills. 'Do you have plans right now?'

'Er... no?'

'In that case, you have a luxury massage and facial booked in the spa, courtesy of the hotel. We are very sorry for what you have had to go through. I know pampering cannot solve the issue, but I hope that it will make you feel better. What do you think?'

'Hell, yeah!' I shouted.

'So, you hate the idea?' Romeo laughed and those pesky flutters started again.

'Hours of pampering in a luxury spa? It sounds *horrendous*!' I joked. 'But if I say no, you'll get in trouble, so yet again, I'll agree, just to help you out.'

'*Grazie*. How will I ever repay you for your kindness?'

'I'm sure I could think of something.' I winked then slapped my forehead. 'Sorry,' I winced. That sounded sexual and as I reminded myself earlier, my mind was supposed to only contain pure, moral thoughts. 'That came out wrong. Foot-in-mouth-itus strikes again! Can you give me ten minutes?'

'Sure. Go to the spa whenever you are ready. Your Relaxation Facilitator will be there waiting for you. Enjoy your treatments.'

'*Grazie*! I will.' I shut the door, let out a happy squeal then ran back to the phone. 'Stell? You still there?'

'Oh my God, was that your Romeo?'

'He's not *my* Romeo! But yes, that was my Love Alchemist.'

'His accent is fucking dreamy! And you two seemed to get on well. Do you have any photos of him?'

'No, course not! Why would I? I'm here for *Edward*.'

'Oh, yeah. I forgot about him. Just like *he* forgot about *you*. Arsehole.'

'Stell!' I gasped. 'You can't call him that. He's got a family emergency! His poor granny could be ill in hospital. Where's your heart?'

'It only takes two seconds to message to let you know.'

'He was probably stressed because he was racing to the airport.'

'*Whatever.* Still think he's rude. I don't like it when people don't treat my bestie with the respect she deserves. But men who organise a massage and facial for her *and* have a knicker-melting, sexy Italian accent get a big thumbs up!'

'He's just doing his job!' I rolled my eyes. 'His boss Victoria probably ordered him to butter me up so I don't go on social media and rant. Romeo's just the messenger. I'd better go. Glad that the designs were a hit with your new client too.'

'Thanks. Call me tomorrow, or when you have any news on *Evasive Edward.*'

As I hung up, my shoulders loosened.

Being left alone by my perfect match wasn't how I would've chosen my day to start. But being indulged with a luxury massage and facial wasn't a bad way to end it.

18

SAMMIE

It was now Tuesday and I was in my room getting ready to go on today's excursion to a secret destination.

There was still no news from Edward, but right now I was too relaxed to care. The massage and facial Romeo had arranged for me yesterday was out of this world.

My Relaxation Facilitator (another crazy job title) had magic hands. During those treatments, all of the stress and worries about being here on my own, what would happen with Edward and everything else melted away.

Once my treatments ended, I floated back to my room. And you could've knocked me over with a feather when I saw the bottle of my new favourite prosecco chilling in an ice bucket, next to a box of fancy chocolates, a bouquet of stunning flowers and a card from Victoria and Romeo apologising for the inconvenience.

Talk about knowing how to make a girl feel special.

Romeo had also called to ask if I'd prefer to have room service for dinner, which was kind because I didn't fancy eating alone in the restaurant.

After I'd finished gushing about how amazing the spa was and thanking Romeo, he'd said the chef could make whatever I wanted so I'd ordered spaghetti Bolognese and gelato.

One benefit of Edward leaving was that I didn't have anyone judging my portion sizes. And eating in my room meant I didn't have to worry about getting tomato sauce down my chin. Every cloud had a silver lining.

Yep. That pamper sesh worked wonders. I felt much more positive.

Other than a quick wave, I hadn't spoken to Romeo this morning. Thanks to the massage and sleeping on the bed that was handcrafted by angels, I'd slept through my alarm so hadn't even had time to grab breakfast at the restaurant, so I'd eaten a banana from the fruit bowl in my room instead.

Just as I was about to leave, my phone rang.

'Hi, Jasmine,' I said, surprised that she was calling me directly. Normally we spoke through Stella.

'Hi, Sammie, how are you doing? I heard what happened with your match. I'm so sorry. Fingers crossed he'll be back soon.'

'Yeah.' I blew out a breath. 'I was a bit apprehensive about going on yesterday's trip alone and the trip today, but Romeo's been really sweet.'

'*Romeo?*' she said, her voice tinged with concern. 'I didn't realise he was still there.'

'Why wouldn't he be?'

'Last time Victoria spoke about him, she said there'd been a couple of *incidents* with guests.'

'Incidents? Like what?'

'I shouldn't really say anything. Especially when I don't know him personally.'

'I thought we were friends? I promise whatever you say will stay between us. Well, and Stella too.'

'Okay.' She let out a sigh. I knew Jasmine was professional, but I wanted to know more. 'I heard that Romeo can be overly flirtatious with the guests.'

'What? Like sleazy?'

'No, no. Nothing like that. If the Love Hotel thought he was dangerous, there's no way that they'd keep him. The safety of guests is paramount. No, more just some complaints from male matches saying he was flirting with their partners. And there was an incident last month with a woman that Victoria didn't go into. Not sure what happened but he's still there so it's probably fine. All I'm saying is just be careful. I don't want him leading you on or anything.'

'Thanks, but I'm here for Edward. Not to hook up with my Love Alchemist.'

'Good. Single employees are allowed to date, but Love Alchemists hooking up with matches is an absolute no-no. Guests pay a lot of money, so the last thing they want is for their match to run off with the staff. That'd be a disaster!'

Which was exactly why I had shut down any attraction I felt towards Romeo. Especially now it seemed like he flirted with every guest.

'Got it. It's not relevant anyway. I'm sure Edward will be back soon and we can get back to building a relationship together.'

'That's the spirit! I'm keeping everything crossed for you. And if you have any queries or concerns, just call. I know how much you've been looking forward to going to the Love Hotel so I want to make sure you're looked after.'

'Thanks. I'd better go,' I said as I stepped out of my room door. 'The coach is leaving in less than five minutes for today's excursion.'

'Okay. Have fun!'

I ended the call, then raced to reception. After climbing the coach steps, I found an empty seat and sat down. Seconds later a delicious scent surrounded me.

'*Ciao*, Samantha.' I looked up and saw Romeo in the aisle.

Jesus, he looked...

Never mind. It didn't matter how he looked.

I had no intention of noticing the fact that his olive skin was glowing, how neat his dark beard was or how his branded shirt clung to what I was sure was a very muscular chest.

Nope.

I definitely hadn't noticed any of that at all.

'Hi!' I said a little too enthusiastically. 'You okay?'

'I am good,' he replied in a ridiculously delicious accent which once again had *zero* effect on me whatsoever. 'You did not come for breakfast this morning.'

'I overslept. I was so relaxed after the spa yesterday. And what do you put in the mattress and pillows? And do you pump sleeping gas into the rooms? I've been here three nights now, and I've never slept better. Don't tell the management, but I'm considering stuffing a pillow in my suitcase to take home!'

'I am glad you had a good rest.' Romeo chuckled and the sound made my body... *Nope.* The sound of his deep, gravelly sexy laugh did absolutely nothing to me. *Nada.*

And if I knew the Italian for *nothing*, I would've added that to my denial list too.

Jasmine had just warned me to be careful with Romeo and I was going to listen.

'The best!' I replied. 'Not ideal for waking up though, but *sorry, not sorry!*'

Romeo laughed again. I liked that he appreciated my sense of humour. Not everyone did.

'Today we are going to a place which involves a lot of walking, so you will need energy. I have something that I think you will like. One moment.'

Romeo disappeared down the aisle towards the back of the coach.

Seconds later he was clutching a takeaway coffee cup and a small white box.

'Here.' He handed the box to me, then pulled the fancy chrome tray table down from the seat next to me and rested the coffee cup in the holder.

I quickly opened the box, eager to see what was inside.

'Wow, what's this?' It looked like a circular shortcrust pastry pie which was roughly the same size as a cupcake.

'This is a *pasticciotto* – it is very typical to eat for breakfast or a mid-morning snack in Puglia. Inside is like a vanilla egg custard. The Cuisine Champions said you like a cappuccino, but I have orange juice in the fridge if you prefer?'

My heart inflated and those crazy butterflies erupted in my stomach yet again.

'You did all this for *me*?' My eyes widened, then I cringed. It was a dumb thing to ask considering he'd just handed me the cappuccino and dessert box and not someone else. 'I mean, that was really kind of you, *grazie*.'

'*Prego*. We like to take care of all of our guests at the Love Hotel.'

'Oh... course!' I added, feeling like an even bigger plonker.

He was just doing his job. I wasn't getting special treatment. Maybe this was all part of his flirty routine. It was still kind of him though.

'I hope you enjoy. If you need anything else, I will be at the front of the coach.'

'Great!' I squeaked. 'Thanks again.'

Romeo continued up the aisle, checking on the guests, and I tore my gaze away and back to the pastry in front of me.

I lifted it out of the box, then up to my mouth before taking a bite.

'Oh my God,' I groaned a little too loudly. It was bloody delicious.

What was it about the food in Italy? How did everything taste so good?

I inhaled the pastry so fast, I was glad that the couple adjacent to me were deep in conversation, so they didn't see me gobbling it up.

Whilst Romeo chatted to other guests, I snuck to the back to see if there were more pastries left, but there was just some fruit.

For the rest of the journey, I took in the sights from the window and pulled out my Kindle to start reading a new romance book. I'd barely read two chapters before Romeo announced that we'd arrived at our destination. Apparently wherever we were going had restricted parking, so we needed to walk the rest of the way.

I gasped as I took in the magnificent views in front of me. And this time I wasn't talking about Romeo's face and body.

'*Benvenuti a* Matera,' he said. 'This is not just the oldest city in Italy or Europe: it is one of the three oldest continuously inhabited cities in the world.'

'Wow,' a lady opposite me said.

The city was carved into the limestone cliffs and was breathtaking.

'Instead of using a guided tour, we have prepared a list of recommended places, because we think it is better for you to discover the city together.' Romeo handed out a glossy brochure and tickets which I assumed gave everyone entrance to key sites. 'But if you get lost or would like recommendations, call me.'

'Will do!' a lady, whose name I think was Kim, said.

'Edward, Samantha's match, has unfortunately been called to attend a family emergency in London. Hopefully he will return soon. But in the meantime, sadly Samantha will be stuck with me accompanying her around the city.'

'Lucky lady!' Kim said and her partner's eyes bulged. 'Only joking, sweetheart.' She pecked him on the cheek affectionately.

'This place is stunning,' I said as we wandered down the cobbled streets. 'I've never heard of it before.'

'It is another UNESCO site and has been featured in many movies.'

'Yeah? Which ones?'

'*Wonder Woman* and the James Bond movie *No Time to Die*.'

'I've seen both of those. Wait!' I shouted out as my brain scanned the different scenes in my memory. 'Is this the place where James Bond drives his Aston Martin down the streets at the start of the film?'

'*Sì*.'

'No way! Never did I think when I was watching it that one day I'd be here!'

'Life is that way sometimes.'

'I get excited when I see landmarks like Tower Bridge or Big Ben in films because it's my home city, so everything's familiar, but now I can say I've visited an *international* film location. Very cool,' I smiled. 'Have you ever been to London?'

'*Sì*. My brother, Giorgio, lives there. And my mother's family live in Kent.'

'I didn't realise you had a brother.'

'I have a brother and a sister. Both younger. My sister, Mirabella, is in Rome and my brother lives with his boyfriend in a place called Brixton.'

'That's not far from where I live!' I said.

'Really?'

'Yep! I'm in Tooting. It's literally a short Tube ride away. Small world!'

'It is. London is a great city, but the weather...' He winced. 'I do not know how Giorgio does it. After living somewhere with such good weather and beaches all of my life, I could not live somewhere that is so cold and grey. I love the sunshine too much.'

'Can't argue with you there!' I laughed.

'What do you do in London for work, Samantha?'

'I'm a receptionist for a pharmaceutical company.'

'That is interesting. Does your company make anything exciting?'

'You mean like Viagra?' I blurted out and Romeo's eyes bulged.

Jeez. My foot-in-mouth levels had already peaked and we'd only just arrived.

'No, strangely that was not what I was thinking, but now that you have mentioned it, do they?' He raised an eyebrow.

'No. Our bestselling products are haemorrhoids cream and diarrhoea tablets.'

'I see,' he smiled.

'Admit it. You're disappointed about the Viagra.' I laughed. I shouldn't have mentioned it again, but I couldn't help myself. Strangely, despite my inability to say things I shouldn't, Romeo seemed really chill about it.

'It is not something I have ever needed...' His voice trailed off and our eyes locked.

Yeah. I kind of imagined that Romeo wouldn't have any problems getting it up. Not that I was imagining his cock or anything, because that would be inappropriate and I was an absolute angel.

'Lucky for you,' I smiled. 'And your girlfriend, of course.'

'I do not have a girlfriend.'

'Wait, what?' I stopped in my tracks. 'So you're in charge of helping people like me find love, but you haven't found your own Mrs Right?'

'I prefer to be single,' he said.

'So you can be *ready to mingle*?' I teased, my thoughts returning to my earlier conversation with Jasmine.

'No, because...' He paused.

'It's okay,' I jumped in. 'I shouldn't have asked. I was just making conversation.'

'It is fine. I am just not looking for a relationship. Bringing other couples together is enough for me. Did you hear anything from Edward this morning?'

Hearing his name made my stomach twist. Not because I missed him. We weren't together long and when we were, I didn't feel the connection I'd hoped for.

I wasn't giving up though. When Edward got back, I'd still give it my best shot.

'Nope.'

'I am sorry.'

'It's not your fault.'

'I know, but you said he was your dream man, so I wanted it to work.'

'I didn't say he was my *dream man*,' I added quickly. 'I said he ticked a lot of boxes. On paper he has the qualities I was looking for. He doesn't seem like the fuckboys I normally go for, so that's an improvement.'

'A fuckboy is a man who has many women?' His brows furrowed.

'Yeah. Like a *player*. It can also mean a man who doesn't respect women and messes them around.'

'Understood.'

'I know Edward isn't like that, but I was just hoping for more of a... spark. Y'know, like when you look at someone and get those butterflies.'

Romeo's eyes met mine and right on cue, the flutter of a thousand butterflies filled my stomach and goosebumps erupted across my skin.

I warned my belly to calm the hell down, but the disobedient fucker ignored me and kept fluttering anyway.

'I... I understand.' Romeo still held my gaze. 'But sometimes, it is not all about fireworks. Sometimes the attraction takes time to grow. And sparks can be dangerous. Sometimes when there is too much fire, you can get burnt.'

As his eyes flicked to the caves beside us, I wondered if he was talking from personal experience. Had Romeo had a bad breakup? I couldn't see how. No woman in their right mind would kick him out of bed.

'Yep. I've been burnt a lot. I've thought about giving up on finding the one so many times, but then I look at my parents and they remind me that true love really exists. They've been married for almost forty years and they're like newlyweds. Seeing them kiss and hug used to make me cringe, but now it gives me hope.'

'That is beautiful.'

'Yeah. *That's* the kind of love I want. And that was what I was hoping to find when I came to the Love Hotel...'

Romeo's face fell and I felt bad. I knew it wasn't down to him or the hotel what had happened to me, so I hated that he felt guilty.

'Perhaps there is still time for the hotel to work its magic.' He gave a half smile.

Fingers crossed that Romeo was right...

19

ROMEO

If there was one thing I hated it was lies.

They caused pain, hurt and disappointment.

Ever since my ex crushed my heart five years ago, I vowed to always do my best to tell the truth. Which was why when I told Samantha that I believed there was still hope for the hotel to work its magic, I felt bad, because I did not believe it.

Victoria and I had tried contacting Edward several times and he had not returned a single call or message.

Perhaps he was with his family, but from what I had seen of him, he did not seem like a caring person.

Samantha said she did not think that Edward was a *fuckboy*, but that was because she did not know how disrespectful he had been towards her.

When she said that she did not feel that spark with Edward, relief washed over me because I thought she liked him and I knew she deserved better.

And when Samantha spoke about butterflies, my body immediately reacted. I had noticed that when Samantha was nearby a warm feeling flooded my stomach, which was a sensation that I had not felt in a very long time.

For the next few hours we wandered down the cobbled streets of Matera, visiting Palombaro Lungo, the city's historic underground cistern where they used to store all the water for the city and the Church of Santa Maria de Idris, which dated back to the fourteenth century and was carved into the rock face. I loved how Samantha's face lit up whenever I told her something about the history or she saw something interesting.

Just as we had finished grabbing lunch, my phone rang.

'*Ciao*, Kim,' I said. It was one of the guests asking if I could show them the best spot to do some hiking with great views. '*Sì*. Tell me where you are and I will find you and take you to Ponte Tibetano della Gravina.' Kim explained where she was and sent a pin to my phone.

'I will show Kim and her match, Timothy, a special place,' I said to Samantha.

Disappointment washed over me. I was sad that I would no longer be alone with Samantha, but that was ridiculous. I barely knew her. And she was a guest. I should be relieved that I now had a reason *not* to be alone with her.

Once we met up with Kim and Timothy, the four of us hiked down into the ravine, crossed the suspension bridge then hiked up the other side. I was glad that they all seemed fine with the heights.

'We just have to climb a little bit to get to the old caves with the best views,' I said as I scaled the rock.

'Up *there*?' Samantha's eyes widened. 'Looks a bit slippery.'

'Your shoes are good and it is safe. You will be fine.'

'Mind if we go ahead?' Timothy asked as he lifted Kim up. 'We're excited to see it.'

'Go for it!' Samantha said. 'We'll catch you up.'

'Would you like me to help you?' I asked.

'Please. Just to be on the safe side.'

I stretched out my hand and Samantha took it. As her palm connected with mine, a bolt of electricity shot through me.

I felt the same sensation in Alberobello yesterday in the gift shop when our fingers had brushed.

Samantha's eyes locked with mine. Had she felt it too?

We stood there, with our hands interlocked, neither of us moving.

She had very beautiful light brown eyes.

My gaze travelled down to her full lips. I wondered how they tasted.

'We found it!' Kim called out, breaking the spell.

What the hell was wrong with me?

It did not matter what I thought of Edward. I was not the kind of man to take someone else's lady. And especially not one that was a guest.

It did not matter that Edward was away. Samantha was his match, which meant she was strictly off limits.

And the sooner I understood that, the better.

20

SAMMIE

Earlier I'd spoken to Romeo about sparks and butterflies. But those sensations didn't compare to the fireworks I felt when he held my hand to help me up the rock.

Fuck.

I thought I was worried about slipping, but when our palms connected, my brain short-circuited and my knees weakened. The heat from his hand lit my body up from the inside and when our eyes locked, it was like I was under some kind of spell.

It was a good thing that Kim shouted out, otherwise I'd still be staring into his eyes now.

This was very, very *bad*.

I was not a cheater.

Although me and Edward weren't officially dating, we were still supposed to be together, so I couldn't let these crazy feelings for Romeo swim around my mind.

Romeo was just eye candy. Yeah, he'd been kind to me, but only because he was protecting the hotel's reputation.

I couldn't let my attraction to him cloud my judgement.

Romeo was the kind of guy you went to for orgasms, not for everlasting love.

I mean, could the man be any more of a red flag?

Not only was he a hotter version of the good-looking guys who always ended up breaking my heart, based on what Jasmine had heard and what I'd seen he was also a flirt. The guy was called *Romeo* for God's sake.

Romeo by name, Romeo by nature, right?

Ordinarily, flirting wouldn't be a crime, but at the Love Hotel, unless it was with your match, it was bad news.

I needed to remember that saying: *insanity is repeating the same actions and expecting a different result.*

I couldn't keep being attracted to the same guys. I had to break the cycle.

Anyway, what the hell was I talking about? It wouldn't even get to the stage of Romeo fucking me over because he wasn't interested in me.

'The views are incredible!' Kim said as she poked her head out from the cave.

I strode towards her and Timothy, making sure my gaze was firmly fixed on the path in front of me and *not* on Romeo.

When we reached the cave and saw the views of Matera on the opposite side of the ravine, I gasped.

'Bloody hell!' I said as I reached for my phone and started snapping away. 'I don't know if I've ever seen anything so beautiful.'

The view stretching out in front of me didn't even look real. The sky was perfectly blue and the limestone buildings looked like the most intricate historical painting hanging in a museum. It really was incredible.

'Want me to take a photo of you two?' Kim asked.

'Oh, no,' I jumped in. 'Romeo's only babysitting me. The memory book is for photos with my match, Edward.'

'But Edward's not here and Romeo is.' Kim raised her eyebrow.

'And a memory book is for memories of this whole trip, right?' Timothy added. 'This will be a pretty phenomenal memory, so it'd be a shame not to capture it.'

'Course. It's just... it's better if you take a photo of me on my own. Romeo doesn't want to be roped into it. He's already helping me out enough.'

Sweat pooled on my forehead. This was so damn awkward.

'Go on, Romeo!' Kim insisted. 'Be a gentleman and get in the photo with Samantha so she doesn't look lonely.'

Romeo hesitated and his eyes darted from me to Kim and Timothy.

'We should take a photo of the four of us together, no?' Romeo said.

Oh. Seeing as he was supposed to be such a flirt, I thought he wouldn't have missed a chance to snuggle up in a photo. Clearly I wasn't his type, which was fine.

'Spoilsport!' Kim said. 'Come on then.' She stood next to me and I thought Romeo would stand on the other side, but instead he stood next to Timothy.

Jeez. Did I have BO or something? I didn't realise the idea of being close to me was so repulsive that he had to create as much distance as possible.

'Say cheese!' Kim said as I plastered on a smile.

After the stuff I'd heard, I should be grateful that he'd acted so professionally.

Jasmine warned me to be careful around him which was what I was doing. And so far Romeo had been the perfect chaperone. He hadn't been flirtatious or shown any interest in me, which was exactly what I'd wanted.

So why did I feel disappointed?

21

ROMEO

'The views are amazing!' Samantha said as she took in her surroundings. We were at Belvedere di Piazza Giovanni Pascoli, a popular terrace in Matera.

After we had finished taking photos with Kim and Timothy, I had invited them to join us (I wanted to create some distance between me and Samantha) but they said that they wanted to spend some time alone.

'*Sì*, it is another great place to get a good view of the cave houses.'

'It's really pretty. Is this where you take all the girls then?' Samantha grinned.

'No.' I rolled my eyes. 'Why do you think that I have had a lot of women?'

That was the second time today that she had made a reference to me being a womaniser or as she would call it a *fuckboy* and I did not understand why.

'Er, *hello*. You're not exactly ugly and no offence, but your name's Romeo, so...'

'Wow. Remind me to add "I am not exactly ugly" to the top of the list of my best qualities.' The corner of my mouth twitched.

'Well, I'm not about to say you're good-looking, am I? If I said that, your head would never fit inside these caves!' She laughed and I shook my head whilst I tried to fight the smile that had formed on my lips.

'I did not choose my name, you know that, right?' I cocked an unimpressed eyebrow.

'No?' She did a dramatic gasp. 'You mean you didn't come into the world and demand that you be given a name which implies that you love the ladies?'

'Strangely not. It was of course my father that chose it. Originally he wanted me to be called Casanova.'

'No way!' Samantha laughed as I led her away from the terrace. We would return here later to watch the sunset with the rest of the group. In the meantime there were more places to explore, so we continued walking.

'It is true, but Mamma said no. She was not keen on Romeo either because like you, she assumed it meant a man who was a womaniser, but Papà told her that it was given to someone who came from Rome and because that was where I was conceived, she thought it would be fitting. But I still think that Papà chose it because he wanted me to follow in his footsteps in all aspects.'

'So was *he* a womaniser?'

'Unfortunately.'

'But you're *not*?' Samantha pressed.

'Believe it or not, I was happy to just stay with one woman for the rest of my life, but then she betrayed me.'

I squeezed my eyes shut, partly because it was a painful memory, but mainly because it was not really something that I should discuss with a guest.

'What happened?' Concern washed over Samantha's face.

'Sorry. I'm just being nosy. Tell me to mind my own business if you want.'

'It is okay.'

Maybe if I told her, she would realise I was not the man she seemed to think I was. Her opinion should not matter to me, but for some reason it did.

Perhaps it was because I had a feeling that Edward was not a good man and I wanted to show her that not all men were dishonest.

'I had a girlfriend, Greta.' I took a deep breath. Just saying her name made anger simmer beneath my skin. 'We started dating when I was twenty-four. It was serious. Well, I thought it was. We dated for four years and I had an opportunity to travel to the US for three months as part of an exchange programme. It was an opportunity of a lifetime, but Greta said she did not want me to go. She wanted us to settle down. Move in together and think about marriage and children. I loved her, so even though I really wanted to go, I gave up the opportunity because I wanted to make her happy. Then I worked night and day to afford the apartment that she wanted.'

'Where were you working?'

'In hotels, mainly. The company I worked for was part of a chain with locations around Italy. They asked me to cover some shifts in Rome and I accepted. The money was good because I would be doing lots of late nights. I was supposed to work for a week, but in the end they only needed me for six days, so I came home early to surprise Greta. But *I* was the one that got the surprise.'

'Oh, no.' Samantha's face fell. 'What happened?'

'When I got home, she was in bed. With my best friend.'

'Fuck!' Samantha's jaw dropped. 'That's awful.'

'It was the worst. When I asked him to look out for her whilst

I was away, I did not expect that he would do *that*. I trusted them and they both betrayed me. Later I realised that Terzo – the man who had been my friend since we were seven years old – did it deliberately.'

'What? Why?'

'He was convinced that I had done something with his girlfriend. She used to talk a lot to me and ask for advice and he did not like that. He was convinced that the reason she broke up with him was because she was in love with me. I told him I had done nothing to encourage her and had no interest in her, but he did not believe me. So the minute my back was turned, he slept with my girlfriend as revenge for something I had not even done.'

'What a dick.' Samantha shook her head.

'*Sì*. I found it hard to deal with the betrayal, so I did not go to work and I lost my job and so all of the money I had saved went straight to pay the rent and bills and I gave up the opportunity of a lifetime all because of a woman. Just because I wanted to make her happy. That is why I cannot make that mistake again.'

'I'm so sorry that happened to you,' Samantha said sympathetically. I had definitely shared more than I should with a guest, but she was easy to talk to. 'I've been cheated on too and it's the worst.'

'It is. So going back to your original comment, it is true that when my ex cheated, once I had dragged myself out of my hole, there was a point that I did sleep around. I trusted Greta. I thought that we were forever and I thought, if I cannot trust her, then I cannot trust anyone. So I just had one-night stands. I did not want to ever get close to anyone again.'

'But you can't stay like that forever, right?'

'Perhaps not forever, but certainly for the next few years. Being single works for me. I am too busy working to have time to date anyway. And there is also an exciting career opportunity coming up and it is important that I stay focused for that.'

'Ooh, that sounds amazing! What is it?' Samantha's eyes widened with interest.

'The Love Hotel is expanding. Soon they will open a resort in California, which will be their biggest and most prestigious and if I continue to do well here, Victoria said that there is a chance that I could apply to work there for a few months.'

'That's amazing!'

'*Sì*. I have always wanted to work abroad. It is my dream. They will open applications soon and because there are only three Love Hotel resorts, I have a good chance of succeeding. Once the business expands, it will become almost impossible, so seizing the opportunity now is important. That is why it is easier to be by myself, so that I am free and do not have to answer to anyone. This time I will not let anything stand in my way.'

'Fair enough,' Samantha nodded.

'Come,' I said, changing the subject. I needed to steer the conversation back to professional ground. 'There is one more place I want to show you before we meet the others.'

'Okey dokey!' Samantha chirped and I couldn't help but smile at her interesting saying. I had noticed I smiled a lot when I was around her. 'Lead the way.'

22

SAMMIE

I slid my feet into my sandals, then headed down to the restaurant for breakfast.

It was now Thursday and there was still no word from Edward.

Since he'd left three days ago, I'd sent him loads of texts and voice notes asking if he was okay, but hadn't heard anything back.

I knew he'd seen the first few WhatsApp messages, but the one I'd sent yesterday was still unread.

I'd been trying my best to be understanding, but I was starting to lose patience. I totally got that he was going through a hard time, but couldn't he at least have sent me a quick message to update me? Even if it was 'sorry but I won't be coming back', at least I'd know where I stood.

As hard as it was, I had to try to stay positive. There were eight full days left here, so there was still time for him to come back.

The last couple of days had been surprisingly good.

After we'd got back from Matera on Tuesday night, I'd just

ordered room service. On Wednesday we had a picnic on a gorgeous beach, so it wasn't too awkward because whilst all of the other couples stared into each other's eyes, I went for a swim or buried my head in my Kindle.

Kim and Timothy were really nice, checking on me throughout the afternoon. Romeo checked on me too, asking if I was okay sitting on my own. I told him that with my Kindle I was immersed in a world with loads of imaginary friends, so I was fine.

I was grateful that I didn't spend too much time with him, because after I felt those sparks at Matera, I knew I had to keep my distance.

When he opened up about his ex, I was surprised. I was convinced Romeo was a player, but after hearing about his long-term relationship and spending more time with him, I wasn't so sure he was a big flirt.

But if that was true, then what happened with that guest that Jasmine mentioned? And why did he get complaints from male matches? I was dying to find out, but it seemed rude to ask and anyway, I was supposed to be keeping our interactions to a minimum.

Yesterday we took a trip to a pretty clifftop town called Polignano a Mare. We also visited Arco delle Meraviglie, a romantic bridge with a beautiful stone arch which legend says was built to connect the houses of two lovers who were forbidden from dating so they could see each other in secret.

During the visits, I was able to hang out for a bit with Kim again, but something told me that being able to keep Romeo at arm's length again would be a challenge.

Today's trip wasn't until later because we were going out for dinner, so I'd taken advantage by having a lie-in and was arriving later than usual.

'*Ciao*,' Tommaso, the maître d', oops, I meant, the *Dining Director* greeted me as I stepped through the door.

'*Ciao*,' I said, a little disappointed not to see Romeo.

I'd gotten so used to seeing him as soon as I stepped into the restaurant that it was strange that he wasn't here.

It wasn't that I missed him or anything. The fact that he wasn't here was good, because I was supposed to be keeping my distance.

After Tommaso showed me to my table, I placed my order. I was about to pull out my phone to text Stella, when I saw Romeo striding towards me.

Excitement fizzed in my stomach and when he flashed me a full, warm smile that was straight out of a toothpaste advert, my pulse quickened.

'*Ciao*,' he said when he reached my table. 'I was just going to call your room to check that you were okay. Everything good?'

'Yeah, great! Perfect!' I blabbed, trying not to be affected by his smile, his scent, his... bloody *everything*.

'You have ordered?'

'Yep!' My voice went high-pitched. 'The usual. I was gutted that they didn't have any of those *pasticciotto* pastries left. That'll teach me to come to breakfast late!'

'One moment.' Romeo disappeared into the kitchen. When he returned a few minutes later, he was clutching a plate and when I saw what was on it, my mouth fell open. 'Here.' He placed it on the table. 'I knew you liked them, so I saved these for you. One is the traditional custard and the other has Nutella.'

'Oh my God, thank you!' I gushed. That was such a kind gesture.

Romeo waved his hand dismissively like it was no big deal, but it really was.

'I've been thinking about these pastries ever since I tried one on the coach. I even went to the back to get another one, but they were all gone. I wasn't surprised though. Everyone probably saw them and took them straightaway.'

'No.' Romeo shook his head. 'You did not find any more because there was only one. I brought that from the buffet to the coach just for you.'

Wait, what?

Our eyes met and I swear my heart doubled in size.

'I should go.' Romeo broke the silence. 'I hope you enjoy them. See you tonight.'

'Yeah,' I said softly, still trying to compose myself. 'See you later.'

I was supposed to be waiting for Edward to come back.

I was supposed to be keeping my distance from Romeo.

He wasn't just my Love Alchemist. Romeo was a guy who openly said he wasn't looking for a relationship. Plus, not only did he live in another country, he was planning to travel even further away to the US.

There were dozens of other reasons why I shouldn't have this growing attraction towards him. But no matter how many times I warned them, my mind and my body didn't want to listen.

Shit.

23

ROMEO

As I saw Samantha walking towards the coach, my breath caught in my throat.

Mamma mia.

She looked absolutely incredible.

Her lemon-coloured dress clung to her curves, her beautiful curls hung loosely over her shoulders and those pretty brown eyes sparkled.

When she saw me, her face broke into a smile and it felt like a fire had just been lit inside me.

I had been trying to deny and fight it ever since I first saw her, but it was time to stop lying to myself and admit the truth.

I liked Samantha.

A *lot*.

And this was bad, because Samantha was off limits.

There were so many reasons why this attraction was dangerous.

Firstly, she was a guest. And as Victoria had reminded me dozens of times, getting involved with guests was not allowed.

I would not risk my opportunity to go to California or jeopardise securing the savings I needed to give Mamma the chance to make a fresh start for some stupid infatuation.

Secondly, she was Edward's match. Whilst it was unlikely, there was still a chance that he could return. Even though he did not deserve her, Samantha was still his partner, so getting involved would be like stealing another man's woman.

It did not matter that they had only been matched for a week. I remembered the betrayal I felt when I was cheated on and I refused to put anyone through that.

Thirdly, she was from London and I lived here, so it would never work.

And fourthly... well, I could not think of a fourth reason right now, but I would find one if I thought hard enough.

The point was, I had to stop thinking about her in that way.

But I did not know how to.

The sensation of her hand in mine when we were at Matera still played on repeat in my head.

I enjoyed our conversations.

I loved her laugh, her smile and her sense of humour. She did not take herself too seriously and I liked that.

And of course, she was as sexy as hell.

'Hi,' she said as she reached me. He sweet citrus scent surrounded me and I reminded myself again to act professionally.

'*Ciao*,' I replied, resisting the temptation to tell her how beautiful she looked.

'You gonna tell us where we're going tonight?' She cocked her head to the side.

'It is a surprise,' I said.

'Ooh, I like surprises! Good ones though. Not like when you walk in a room and a spider jumps out. Or when you come home and your boyfriend tells you he's met someone else! Those are very bad surprises. It won't be anything like that, will it?' She laughed, but I saw a flicker of sadness in her eyes.

Had her ex cheated? I wanted to know more about her story. I wanted to know everything about her. But it was not my place to.

'I promise that it will be the kind of surprise that will put an even bigger smile on your beautiful face,' I said, then groaned internally as I realised what I had just said.

I was not supposed to say that out loud. Now she would think I was a creep.

'Such a charmer.' She touched my shoulder gently and heat blazed beneath my skin. 'You really know how to make your guests feel special. I'll be sure to give you a five out of five rating,' she grinned.

As I watched her board the coach, I tried not to look at her arse, but failed.

She had a really great arse. Full, round and perfect for...

'*Ciao*, Romeo!' Miranda, one of the guests, approached, jolting me out of my inappropriate thoughts.

'*Ci-ciao*,' I stuttered. 'How was your day?'

'Great, thanks.'

After I'd chatted briefly with Miranda then checked that all of the guests were onboard, the driver set off.

During the journey, I did my usual rounds, speaking with each of the couples, asking them about their days and making mental notes of important things they had mentioned about their likes or dislikes that I could use to bring them closer together.

When I got to where Samantha was sitting, she had her headphones in and her eyes squeezed shut as she danced in her seat to the music.

For a moment I just stood and watched her, a smile tugging at my lips.

I loved how free she was. Samantha was on a coach full of people, but she was dancing like she was alone in her bedroom.

Just as I was about to continue walking, her eyes flicked open. They bulged in surprise and then a wide grin spread across her face, causing my heart to expand.

'Hey, you!' she said enthusiastically.

'Good song?' I asked.

'Yep! How did you guess?'

'From your very enthusiastic dancing.'

'Is *enthusiastic* your Italian for shit?'

'No,' I laughed. 'Not at all. It was very *interesting* dancing.'

'Interesting is probably more of an insult than shit!' She laughed. 'If you think my seat dancing is rubbish, you should hear me sing.'

'I am sure you sound like an angel.'

'Yeah! One that's being tortured by the devil,' Samantha cackled and I could not help laughing too.

This woman.

Her personality and joy were infectious.

If I did not have to work and take care of the other guests, I would happily sit here and chat with her all night.

But that was not possible.

'Well, now that I have confirmation that you are happy and enjoying your chair disco, I will check on the other guests. We will be arriving at our destination soon.'

'Okey dokey!'

Samantha gave me a thumbs up and then went back to dancing. I smiled again as I thought that she was quickly becoming one of my favourite guests.

* * *

Once the coach had dropped us off, I led the guests towards our destination.

'Isn't this the town we came to the other day?' one of the guests said.

'You are correct,' I replied. 'We are back at Polignano a Mare, but we are going somewhere that we did not visit.' When we stepped into the restaurant, the gasps were audible. 'So this is Grotta Palazzese which translates to Cave Palace in English. It is one of the most iconic cave restaurants in the world.'

'Holy crap!' Samantha's mouth fell open. She looked like a child who had just woken up in a toy factory. 'This place is flipping amazing! I've never been to a restaurant that's on the edge of a cliff and built inside a cave before! And the sea's right there!' That was true. Because the cave was open, the sea was directly in front of us. 'I know it's not cool, but is it okay to take photos? I might not get to come to somewhere as fancy as this again, so I can't miss my chance.'

'Sure.' I tried to stifle my grin.

Samantha whipped out her phone and started snapping away at the uninterrupted sea views. The other guests did the same. I could not blame them.

Whilst Samantha was taking pictures, the maître d' started allocating tables to the other guests.

When Samantha had finished, she waltzed over to him.

'So, where do you want me?' she said and the maître d's eyes popped. 'Oops, that came out wrong! I meant to ask what table I'm on? I'm Samantha Gordon.'

'*Sì*,' the maître d' replied. 'Please follow me. Here you are, madam. This is your table. The view is incredible, no?' He stopped at a table for two overlooking the sea.

'It's, wow, thank you! But if you don't mind, can you take away the other plate and cutlery? I only need a table for one.'

'For one?' His brows furrowed. 'I have this table listed for two: you and a gentleman called Edward, no?'

'Yeah, my match, he...' Samantha's face fell and my chest tightened.

'*Scusi,*' I said. 'The reservation should have been updated.' This was my fault. I forgot to call ahead earlier to tell them Samantha would be dining alone. I had been putting it off because I thought there was still a chance that Edward would have returned. 'I will take care of this,' I said to Samantha before I explained everything in Italian.

'I understand,' the maître d' replied, giving Samantha a reassuring smile.

'This place is stunning!' Kim said as she pulled out a chair at the table near where we were standing. 'You sitting here?'

'I think so,' Samantha replied. 'They're just going to clear away one setting as it's just me, but they have a reservation for two.'

'Why don't you join Samantha, Romeo?' Kim asked and my brows shot up to my hairline. 'You can't let the poor girl sit at this beautiful place alone. They've probably already catered for ten couples and you gotta eat, right? Can't let the food go to waste.'

Although she was right that the booking was made for ten couples, there was no way that I could have a candlelit dinner with one of the guests.

Especially not one that I was attracted to.

'The booking is for guests. I do not normally eat here. The meals are very expensive. But of course, worth every euro.' I smiled at the maître d'.

'The hotel's probably going to have to pay for the meal

anyway, so you might as well enjoy it,' added Timothy. 'You don't mind, do you, Samantha?'

Now it was Samantha's eyes that were bulging.

'Course not!' she said, quickly.

Her reply seemed genuine.

I should not want to have dinner with her.

I should dread the idea of sitting with a guest for hours, but the truth was I would love to spend more time with Samantha. She made me smile.

But this was different to walking around a town with her or checking on her during a beach excursion.

'I will have to check with Victoria,' I said. 'It is very unusual for a Love Alchemist to dine with a guest in this kind of setting.'

A group dinner where we were all sat together on one large table like at the trip to Alberobello would have been fine. But a table for two meant staring into Samantha's eyes. It was significantly more romantic. And that was the point. This dinner was designed to stimulate romance between the guests.

The last thing I needed was to encourage any extra feelings between me and Samantha. Unfortunately, I was managing to do that all on my own.

'Yeah,' Samantha said. 'That's best. So she doesn't get the wrong idea.'

'Excuse me one moment.' I nodded.

Given the fact that I was already on thin ice with the management and Victoria was worried about me flirting with female guests, she was sure to say no. I'd be disappointed when she did, but it was the sensible option.

I dialled Victoria's number. The phone rang out and just as I was about to hang up, she answered.

'Romeo?' She seemed flustered. 'What is it?'

'I am at Grotta Palazzese. They still have a table for two for Samantha and'

'I can't... I'm in the middle of something,' Victoria said and I realised she must have someone else on another line. 'Sorry, Romeo. I'm dealing with a personal issue. What did you say?' I explained the situation again. 'So she'll be sitting there, alone?'

'*Sì.*'

'And is she upset?'

'She is a little embarrassed and the other guests have said it's not nice that she has to sit alone and...'

'Shit. So not only is Samantha upset, the other guests are noticing how bad it is too? I don't need a revolt on my hands. I don't need... I said I'll sort it!' Victoria was clearly still having a conversation with whoever was on the other line. 'Sorry, I can't deal with this right now. I need you to resolve this. What do you suggest?'

'Get the waiter to clear away the second plate and cutlery?' I suggested, even though I knew that would not make Samantha happy. It was the safest choice though.

'What? And make everyone feel sorry for her? No! Just sit with her, for God's sake. Do whatever you need to make her happy so she has a good experience.'

'But I thought you did not want me to spend too much time with female guests?'

'Yes! I'm still here!' It sounded like I had lost Victoria again to her other conversation. 'No! I can't just drop everything just because... hold on! I have one of our Love Alchemists on the other line. Just give me one second! Romeo, I need to go. Just sit with Samantha, smile, play nice and tell the other guests that this is a sign of the Love Hotel going the extra mile and doing whatever is needed to delight our guests. It's not like Edward can complain about you flirting when the bastard's done a disappearing act! Speak tomorrow, okay?'

'*Va bene.*' I hung up.

So that was settled then.

I would be having dinner with Samantha.

I had never shied away from a challenge, but something told me that staring into her beautiful eyes, sharing delicious food and chatting to her for hours without becoming more attracted to Samantha would be impossible.

24

SAMMIE

As I watched Romeo at the other end of the restaurant talking on the phone with his boss, I prayed that Victoria would ban him from sitting with me.

It wasn't that I didn't like him. Now the problem was the complete opposite.

I fancied the bloody pants off him.

God, I should *not* have thought about taking his pants off...

It wasn't the first time today that I'd thought about him, but I couldn't help it.

Not only had he bought that pastry for me to have on the way to Matera, he'd also saved two for me this morning because he knew I liked them.

How was this man still single?

At one point I forced myself to think of Edward and what nice things he'd done for me during the short time we'd spent together and I came up with a big fat zero.

The only things I could remember were negative. How he'd food shamed me, how he'd reacted when I told him about the company I'd worked for. How he'd snarled during that volleyball match. And how he hadn't even bothered to tell me he was leaving or message me since then.

Romeo, on the other hand, had been nothing but attentive. Always looking out for me, checking on me, encouraging me to enjoy my food, bringing me food he knew I'd like. He didn't ridicule my job. He was interested. He didn't make me feel stupid.

It's his job! my brain screamed at me.

That was like swooning over a chef because he cooked a meal that you paid for.

Gah. Get it together, girl.

Romeo ran his hand through his dark, shiny hair, causing his bicep to bulge and the sexy thoughts whooshed straight back into my mind.

I knew I was supposed to be curbing my thoughts, but cut me a bit of slack. The man was the fittest guy I'd ever seen in real life.

No actually, scrap that. Name any hot Hollywood film star, musician or model and I can guarantee you that Romeo was ten times hotter.

At least.

The man must work twelve-hour days, but he always looked utterly gorgeous. His deep olive skin glowed like it'd been freshly kissed by the sun. Looking that good should be illegal.

And despite whatever supposedly went on with a guest and his reputation, something told me that he was a decent guy. I could just feel it.

Relaxing music played in the background and we were so close to the sea I could hear the waves crashing against the rocks. I tried to focus on the incredible views, but my gaze kept returning to Romeo.

Seconds later he ended his call and started walking towards

me. I tried to act all cool by pretending that I'd been looking at the views and not at him the entire time, but I doubted I succeeded.

He stopped to say something to the maître d', who nodded, then walked away. He was probably getting a waiter to clear away the extra table setting.

But then Romeo pulled out the chair opposite me.

WTF.

'So,' he said and my gaze flicked to him. God, those eyes. I could get lost in them for days. It was a really good thing we wouldn't be having dinner together. I wouldn't survive. It was kind of him to sit down to tell me the news though to soften the rejection. Little did he know that I'd be relieved to not be dining with him. 'I have spoken to Victoria and she has agreed for me to keep you company this evening.'

'What?' I said a little louder than I'd intended.

'But only if you feel comfortable. If you prefer to dine alone it is not a problem.'

'No, I...' Shit. What was I supposed to say now? If I said that I didn't want to eat with him, I'd sound ungrateful and might hurt his feelings. But if I said yes, I'd end up fancying him more. And I was guaranteed to put my foot in my mouth at some point. I always did. 'It's fine!' I squeaked. 'That is if you don't mind. You're babysitting me so much, soon I'll have to start calling you Daddy!' I cackled, then cringed.

Oh. Dear. God.

When I'd said that I was guaranteed to put my foot in my mouth, I wasn't expecting to do it so soon.

'It would not be the first time that a woman has called me that.' Romeo's eyes darkened, and the corner of his mouth twitched.

A bolt of desire shot between my legs.

Jesus.

'Oh, yeah?' I raised an eyebrow. 'That sounds like an interesting story...'

'Have you looked at the menu?' he asked.

'Not yet,' I replied, getting the hint that he wanted to change the subject.

I wasn't surprised. The man had barely sat down before I'd brought the conversation straight to the gutter.

'So, you two are dining together! Excellent!' Kim called out from the table behind us.

'Victoria agreed that it is important to ensure that all of our guests are looked after, so although this is not something our Love Alchemists would normally do, because of the difficult circumstances, we wanted to make an extra special effort to make sure that Samantha is happy.'

'Well, I think that it's very good of the hotel to agree to that,' Timothy added.

'And if there's anyone that can make Samantha happy, I'm sure it's you,' Kim smirked, then winked at me. So cheeky, but she was probably right. 'Enjoy your meal.'

'In all seriousness though,' I said, turning back to face Romeo, 'you don't have to sit with me if you don't want to. Wouldn't be the first time I've eaten alone and I'm sure it won't be the last.'

'No. I have been told to make sure that you enjoy yourself and I will not fail.'

The waiter brought over a platter of different breads and some olive oil and rested it on the pristine white tablecloth then took our order. Soon afterwards he brought over a bottle of wine and poured it into our glasses.

As I took a sip, I squeezed my eyes shut.

'Oh my God!' I sighed. 'This is amazing. I think I'm going to have to buy an extra two suitcases when I go back. One to steal the pillows and the other to fill it with this wine and my favourite prosecco. It's the best booze I've ever tasted.'

'Surely not better than the many bottles of wine you drank on the plane.' Romeo flashed a cheeky smile.

'Oi!' I slapped his arm playfully. Blimey, I'd forgotten how firm it was. 'I told you, it was only *one mini* bottle of wine. Not *bottles*, plural. And I didn't even drink all of it!'

'Of course, I believe you,' he said. 'By the way, how is the jet lag? Have you recovered yet?'

'You are terrible!' I grinned, then hid my face behind my hands. 'I didn't mean to say I had jet lag,' I winced.

'I know. You only said it because of all the bottles of wine, *plural*, that you drank on the plane.' This time Romeo laughed and I chuckled with him.

'Honestly, I can't believe some of the crap that comes out of my mouth sometimes. It's so embarrassing.'

'Do not be embarrassed.' Concern washed over his face. 'I hope I did not offend you.'

'Course not!' I grinned. 'I love a bit of banter. And *Banter Romeo* is much better than *Grumpy Romeo*.'

'*Grumpy Romeo*?' His brows furrowed.

'Yeah. When we first met, you acted like you didn't want to be there. I thought everyone who worked at the Love Hotel would be like a ray of sunshine and then I met you and you were all grumpy, like you didn't enjoy your job at all.'

Romeo blew out a breath.

'I enjoy my job. It is just that day my... Never mind. You would not understand and you are a guest. I cannot burden you with my troubles.'

'Go on. I need to understand why you acted like such a judgemental dick.'

'A dick?' He frowned. 'There is nothing wrong with my dick.'

'No! It means...'

'I am pulling your leg. I know what it means! You thought I was a dick?'

'Only when we first met.'

'*Scusi.*' His face fell and now I wondered if I was the one who had offended him. Maybe calling him a dick was a bit strong. Especially considering the fact that he'd been helping me out all week.

'Just before you arrived I got the news that Biscotti, my family's dog, was ill and was about to be operated on. They were not sure if she would make it so I was upset. I know that might sound dramatic because she is a dog and not a human but...'

'I'm so sorry.' I reached out and rested my palm on his. As soon as my hand connected with his skin, my whole body lit up like a fireworks display.

'I get it. We had Tyson, our dog, for years. He was part of the family. And when he passed I was so cut up. I loved him more than I loved most people.'

Romeo's eyes widened.

'That is exactly how we feel about Biscotti. She is so much more than just a pet. We adore her. She gives us so much love.'

'How is she now?'

'She is better, *grazie*. It was close, but she is a fighter.'

'I'm so happy to hear that.'

Romeo looked down at my palm on his and embarrassment washed over me.

'Sorry.' I pulled my hand away. 'I didn't mean to... I just... I hate hearing about any animals suffering and I could see you were upset and...'

'It is okay. You do not have to explain. I appreciate your

concern. It means a lot. I hope to visit Biscotti this weekend when I go to see Mamma.'

My heart fluttered and a wide grin spread across my face.

Earlier, I'd thought my interest in Romeo was purely because of his looks, but we hadn't even started eating yet and I could already see that there was more to him than just a pretty face.

'What?' Romeo's brows furrowed.

'Nothing!' My grin widened. 'You're just full of surprises.'

'Why?'

'The grumpy Love Alchemist who has a soft spot for animals and goes to visit his mamma? How are you still single?'

'I told you, I do not date.'

'Oh yeah, I forgot.'

That was a lie. I knew he'd said that in Matera but my stupid brain brought it up anyway.

The waiter delivered our starters and we both thanked him before getting stuck in.

'By the way, how old are you?' I asked.

'Thirty-three. Why?'

'Just curious. And what do you do when you're not working?' I asked.

'I go to the beach to swim. I love the water. I have a boat that I take out sometimes,' Romeo said.

'Really?' I perked up. 'That's cool.' I slid a forkful of ravioli into my mouth and nearly keeled over on the spot. It was *so* good.

'Taking it out is very relaxing. It is just me and the water.'

'Sounds amazing! The only boat or should I say ferry that I've been on is one from Dover to Calais when I was on a school trip.'

'Ah, that is very different. A smaller boat is much more peaceful.'

'I bet. What else do you like doing?' I asked.

If he was this big flirt, then he'd probably enjoy partying or drinking or some other activity that involved him interacting with lots of women. Yeah, he said he wasn't looking for a relationship, but that didn't mean he didn't have hookups.

I took another glug of my wine.

'I like pottery,' Romeo said casually and I spat a mouthful of wine in his face.

'Shit! I'm so sorry!' I winced, whipping the thick napkin from my lap and handing it to him.

Romeo squinted, wiped his eyes with the back of his hands, looked at me and then burst out laughing.

'Samantha, Samantha.' He shook his head whilst his deep chuckle continued to vibrate from his chest. 'You are one of the most amusing women I have ever met.'

He wiped his damp cheeks with the napkin, then licked around his lips, catching the remaining droplets of wine with his tongue.

I was sure he didn't intend it to be erotic, but seeing his tongue moving so skilfully was hot as fuck and had me thinking about what else he was good at licking.

'Please, call me Sammie,' I said as I tried to divert my dirty mind from straying down Filthy Thoughts Street. 'Samantha's what my mum calls me when I'm in trouble. My friends call me Sammie.'

'So we are *friends* now?' Romeo quirked an eyebrow.

'Course! I don't share my second-hand wine with just anyone.'

Romeo snorted.

'I cannot believe you spat in my face.' He shook his head good-naturedly. 'I offer to keep you company at dinner and *this* is how you repay me.' He gestured to his damp face and continued mopping it up.

He was being a good sport about it though. If someone spat in my face, I'd go straight to the loo to rinse it off. But if it was Romeo's spit, I'd just leave it.

'I really am sorry,' I winced. 'It's just that when I look at you, nothing says *this is a guy who enjoys making shit with clay.*'

'Appearances can be deceiving.' His eyes darkened.

'Yeah,' I said, my heart beating faster.

Was it me or had the temperature just shot up ten degrees?

I couldn't even blame the sun because it was almost ten at night.

The air crackled between us and as our eyes locked, I wondered what else there was to discover about Romeo.

Because as much as I knew I shouldn't, I wanted to know *everything.*

25

ROMEO

'Did you enjoy your evening?' I said as Sammie got off the coach.

The other guests had already left and the driver had pulled away, so now she was the only one around.

'I had a fantastic evening!' Her eyes sparkled. Seeing her so happy made my chest inflate several sizes. Making Sammie smile was becoming one of my favourite things to do.

Sammie.

I liked that she asked me to use her nickname and said that we were friends.

Although I would be lying if I said friendship was what I wanted from her.

'The activities you organise are really cool.'

'We try. The location helps. We have so many beautiful places nearby. We are always looking for new ideas to add to the itinerary though.'

'Oooh! If you're looking for stuff to do at the hotel to help couples bond, you could try a games night on the beach. You could do board games or just play question-related games, like

Two Truths and a Lie, where they say three things and the other person has to guess which is the lie, or Never Have I Ever, or This or That.'

'This or That?' I frowned.

'Yeah, like starter or dessert.'

'*Always* dessert,' I replied.

'Same!' Sammie held my gaze for a few beats. 'I... I have loads of other ideas. Sometimes my boss lets me organise the teambuilding activities at work and any parties we have. I really enjoy it.'

'Those are great ideas. I will pass them on to Victoria.'

'Yay!' she said.

'And I am glad you enjoyed your evening. I should not be surprised. The food was delicious, the setting was magical and you got to drink some good-quality wine.'

'Yes! And don't forget about the company. That was okay too.'

'Okay?' I glared. 'First you compare me to a man in his seventies, then you spit in my face and now you call my presence *okay*? Do you like insulting me?'

'Oops!' She covered her mouth with her hand. 'I forgot about that Mr Bean stuff!' She burst into a fit of giggles.

'And now you laugh at me!'

'I'm not! Well, sort of. It's just that when we met and I said you looked like someone, you rolled your eyes, like, "Mamma mia! Not this again."' Sammie started talking in a terrible Italian accent. '"It is so tiring to be compared to a hot, sexy actor all the time!" So, I wanted to teach you a lesson.'

'That was a terrible impersonation. Is that how you think I sound?' Now it was my turn to laugh.

'It wasn't *that* bad!'

'No, it was worse!'

'*Scusi*,' she said and the sound of her genuinely trying to talk in Italian sent electricity shooting through my veins. 'Obviously you look nothing like Mr Bean.'

'No, because I look like Sheldon.'

'Sheldon is an attractive man. But no, you don't look like him either. You look *much, much better...*'

Sammie's voice trailed off and she bit her lip.

As our eyes locked I noticed there was something burning in hers.

Was it desire?

Was Sammie attracted to me?

Usually, if a woman was interested she would flirt openly or touch my arm like some of the guests had done.

But ever since we had met, Sammie had done nothing but joke with me or take pleasure in letting me know that she did not think I was anything special.

A woman who is attracted to you does not compare you to a senior citizen.

It is true that earlier when she had touched my hand, I had felt a spark again, but she was just trying to comfort me after I told her that Biscotti was unwell.

But it was more than just the physical attraction. I felt a connection.

The conversation tonight flowed easily.

She made me laugh more than any other woman ever had.

Sammie was strong, confident and fearless.

She said what she felt without caring what others would think, which was a breath of fresh air.

Many of the women that were interested in me were always so worried about looking a certain way or saying the right thing to impress me that they did the exact opposite. They did not have their own opinion. They dumbed down their personalities to be the person they thought I wanted them to be.

But not Sammie. She was unapologetically herself and I loved that.

'*Grazie*.' I broke the silence.

We stood there for a few more beats, neither of us saying a word.

I should go. I should wish her goodnight and go straight to bed. But I was not ready for the night to end.

Of course, I was not suggesting that anything should happen between us.

Even if Edward had disappeared, Sammie was still his match.

And I was still her Love Alchemist.

That was when I remembered that the hotel grounds had cameras. If my bosses saw me gazing into the eyes of a guest, they would not be happy.

My gaze drifted to the reception entrance.

'Are you okay to get to your room or would you like me to come with you?'

'Oooh, you cheeky little thing!' Sammie cackled. 'I would've said that you should've at least bought me dinner first, but you've already done that.'

'What?' I frowned. 'Oh...' I said as I realised what she meant. If only she knew how much I would very much like to *come with her*. 'Let me rephrase: would you like me to walk you to your room?'

'I'm just pulling your leg! *Grazie*, but I'm a big girl. I can walk there myself.'

At that point, I thought she would say goodnight, but she did not move. We stood there again just staring at each other.

I was not sure before, but now I saw it. The attraction was mutual.

For the first time in years, I had a connection with a smart, sexy, funny woman.

And there was absolutely nothing that I could do about it.

26

SAMMIE

There was something wrong with my feet.

For the last five minutes I'd been telling myself that I needed to stop staring into Romeo's ridiculously beautiful eyes and get my arse to my room and away from temptation. But here I was, my feet still rooted to the ground like they were covered in concrete.

And I could tell I was staring at him with heart eyes.

I couldn't be arsed to crack a joke or pretend that I didn't like him any more. I didn't know if I'd ever been so drawn to someone before in my life.

He was already ahead of the game because of his looks, but these past few days, the more I'd got to know him, the more I'd realised he was a good guy too.

But it didn't matter how much I liked him, nothing could happen.

Life was so unfair sometimes.

'I... I should go,' Romeo said as he took a few steps towards reception.

'Yeah. Me too. Er, see you tomorrow and *grazie mille* again!'

As I shot off towards my room, I winced. I'd gone from rooted to the spot to running away like my feet were on fire in the space of twenty seconds.

Once I was in my room, I flopped onto the bed.

What the hell was I going to do? This was an impossible situation.

I pulled out my phone and jumped up with relief when I saw that Stella had messaged half an hour ago.

Without missing a beat, I clicked the call button.

'Hey, Sammie!' she answered. 'How's it going?'

'Bad, but good, but... aaargghhh! I'm so confused! I fancy my Love Alchemist,' I blurted out. I needed to tell someone or my head was gonna explode.

'Shit. And still no word from Edward the idiot?'

'Not a bean. It's so unfair! Edward isn't even here and clearly doesn't give a fuck about me, but I'm feeling the sparks with someone that I really like and I can't do anything about it. And the thing that makes it harder is that I think there's a chance that Romeo feels something too.'

I was gutted. Most people would say fuck Edward and the rules, but I had to do the right thing.

'Yeah? What makes you think he's interested?'

'Well, he laughs at my jokes.'

'I laugh at them too!' Stella chuckled.

'God bless you, sweetie! I mean, he laughs at them, but it's the way that he looks at me when he does. Like he thinks I'm amazing. He even said I was the funniest woman he'd met. Maybe it's just wishful thinking.'

The more I thought about it, the less sure I became. Guys had told me they found me funny before, usually before they friend-zoned me...

'Forget I mentioned it. I'm just fantasising, because I'm

crushing hard on him. In my defence, the man is a freaking smokeshow. No. He's an inferno. He's a blaze of hotness. He's like... you know how much I love Nando's Peri Peri chicken?'

'Yeah.'

'Well, take the extra-hot sauce, multiply it by a million and that's about 10 per cent of how hot he is.'

'Damn.'

'But it's not just about his looks. He's really easy to talk to. He's kind and caring. He loves dogs – he was upset about his dog being ill when I arrived at the hotel – that's why he was so grumpy. And he's super close to his mum. And he does *pottery*! And he's got great banter. And... Oh, God. I've got it *bad*!'

'Sounds like you like him a lot.'

'I really do. And even though Edward has made no attempt to contact me since he pissed off, I still feel bad for thinking about how much I fancy Romeo because I feel like I should only be thinking about my match. That's why I used all my savings to come here. Because I wanted to find my Mr Right, not fall for another Mr Wrong.'

'I'm not gonna lie, even though I can tell you're really into Romeo, the odds are stacked against you. Not only is he your Love Alchemist, he lives in another country. At least with Max, we were both still based in London. Same for Jasmine and Alejandro. They both lived in Spain, but long-distance relationships...'

'I know. They don't all turn out like my parents'.'

My dad was an American studying in London when he'd met Mum. They faced challenges like coming from different countries and some ignorance from small-minded haters (Dad was black and Mum was white), but they overcame it all because they were in love.

Even though it worked out for them, I'd tried the whole long-distance thing in my twenties and it was a disaster.

'So what do we know about Edward? Have the hotel really heard *nothing* from him?'

'Nope. *Nada.*'

'Have you done any online snooping?'

'I tried, but I couldn't find him on socials. But his handle could be anything.'

'Remind me of what you know about him.'

'He's called Edward Barclay, lives in Shoreditch, works for a computer software company, used to date a woman whose name I can't remember but it's something to do with wine, likes the gym and healthy eating. That's about it.'

'We should do some digging. There must be a way to reach him to get closure. We need to know if he's coming back. I'm not saying it's a good idea to pursue anything with Romeo, but I haven't heard you so enthusiastic about a guy since... ever. So even if there's a 1 per cent chance you could be happy with him, you should at least be free to consider it. Until you hear from Edward, you can't move on.'

'You're right. I'm sure the hotel would have his work details. Obviously, they couldn't pass that onto me, but surely they could call his office or something, right?'

'Exactly,' Stella said. 'And in the meantime, we should do our own research. He must have a digital footprint *somewhere*.'

'Yep,' I said, suddenly feeling more optimistic. 'I bet he has a page showing off how good he is at calorie counting. Our next activity isn't until tomorrow evening, so I'll have all day to do some sleuthing by the pool. If Edward's online, I'm gonna find him and finally get some answers.'

27

SAMMIE

As I stepped out of the sea, I exhaled.

The water was heavenly. Swimming here was a billion times better than at my local pool. Especially considering the last time I went, I saw a kid weeing in it.

And I much preferred the salty scent to the heavy chlorine stench that was always in the air at public pools.

Yep. I could definitely get used to this.

I walked over to where I'd left my things and picked up my towel. As I dried off, I thought about what I wanted to do next. Today's group activity was a beach barbecue which started at seven, so I still had a few hours left before I had to get ready.

After breakfast, I'd read by the pool for hours, then once I'd eaten lunch, I'd started searching for Edward online. I'd found his LinkedIn easily, so I'd tried calling his office, but his secretary said he was 'unavailable'. When I'd asked when he'd be free, she'd asked who was calling, so I'd hung up.

My social media searches so far had also come up blank. Stella hadn't had any joy either, but she said Jasmine was great at research, so she'd ask her.

Then I'd decided that as much as I wanted to know what had happened to him, I couldn't waste my holiday thinking about someone who clearly wasn't thinking about me. Which is when I decided to come to the beach for a swim.

I looked out into the distance. The sea stretched as far as the eye could see and this beach looked pretty long too so I wrapped a sarong around my waist, slung my towel in my bag and decided to explore.

My feet sank into the golden sand and I wished for the hundredth time that I could stay here forever. Imagine being able to go swimming in the sea whenever I wanted. That'd be the dream.

It wasn't likely to happen though. When I was younger, I'd thought about living in Florida, which is where my dad was from, but it just never happened. It was hard enough finding a decent job in London, never mind in another country. Moving to a new place and leaving my parents and friends behind was way too scary. Plus, I was so close to getting that head receptionist role, so I couldn't go swanning off. If I did, all my hard work over the past almost five years would've been for nothing.

Maybe one day I'd go for an extended holiday.

'Sammie,' a deep Italian voice called out.

I snapped my gaze away from the sea and saw Romeo walking towards me.

Jesus. The man really was a god.

He wasn't in his uniform. He was wearing a vest which showed off his glorious arms and a pair of swimming trunks.

Romeo's hair was damp and droplets of water slid down his skin.

The urge to step forward and lick them off was strong. But I was happy to report that somehow, I resisted.

'Romeo! *Ciao!*' I said. 'What are you doing here?'

'I am on my break, so I went for a swim. I like to come to this part of the beach because it is quieter.'

'I just went for a swim too. I never walked this far up before. It's lovely here.'

'Sorry I did not get to speak to you at breakfast.'

'It's fine.' I waved my hand away. I'd missed speaking to him though. When I arrived and every time I looked up, he was chatting with other guests or his colleagues. 'Thanks for sending over the pastries though.'

Not long after I'd arrived, one of the Cuisine Champions came over with a plate of cherry-flavoured *pasticciotto*, which she said were courtesy of Romeo.

'*Prego*,' he said. 'Now that you have tried different flavours, I am interested to know which is your favourite?'

'Oooh, that's a tough one. Maybe the original custard one or the Nutella? You?'

'I like them all, but perhaps Nutella is my favourite. I like chocolate.'

'Me too.'

Our eyes locked.

Prosecco bubbles popped in my stomach and electricity crackled in the air.

'You have...' Romeo stepped closer and brushed away a curl that had fallen onto my cheek.

'Th-thanks.' My breath caught in my throat.

Romeo's gaze dipped to my mouth.

Was he thinking about kissing me?

God, I hoped so.

I wanted him.

Would it be so bad if we did?

At this point, Edward returning seemed unlikely.

This part of the beach was deserted, so his bosses wouldn't find out.

It would just be one kiss. Just so I could know how he tasted.

My lips parted and the thought of locking lips with Romeo caused tingles to erupt between my legs.

Just as I was about to inch my head closer, Romeo stepped back.

Noooo.

I couldn't be imagining this attraction. I was sure that he liked me.

But maybe he just made every woman feel special. I still had Jasmine's words swimming round in my head. I needed to know if he felt the electricity or if I was just another guest he was being nice to.

'Can I ask you something?' I said.

'Sure.'

'Did something happen between you and a guest before?'

'What?' He frowned. 'Where did you hear this?'

'I... er.' I didn't want to drop Jasmine in it. 'I heard some people saying that you flirted with guests and that maybe something happened with one?'

'That is not true.' He shook his head. 'I will explain.' We sat on the sand, facing each other. 'Last month, there was a guest who became a little... *enthusiastic* about me. She would always come to my office. I was concerned that she was becoming too familiar, but I thought that I could handle it. But then she tried to kiss me.'

'No!' I gasped.

'*Sì.*' He rubbed the back of his neck. 'I pushed her away and told her I was not interested and she should be with her match. I reported it to Victoria straightaway, but in the meantime, the woman had told her match that we had kissed and she did not want to be with him any more, because she was in love with me.'

'Bloody hell! Sounds like she was obsessed! What happened then?'

'Of course her match was furious. He complained to management and when he saw me, he tried to punch me.'

'Fuck!' I gasped. 'Was that the only time something like that happened?'

'That was the most extreme. Sometimes guests become too tactile. For example, a few weeks ago, a woman was stroking my arm and her match complained. I try to be polite but firm, but it is difficult because they do not like the rejection. So she also complained.'

'It must be a nightmare being so irresistible that the guests can't stop throwing themselves at you!' I laughed, then winced. I didn't want to sound insensitive.

'I am not looking for sympathy. I just want to do my job. And it is damaging when these rumours circulate and they are not true.'

'It must be,' I nodded, then softened my voice. 'If it means anything, I believe you.'

'You do?' Romeo's eyes widened.

'Yeah. I've spent a lot of time with you this week and I can see you're a good guy.'

'*Grazie.*' Romeo held my gaze. 'That means a lot.'

I meant what I said. He was genuine, kind, caring and God, so beautiful.

'I should get back.' He stood up and brushed the sand off his shorts.

I jumped up too and stood in front of him.

Our eyes locked again.

Electricity sparked between us. I knew I should move away, but I couldn't.

'I am going.' Romeo turned to leave.

'Wait.' I grabbed his hand and jeez, the sensation of touching his soft, warm palm hit me like a wrecking ball. His eyes shot up to meet mine, but he didn't pull away. 'Do you feel it?' I blurted out then instantly regretted it. If he said no it was gonna be a very awkward week.

Maybe I shouldn't have asked him so soon after what he'd just told me about the handsy guests, but in many ways, what he just said proved that he wasn't the flirtatious womaniser people thought he was.

And just maybe it also proved that I wasn't just another guest to him. That somehow I was more.

Even if we couldn't act on it, I still needed to know, one way or the other.

'Feel what?' His gaze dropped to the sand.

'Oh, come on!' I rolled my eyes. 'You know what. Can you feel the connection between us?' I stroked his palm gently.

'*Sì.*' He rubbed the back of his neck. 'I feel it. But there is nothing we can do. You are still Edward's match. Victoria has tried everything to contact him, but there is still no news. And you are a guest here. It is forbidden.'

'I know.' I blew out a heavy sigh.

'But if the circumstances were different...'

'Yeah?' Hope sprung in my chest. 'What would happen if they were?'

'I should go.' Romeo slipped his palm out of mine and I instantly missed the sensation. 'I will see you at the barbecue tonight, *va bene*?'

'*Va bene*,' I replied.

Although I wished I could say that I was okay, I was far from
bene.

I was frustrated because I wanted Romeo.

He'd just admitted that he wanted me too.

But he was strictly off limits.

And there wasn't a damn thing we could do about it.

I'd been at the barbecue for half an hour and was already
thinking about heading back to my room. Being surrounded by
all of these loved-up couples was difficult enough, but then
seeing Romeo and knowing that I couldn't be with him made
things ten times harder.

Just as I was about to excuse myself, my phone rang.

'Jasmine, hi!' I said.

'Hi, can you talk?'

'Yeah. Perfect timing actually. Give me a sec.' I stepped away
from where everyone was huddled on the beach. 'What's up?'

'I've been doing some digging on Edward. I know Victoria
and the team have been on the case from day one. They've
contacted him at work, called his next of kin, sent emails, texts...
you name it, they've tried it.'

'I've lost count of the messages I've sent. I even tried calling
him at work too.'

'He's ignoring everyone and there's something fishy going
on. I can just feel it. And I hate that he's left you in limbo. So,
with Victoria's permission, I tried a different route. Instead of
calling from the hotel, I said I was a new plant-based restaurant
looking for influencers to promote the brand on social media
and asked his PA for his social media handles to see if he'd be a
good fit.'

'That's genius! He'd lap that shit up!'

'He did. His PA was very happy to share them and I found his Instagram.'

'No way!'

'I've just sent you a link to it now. He hasn't posted since the first day he arrived in Italy, so there's nothing suspicious that jumps out, but I haven't time to do a deep dive and I won't get a chance tonight.'

'You've already done more than enough. I'll have a look myself and see what I can find out. Thanks so much!'

'You're welcome. I hope you find something useful. Keep me updated.'

'Will do.'

I hung up, then clicked the link.

No wonder I couldn't find him online. His handle was Shredded Ed followed by a string of numbers (probably related to the exact number of calories he thought women should consume each week) which I never would've found or guessed.

I scrolled through his feed and, like Jasmine mentioned, nothing stood out. Then I started looking at his most recent posts. He didn't have loads of likes, but I noticed there was one person that had liked every single one.

When I clicked on it, I saw it was a woman called Chardonnay.

That was his ex. I knew it was something related to wine.

She had a few more recent posts. One from a few days ago at a restaurant, holding some guy's hand. That post had been liked by Edward.

So he had time to like his ex's post, but couldn't even take two seconds to message me? Twat.

Then I noticed Chardonnay had some stories that were still live, so clicked them straightaway.

But when I saw what was on the screen, my jaw dropped and my stomach plummeted.

It was a photo of Chardonnay.

Touching her bare stomach.

With Edward standing beside her, with his hand also touching her belly.

The caption read:

It's early days, but we're thrilled to announce that we're expecting!

I blinked, then blinked again.

My phone slid out of my palm and crashed onto the sand.

There wasn't a sick family member.

Edward wasn't grieving.

All this time I was worrying about him, feeling like the worst person in the world because I had feelings for Romeo, Edward was with his ex.

His *pregnant* ex.

Anger bubbled in my chest and tears stung my eyes.

I scooped up my phone then started running.

I needed to get out of here.

'Sammie!' I called out as I saw her running away from the beach.

One minute she was speaking on the phone then the next time I looked, Sammie was racing away.

I should call a colleague to cover me, then excuse myself from the guests, but there was no time. I needed to go after Sammie. I had to find out what was wrong.

I sprinted after her and caught up before we reached the pool area.

'Sammie!' I shouted seconds before I grabbed her arm. When I stood in front of her, I saw tears rolling down her cheeks. 'Why are you crying? What happened?'

'That lying motherfucker!' she shouted.

'Who?'

'Edward!' she hissed.

'Did he call you?' I asked.

'No! Jasmine found his Instagram page, then I tracked down his ex's and he was on it. Well, she's not his ex any more. Looks like they're together. There was no sick relative! He went back to be with her and she's fucking pregnant!'

Sammie thrust her phone in my face.

'*Figlio di puttana!*' I swore as I watched the Instagram story.

It was the same woman who was in the photo he had shown me in the restaurant, when he was talking about how much he loved her breasts.

I had never considered myself a violent person, but right now, I wanted to punch Edward.

'I am so sorry. He does not deserve you.'

'Did you know?' Sammie asked.

'Of course I did not know that he had got his ex pregnant!'

'But did you suspect something? When I told you Edward was sick, you insisted on going to see him. And you seemed to be angry. At first I thought you were being a dick, but now I'm wondering if you suspected something.'

I opened my mouth to speak then closed it again. I did not want to upset her more, but I could not lie to her either.

'I had my suspicions.' I scrubbed my jaw. 'I saw Edward the night before he left and his ex called. And when I went to his room the next morning, he had a hangover, he was not sick. He did not care about leaving you alone and I did not like that.'

That was enough for Sammie to know. I did not see any benefit in sharing the disgusting comments he had made about her.

'They always leave me.' Sammie slumped onto the sand.

'What do you mean?' I sat down next to her.

'Edward left because he didn't like me and the same thing happened with my ex. I wasn't enough. We were together for three years and whenever I discussed any kind of future that involved marriage or having kids, the blood drained from his face. I stayed, hoping that he'd change, but he never did. Then the bastard had the audacity to tell me that he'd met someone. And miraculously eight months later, they got engaged. He said he wasn't ready to commit but what he meant was that he just wasn't ready to commit to *me*.'

Sammie was always so strong and unaffected by other people's opinions of her. So seeing her so upset and vulnerable was like a knife to my heart.

'He was not the right man for you. Neither was Edward.'

'But it wasn't just them. The same has happened with all my dates. Anyone I was ever interested in always ghosted me or said they didn't feel that "connection".'

'That is because they were not your soulmate either.'

The tears continued streaming down her cheeks and each one that fell was like a fresh cut to my skin.

I wanted to take Sammie in my arms, wipe away her tears and hold her until she felt better, but I could not. All of the guests were on the beach, just a few hundred metres away. I doubted they could see us, but it was still too risky.

'Well, then who is?' she shouted in frustration. 'I thought that by paying all this money to come here, I'd be safe from rejection and having men disappear off the face of the earth. But I ended up getting ghosted when we were staying in the same hotel!'

As Sammie's sobs grew louder, the pain in my chest became unbearable.

I could not take it any longer.

'Do not cry.' I gently wiped away her tears with the back of my hand. 'Come here.' I pulled her into me and she rested her head on my chest. 'I promise, there is somebody better waiting for you. Someone who will love the way your eyes sparkle when you smile. Someone who will appreciate the way you make them laugh because you've said something funny or because you have put your foot in your mouth. Someone who will love your confidence.' I stroked her curls and inhaled her sweet citrus scent. 'Someone who will value your kind heart. Someone who will recognise how beautiful and sexy you are.'

Sammie's head bolted up and her gaze met mine.

'Is that what *you* think about me?'

'*Sì*.' I cupped her chin. 'You are one of the most amazing women I have ever had the pleasure of meeting. Edward is a fool. Do not waste a single tear over that *bastardo*.'

Our eyes locked and our faces inched closer.

I knew I should not kiss her.

I knew that the guests were nearby and I was supposed to be taking care of them, but the pull between me and Sammie was too strong.

I was powerless to stop it.

Sammie parted her lips and her sweet, warm breath tickled my skin.

Just as I was about to close the gap between us, I heard my name being called.

'Romeo!'

'*Merda*.' I sprang back.

It was Victoria.

29

SAMMIE

Romeo had only managed to move a few inches away from me when Victoria turned the corner and found us.

Shit.

'What's going on here?' She put her hands on her hips. 'Why are you with Samantha whilst all of our other guests have been left alone?'

'Sammie... Samantha,' Romeo corrected. I supposed he thought using my nickname wasn't appropriate right now. 'Samantha was upset and I was just... comforting her.'

'Romeo! I warned you! I told you not to—'

'I found Edward!' I jumped in.

There was no way I could let Romeo get in trouble for this.

I should be glad that Victoria had found us now and not a minute later, because Romeo and I were finally about to kiss.

Even though every part of my body was weeping, I had to focus on what was most important: Romeo keeping his job.

Edward had already royally fucked me over. There was no way I could allow him to screw with Romeo's career too.

'What?' Victoria frowned. 'Did he call you?'

'No. Jasmine found him on Instagram. And when I did some digging, I saw him with his *pregnant* girlfriend and I was upset. Romeo came after me to find out what was wrong. He's been nothing but a gentleman. It's *Edward* you should be pissed with, not Romeo. Look.' I thrust my phone in front of Victoria and when she saw the story, the blood drained from her face.

'I... Shit. Samantha, I'm so sorry.'

Now so much made sense. When Edward spoke about his ex, he said how amazing their chemistry was and the only barrier was that she didn't want kids, so now she was knocked up, that obstacle had been removed.

'On his application he told us they had been separated for over a year,' Victoria insisted. 'That is one of the key things we look at during the selection process to avoid any rebounds. We trust applicants to tell the truth. The matches are based on the information we're given. If we'd known that Edward had recently reconnected with his ex, there's no way that we would've invited him here.'

'I know it's not your fault and you did your best, but the hotel shouldn't just rely on the applications. You should add another layer of checking, like video interviews so you can see how people react when they talk about their exes. That way you might be able to see whether they're still hung up on them.'

Now that I thought about it, when I'd told Edward about Stella getting back with Max, her ex, he wasn't as shocked as people usually were. I think he even said something like, 'It was clear that they were meant to be.'

All during that conversation he knew that he still had feelings for his ex and had slept with her. What an arsehole.

'That is a good idea,' Romeo said.

'Yes,' Victoria added. 'We will certainly look into that.'

'And maybe do in-person events, like an open day so you can

see how potential guests interact with each other,' I added. 'I get that some people are introverts so they might hate that, but it's good to see people's personalities in real life instead of just relying on what they put on a form. Anyone can lie when they're filling out a questionnaire. Some things you can only tell about a person when you meet them in the flesh.'

Maybe if someone had met Edward in advance, they might've realised that he was a lying bastard.

'Another good suggestion, thank you.'

'I'm tired and don't feel like socialising, so I'm going back to my room.'

'Of course,' Victoria said.

'You will be okay on your own?' Romeo asked.

'Thanks. I'll be fine. At least now I know he's not bloody coming back!' A weak laugh fell from my lips. 'Night,' I said, as I headed to my room.

* * *

I sat up in bed and stretched my arms to the ceiling.

Considering what happened last night, I'd slept surprisingly well.

Now that I wasn't in limbo any more with Edward, I wondered what would happen to me. Was there any point in staying if I didn't have a match?

Based on what Stella had told me, now that I'd been here a week, today I'd leave this room and get transferred to a couple's villa. But I wasn't sure if moving to a bigger place was a good idea. It'd just remind me that I was there alone, whilst everyone else was happily matched up.

I knew that what Romeo said was true: I shouldn't waste any

more time thinking about Edward, but I couldn't help feeling shitty.

It wasn't about Edward per se – if I was honest, I didn't feel the connection with him from the start. It was just I was tired of the constant rejection. The feeling of never being good enough.

Romeo was kind to say all of those sweet things about me, but in a way, it only made things worse. It didn't matter if he thought I was funny or smart and sexy (I still wasn't sure if he meant that or was just trying to make me feel better), because even with Edward out of the picture, it didn't resolve the issue of relationships with guests being forbidden.

Yes, I fancied Romeo like crazy and I'd wanted to kiss him, but I saw how angry Victoria was when she saw us together. Imagine if she caught us doing more? I wasn't going to be responsible for Romeo losing his job. I didn't need that kind of karma.

Especially given what he'd told me before about how determined he was to secure the opportunity to work in the US. That was his dream and he'd made it very clear that he wouldn't let anything, especially a woman, jeopardise that.

And even if Victoria declared that as compensation for Edward screwing me over, she'd allow me and Romeo to fuck once to get it out of our systems, it wouldn't solve the issue. I was tired of hookups. I wanted more. And as much as I felt the connection with Romeo, he couldn't give me a committed, long-term relationship.

Now that I thought about it, I was glad that Victoria had interrupted us.

She'd stopped us both from making a terrible mistake.

I had no idea what I was going to do for the rest of my stay here, but one thing I knew for sure was that it definitely would *not* involve kissing Romeo.

30

ROMEO

As I finished clearing away the chairs from this morning's briefing, my heart hammered in my chest.

Victoria had summoned me to her office, which could not be good. Especially after she caught me with Sammie yesterday.

Although Sammie had told Victoria that it was innocent and I had been a gentleman, I knew the truth.

There was absolutely nothing gentlemanly about the thoughts going through my head about what I wanted to do with Sammie just seconds before Victoria had arrived.

Until I received that message from Victoria ten minutes ago, I thought I had been lucky and that my job was safe.

After Sammie returned to her room last night, Victoria was about to talk to me but she got called away. There would be no more hiding now though. It was time to face the music.

I strode to Victoria's office, frustrated that my plan to check on Sammie had been disrupted. She had not come for breakfast and she had also missed the last morning briefing.

Now that it was Saturday and the guests had been here for a

week, they would be moving from their individual rooms to share a villa with their match.

There would be no more daily group activities. They would be in charge of organising their own excursions with my help.

I hoped Sammie was okay. As soon as I'd met with Victoria, I would go straight to check on her and bring her the *pasticciotto* pastries I had saved for her.

I knocked on the door.

'Come in,' Victoria replied. I sat in the chair opposite her desk, straightened my shoulders then puffed out my chest.

If Victoria wanted to punish me for comforting Sammie, then I would take it. After finding out about Edward's lies, it was understandable that she was shocked, angry and sad. I couldn't just sit there and do nothing. If I could go back in time, I would do the same thing all over again.

'I've spent most of this morning on the phone with head office and speaking to Edward.'

'You spoke with him?' My nostrils flared. If I ever saw that *stronzo* again, the only way I would want to communicate with him would be with my fist. I knew he was bad from the beginning. I should have trusted my gut.

'Yes. The office was closed, but I found his PA's mobile number and when I told her that we were considering legal action, it was amazing how quickly Edward returned my call.'

'You can take him to court?'

'Truthfully? Probably not, but I hoped it would get his attention. And I only said that we were *considering* it, not that we were going to do it. Anyway, the little weasel said that when his ex heard that he'd applied to come here, she came to see him and they'd ended up screwing a few times and hey presto, now she's expecting. Apparently, she called and told him the news the night before the Alberobello trip and he decided that he had to go and see her and talk about it properly.'

'And instead of telling us the truth, he lied and said that someone was sick.' I ground my jaw.

'According to him, he didn't lie. He said that he'd told us it was a family emergency and he insists that was true.'

'And did he also have excuses for why he did not think it was important to tell his match personally instead of ignoring the many messages she sent to him?'

'He was "busy", but said he will apologise to her soon.'

'*Figlio di puttana!*' I scowled.

'Ordinarily, I would tell you that it wasn't appropriate to swear and call a guest a son of a bitch.' She clasped her hands together and leant forward in her seat. 'But in this case, it's entirely justified. I've been calling him a lot worse in my head. He's left us with a big mess to clear up.'

'What will happen with Samantha?' I said, remembering to use her full name.

'Obviously we'll give her a full refund. It's up to her whether she stays, but I think it'd be best if she doesn't leave on such a low note. If she stays we could show her how sorry we are and prove that the Love Hotel will do whatever it takes to ensure she's well looked after. Which is where you come in.'

'What do you mean?' I asked.

Ordinarily, I would be more than happy to make sure my guests were well looked after. But I was sure that the way I wanted to do that with Sammie was not what Victoria had in mind.

'Based on how Samantha defended you last night, she trusts you. So, I need you to ask her to stay. At least for a few more days. We've reserved one of the best villas for her, we can provide her with a chauffeur-driven car to take her to wherever she'd like to go and pay for any excursions. The objective isn't just her happiness. It's damage control. In an ideal world, the media won't find out what happened, because only you and I and a few of the management know what Edward did, but if it does, we need to be able to show that we went above and beyond the call of duty to rectify the situation. Understood?'

'*Sì*. I will go and speak to her now.'

'Good. Report back to let me know what she said, straight-away. And Romeo?'

'*Sì*?'

'Be careful.' She raised an eyebrow.

I nodded in acknowledgement, got up, left her office, went to the restaurant to collect the *pasticciotto* I had put aside, then rushed to Sammie's room. I needed to make sure she was okay.

Sammie opened the door and when I saw her tear-stained cheeks and red eyes, my heart shattered.

'*Ciao*, Sammie,' I said softly. 'I came to check on you. You did not come to breakfast or to the briefing. I brought you these.' I handed her the box of *pasticciotto*.

Her face instantly lit up when she opened it and relief washed over me.

'*Grazie*,' she replied solemnly.

I missed her smile and bubbly personality.

I hated Edward for doing this to her.

'I wanted to talk to you about the rest of your stay.'

'Are they kicking me out?'

'No! We want you to stay. I want to explain what we have in mind for you.'

'Okay. Do you want to come in?'

'I...'

Of course I wanted to, but I was not sure if I should. Even though I could tell she had been crying and was dressed in the hotel's bathrobe, she still looked beautiful. If I came inside her room and we were all alone, I was not sure I would be able to resist the urge to kiss her. That would be wrong at any time, but especially right now when she was upset.

'Don't worry,' she said. 'I promise not to jump you.' A small smile touched her lips.

'Are you sure? Because I heard you are obsessed with Mr Bean and seeing as I am basically his twin, I am worried that you will not be able to resist me.' I smirked.

'Shit. I knew I shouldn't have mentioned the Mr Bean duvet and pillow covers I have in my bedroom or the fact that I kiss the posters I have of him next to my bed every night before I go to sleep on the Love Hotel questionnaire!' Sammie laughed and the sound warmed my chest.

That was the Sammie I knew and loved.

When I said 'loved' of course I did not mean literally.

'I will sit on the opposite side of the room, just in case.' I grinned.

Sammie opened the door wider and gestured for me to come in.

'Excuse the mess.' She gathered a pile of clothes off the sofa, put them on the bed, opened the curtains, then returned to the sofa and patted the seat beside her. 'I wasn't expecting company and obviously I haven't been feeling my best.'

'Do not worry. So.' I inhaled deeply. 'Victoria spoke to Edward.'

'What?' She almost leapt off the sofa in shock. 'What did that tosspot have to say for himself?'

As I explained everything Victoria had told me, Sammie's facial expressions jumped from disbelief to anger then rage.

'What an arsehole!'

'*Sì.* But although we did not find you a match, we do not

want all of your memories of the hotel to be negative, so we would like you to stay.'

I told Sammie all about what we would like to offer her and she nodded along.

'Okay. Do I have to move to the villa right now?'

'No. Whenever you like.'

'Could I maybe move there later today or tomorrow? I don't feel like packing and moving right now.'

'Would you like someone to come and pack for you?'

'Thanks, but no, I can do it. Can't I just get the key from reception when I'm ready?'

'Normally I take the guests to the villa to show them around personally.'

'You've already done enough. I don't mind. I'm sure I'll figure everything out.'

'If you are sure?'

'Yep. Now I just need to work out what I'm gonna do all week.' She blew out a defeated breath.

'There are many places to visit. Some of the beaches in Salento are so beautiful that they call them the Maldives of Italy. And you could go on a guided tour of the illuminated caverns at Grotte Di Castellana... I could make a list.'

'To go on my own.' Her shoulders slumped and an uncomfortable silence filled the air.

'I could go to some places with you,' I blurted out and her face instantly brightened.

That was a very, very bad idea. But I could not help it. Sammie looked so defeated and for some reason, making her smile was becoming one of my favourite things to do.

'You'd do that?' Her eyes filled with hope. 'Would you be allowed? I mean, wouldn't you be working?'

'During the second week guests organise their own activities, so I am able to have more time off.'

'If you're sure, then I'd really love that. I enjoy spending time with you.'

'The feeling is mutual,' I said.

Our eyes met and just like last night, I had an overwhelming urge to kiss her. My gaze dropped to her lips.

I wondered if they felt as soft as they looked.

I wondered how they tasted.

And I wondered if once I started to kiss her, I would be able to stop.

If she let me, I would kiss her beautiful breasts.

I would kiss every inch of her, then beg Sammie to let me bury my head between her legs.

As I pictured myself licking her pussy, my cock thickened.

Cazzo.

I wanted Sammie so much.

When my eyes returned to hers, Sammie's lips were parted and desire burned in her eyes.

She inched forward and I stroked her cheek, then traced my finger over her bottom lip.

Sammie groaned with pleasure and the sound made my dick strain against my shorts.

'Kiss me,' Sammie moaned softly.

Hearing her give me permission caused a bolt of electricity to shoot through my veins.

I should not accept her invitation.

There was still time to walk away from this.

But I did not want to. I wanted to kiss her.

And no one would know.

Victoria told me to come and see Sammie. Not to cross the

line with her obviously, but this would just be a secret between me and Sammie.

If I was going to kiss her, now was the perfect time.

I inched forward again and cupped her face.

Just as I was about to close the gap between us, the shrill ring of Sammie's phone sounded.

'Bloody hell!' Sammie jumped back, clutching her chest. 'That scared the shit out of me!'

'You should get that.' I stood up. 'And I should go.'

'I don't want you to.'

'I need to let Victoria know that you will be staying and check that your villa is ready. I will call you when I have some news.'

'Okay,' she said.

I rushed towards the door, then stepped outside.

That was close.

Maybe being interrupted was a warning to stop me from making a big mistake.

But if that was true, why was I not glad about it?

31

SAMMIE

'This place is *incredible!*' I said as I stood at the front door of my villa and took in the view of the swimming pool that I'd just spotted out on the patio. 'Oh my God!' I screamed down the phone before racing through the open-plan living room to take a closer look.

'Ouch,' Stella replied. 'My eardrums!'

'Sorry, but I've got my own pool *and* hot tub!' I said as I ran along the patio towards it. 'And the living room is huge! To think I was considering going home!'

'So, you're staying?'

'Too right! They're gonna give me all my money back and a driver to take me anywhere I want. I mean, I'd have to be an idiot to turn that down.'

'And will you be going to these places *alone?*' Stella asked suggestively.

I stepped into the huge bedroom and slid the patio doors shut. Even though it was a detached villa, I didn't want to risk anyone overhearing my conversation.

'Well, Romeo said that maybe we could go to some places *together*.'

'I didn't know Love Alchemists could take a guest on an excursion by themselves.'

'We almost kissed. *Twice*.'

'What?' Stella shouted.

'Ouch! My eardrums!' I joked, repeating her earlier comment.

'When did *this* happen?'

'The first time was after I'd found out about Edward and was upset. Then earlier today when he came to tell me about Victoria speaking to Edward and what the hotel wanted to offer me, we had another moment and I asked him to kiss me.'

'You *asked* him?'

'Yeah,' I shrugged, even though she couldn't see me. 'It just felt like the attraction was mutual and I knew he wouldn't make the first move because he'd be worried about taking advantage of me, so I wanted to let him know that it was okay. That I wanted him too.'

'So, why'd you stop?'

'You called.'

'Oh, shit! That's why you didn't answer straightaway. I can't believe that I was the person responsible for a dreaded kiss-interruption call!' She laughed.

Once Romeo had left, I hadn't called Stella straight back as my mind was still racing from our almost kiss and when I phoned her half an hour later, she was busy.

'Don't worry. I'll get you back one day,' I chuckled.

'Maybe it was for the best?' Stella asked. 'I mean, you've gotta admit, it would make things complicated. Not just because of the whole Love Alchemist-guest dynamic, but you've only got six more full days there and then what? I want to tell you to go for it and enjoy yourself, but I don't want to see you get hurt.'

'Same. Anyway, it's kind of out of my hands. Since Romeo told me about the villa earlier this morning, I haven't heard from him. So, I'm just gonna chill by my pool, read for a bit, go for another swim in the sea, then see what happens.'

'Good plan.'

'Oh my God,' I gasped as I looked at the screen. 'Romeo's calling.'

'You gonna answer?'

'No. I'm talking to you. I'll call him back afterwards.'

'I've already cockblocked you once, so I'm not doing it again! Let's speak later.'

'You sure?'

'Positive. Just... oh, what the hell. Just enjoy yourself and be safe.'

'Hold your horses! I don't even know why he's calling!'

'Only one way to find out! I'm hanging up now.'

Stella ended the call and I quickly pressed the accept button.

'*Ciao*, Romeo,' I said, trying to sound casual.

'*Ciao*, Sammie. What are your plans for tomorrow?'

'I'll probably just chill at the villa and go for a swim, why?'

'After I go for lunch with my mother, in the afternoon I will do some pottery at my friend's studio. Would you like to join me?'

'I'd love to!' Excitement bubbled in my chest.

'Okay. I will send you the details of the town his studio is in. Ask the driver to take you to the centre and I will pick you up there. Tell them you do not know how long you will be so you will call when you are ready to leave. And of course, please do not tell him that you will be meeting me.'

'Got it. Mum's the word.'

'See you tomorrow,' Romeo replied, then hung up.

Seconds later, my phone pinged with the name of a town I couldn't pronounce and my stomach fizzed with excitement.

I knew it wasn't a date, but it was an opportunity to spend more time with Romeo, so I'd take it.

Tomorrow couldn't come fast enough.

* * *

I waved at my chauffeur, Aldo, as he pulled out from the parking space and drove off.

My heart thumped against my chest. In less than ten minutes I'd be meeting Romeo.

When I spotted him in a black car, butterflies filled my stomach.

As usual, he looked hotter than a bucket of chilli sauce.

Romeo's eyes connected with mine, then his face broke into a wide smile. He jumped out of the car and headed towards me.

'*Ciao.*' He kissed my cheeks.

'*Ciao,*' I said as his manly, woody scent surrounded me.

After opening the door for me we both slid into our seats then Romeo set off.

We chatted easily about what we'd done earlier and less than ten minutes later we pulled outside a cute stone building. Romeo unlocked the front door then invited me inside.

'This is nice,' I said as the scent of earthy clay hit my nostrils.

There were multiple potter's wheels and tables dotted around the room. The shelves were decorated with colourful bowls, plates, vases and other items that I guessed had been made in the studio and there was a large kiln at the back. 'What are you making today?'

'You mean, what are *we* making today,' he corrected.

'I've never done pottery before.'

'There is a first time for everything. Here.' He plucked an apron off the wall. 'I brought you some clothes to change into. It can get messy and you do not want to ruin your beautiful dress.'

'*Grazie*,' I said as he pulled out an oversized T-shirt and an old pair of trousers.

'The bathroom is at the back.'

I went inside, slipped out of my dress, picked up the T-shirt, lifted it to my nose then squeezed my eyes shut and groaned. It smelt delicious, just like Romeo. Once I put it on, I wasn't sure if I'd want to give it back.

I slid it over my head. It was so big that it came almost to my knees. When I tried the trousers on, they were too long. I'd end up tripping over them, so I took them off. The T-shirt wasn't that much shorter than my dress, so with that and the apron I'd be fine.

When I returned to the main area, Romeo was setting things up by the wheel.

'Sit here.' He gestured to the stool. 'I'm going to teach you.'

'Okay!' I sat down. 'So how did you get into pottery?'

'My grandparents used to do it. There is a lot of clay in Puglia and towns like Grottaglie are famous for their ceramic pottery.'

'Cool. So what are *we* making today?'

'I want to make a new bowl for my mamma. I went to see her earlier and I will see her again on Tuesday, so I would like to bring her something.'

'Awww, that's so sweet.' My stomach fluttered. 'We'd better make it good then. How's Biscotti?'

Romeo's eyes widened like he was surprised I'd remembered she was ill.

'She is much better, *grazie*.' His face lit up. 'I appreciate you asking.'

'No worries! I'm glad she's on the mend.'

Romeo put the clay on the wheel and explained how I should try and mould it with my hands.

Unsurprisingly, my first few attempts were disasters. But I was determined that the next try would be a masterpiece. Well, decent enough anyway.

'Like this.' Romeo reached from behind me and laced his fingers with mine. As he showed me how to shape the wet clay, electricity rocketed through my body.

'Mmm.' A moan slipped from my mouth. 'Are you deliberately trying to recreate the scene from *Ghost*?'

'*Ghost*?'

'Y'know, the film with Demi Moore. There's a scene where she's doing some pottery and Patrick Swayze's character comes behind her and helps.'

'And what happens next?'

'They start kissing,' I said, my heartbeat racing.

'*Really*?' he said. 'And is that something that you would like to happen?'

'I wouldn't say no...' Desire bubbled under my skin.

'But does that mean you would say *yes*? I must be sure.'

'Yes,' I said through a ragged breath.

Romeo didn't say a word. The silence seemed to stretch for an eternity and I almost regretted mentioning it because I was worried he'd say it wasn't a good idea.

But when he stepped forward so his hard body was pressed against my back, my brain short-circuited.

'Oh, God,' I moaned as he peppered soft kisses across my neck, then along my collarbone. 'That feels so good.'

His lips travelled up to my cheeks and as his warm, sweet breath tickled my skin every atom in my body sprang to life.

I pushed my bum into him and when I felt his hard length pressed against me, I groaned again.

Romeo moved his hands and body away and I instantly missed the contact. But then he lifted my palms away from the clay, spun me around then crashed his mouth onto mine.

The kiss was hot, hungry and passionate. A desperate collision of lips, like we'd been waiting to do this for years instead of just days.

My mouth parted and Romeo slid his tongue inside. As it thrashed against mine, my arms snaked around his waist, pulling him into me. I wanted to feel him.

His hard-on pressed against my stomach and I swear a dam burst in my knickers.

I gripped his arse.

'Fuck me, Romeo. Please. I want you.'

Romeo's clay-covered hands moved from my back, brushing the fabric of the T-shirt covering my arse before sliding underneath.

'I am glad you did not wear the trousers,' he said as his hands travelled up my thighs, before dipping between my legs. As he slid his fingers over my damp knickers, I bucked against his hand. 'You are so wet, Sammie. I love it. If I did not have clay over my hands, I would slide my fingers inside you.'

'You don't have clay on your dick, so why don't you slide that inside me instead?' I panted.

A mischievous grin touched Romeo's lips.

'Are you sure that is what you want?'

'Positive. But hurry up, please. The thought of you fucking me here is turning me on so much it won't take much for me to come. Do you have a condom?'

'*Sì*, in my wallet, but our hands are covered in clay.'

'Yeah... that probably won't go well with latex. Stay there. I like the idea of you keeping your hands like that, so I'll clean mine.'

I raced over to wash my hands, used some wipes I spotted by the sink then washed them again.

After taking Romeo's wallet out of his shorts pocket, I found the foil packet.

'Permission to undress you, kind sir,' I said in a posh accent as I tried to hide my excitement.

'I am all yours.'

As Romeo stood in front of me, my nipples hardened and a fresh wave of tingles erupted between my legs.

I felt like I was standing in front of an all-you-can-eat dessert buffet. I didn't even know where to start.

I wanted to see his magnificent chest, but I was also dying to see his cock too.

As if he was a mind reader, Romeo whipped off his T-shirt.

Jesus.

Those abs.

Those pecs.

The man's chest was a work of art. Every one of his abs looked like it'd been sculpted to perfection right here in this studio.

He had gorgeous dark hair covering his chest and as I followed the happy trail that led to the waistband of his shorts, I swallowed hard.

I reached forward, unbuckled his belt, undid the button, pulled down the zip, then tugged at the waist.

As his shorts dropped to the floor and I saw his enormous cock straining from his dark black boxer shorts my body lit up like a volcano.

I ran my hands over his long, hard, thick length and Romeo squeezed his eyes shut. Next, I gripped his boxer shorts and slid them down his thighs. As his giant cock sprang free, my jaw dropped.

'Jesus,' I gasped, wondering how the hell that was going to fit. I'd find a way though. There was no way I was letting that go to waste. Once I'd ripped open the condom wrapper, I slid it down him. 'Where do you want me?'

'I am not fucking you yet.' He shook his head. 'You have undressed me. Now it is my turn.'

Romeo stepped forward and held my gaze whilst he slid his arms behind my back, undid the apron, then lifted it over my head. Next, he removed the T-shirt, leaving me standing in front of him in just my underwear. Thank God I was wearing something decent.

I had on a red lacy bra and one of the sexy thongs Stella's mum made which had 'Good Girl' written in diamantes across the back. I had no intention of being 'good' in the traditional sense though. Right now there were so many filthy things I wanted Romeo to do to me.

'*Mamma mia*,' Romeo gasped. '*Sei bellissima.*'

'What did you say?' I panted. Whatever it was sounded sexy as hell.

'I said that you are beautiful. Your underwear is pretty too. I do not want to make it dirty so unless you object, I will find another way to remove it.'

'Fine by me.'

'Get up on the table and open your legs,' he growled.

I did exactly as he asked. I was so turned on that I swear there was fire and not blood racing through my veins.

Romeo stepped forward, dipped his head between my legs, latched onto the fabric of my thong with his teeth, then dragged it down.

'Fuck, that's so hot,' I panted, lifting my bum up so he could pull it down.

'Such a pretty pussy,' Romeo said before leaning forward and licking my clit. 'Mmm,' he moaned. *'Deliziosa.'* He gave another long, slow lick.

My hips jerked off the table and as he circled my clit with his tongue I could already feel the wave building.

'I can't believe I'm going to say this, but that feels too good. If you keep doing that I'll come and I want to do that with you inside me.'

Romeo lifted his head and grinned.

'Va bene. The first time I will make you come with my dick. And then I will make you come again, but with my tongue.'

'Confident little thing, aren't you?'

'Let's see if you are calling me "little" when I put this inside you.' He gestured towards his cock. 'Are you ready?'

'Sì,' I panted.

Romeo grabbed his cock, lined it up at my entrance then slammed inside me.

I cried out. He was right. There was nothing small about the giant pipe that he'd just buried inside me.

'Stai bene?' he asked, checking if I was okay.

'Sì,' I confirmed, gripping his bum cheeks and pushing him deeper.

As I took in the sight of Romeo in front of me and watched as his cock sank into me, I was dizzy with desire.

I'd dreamt about having sex with Romeo for so long and I couldn't believe it was finally happening. And it was even better than I'd imagined.

Our hips moved in perfect rhythm as he filled me up.

Whilst he continued pumping into me, he leant forward and

pulled the fabric of my bra down, exposing one breast, and then moved to the other.

'*Che tette spettacolari.*' He licked his lips. 'Your boobs are beautiful.' He took a nipple in his mouth and sucked it slowly, almost tipping me over the edge.

I was so used to men commenting on how small my boobs were. But Romeo looked at me like I was his favourite topless model.

Romeo ran his hands over my breasts then froze.

'*Scusi*! I forgot about the clay.'

'I don't care,' I said. 'Cover me with it if you want. Just keep fucking me.'

Romeo pounded into me, harder and faster as he squeezed my nipples.

I couldn't believe I was getting fucked on a pottery table by the hottest man I'd ever laid eyes on, with clay all over my tits. Never in my wildest fantasies would I have imagined a scene like this.

Those thoughts alone sent me hurtling close to the edge.

But when Romeo took *my* hand, placed my fingers on my clit and started circling it, I knew I was on the verge of erupting.

'I do not want to get clay on your clit, so I need you to touch it for me,' he growled. 'Come for me, Sammie.'

As he slammed into me again, I tipped over the edge.

'Romeo! Fuck, Romeo!' I cried out as my orgasm ripped through me.

My whole body shook and I swore I saw enough stars to light up the whole of Italy.

Romeo continued pumping before letting out a guttural growl, then collapsing on me.

We both lay there, chests heaving, bodies slick with sweat.

'That was... I don't even have words,' I said.

'But good words, *sì*?'

'Not good words, *amazing* words.'

'I am happy to hear that.' Romeo lifted his head and as I took in the gorgeous sight of him, I chuckled.

'Why are you laughing?' he asked.

'Because you have clay in your hair, on your face and all over your chest. And my hands were clean.'

'But thanks to me, your breasts were covered in clay.'

'That's hot,' I grinned.

'*You* are hot.'

'So, no regrets?' I asked.

'How could I regret burying my cock in the sexiest, funniest woman in the world?'

'Only in the whole world? I was hoping you'd at *least* say the universe,' I grinned.

'You are right. You are the sexiest, funniest woman in the universe.'

'*Grazie.* So, you're not worried about breaking the no-fraternising-with-guests rule?'

'I should. But after that, I am not. Some rules are meant to be broken...'

32

SAMMIE

I was currently sitting in Romeo's car on the way to lunch at one of his favourite restaurants.

Actually, 'floating' was a better description than 'sitting' because I was still on a high from our epic sex sesh yesterday.

Romeo was even more talented than I'd imagined. Those hands, that mouth and his dick... wow. He was easily the best I'd ever had.

After we'd fucked on the pottery table, we'd said that we should clean up and get back to making the bowl. But one thing led to another and before I knew it, we were at it again.

By that point, the clay was everywhere. In my hair, over my breasts, thighs... I even had an imprint of Romeo's palms on my arse.

He was covered in clay too, because after I'd slid on a fresh condom, I thought it'd be fun to put more on my hands so I could also leave my mark all over his gorgeous body.

Romeo was about to make good on his promise to make me come with his tongue, but then his friend had messaged to say he was on his way, so it was a race against time to get the studio cleaned up and scrub as much of the clay off in the bathroom as possible before he got there.

Once we'd finished making the bowl, Romeo had dropped me back in town and I waited in his car until my driver arrived.

When we said goodbye, he'd given me a long, slow kiss and the temptation to invite him back to my villa was strong. But we were already playing with fire. It was best if we just stuck with seeing each other outside of the hotel grounds.

'Did you sleep well?' Romeo asked now.

'Like a baby,' I said, tapping my feet to an Italian pop song that was playing on the radio. 'You know I'm already a fan of the mattress at the hotel, but when you add in a couple of epic sex workouts, there was no way I wasn't gonna conk out as soon as my head hit the pillow.' I grinned as a flashback of Romeo sliding in and out of me popped into my head for the hundredth time today. 'How about you?'

'I also slept very well.' He flashed a cheeky smile and I got the feeling he was having illicit flashbacks too.

'Yesterday afternoon definitely blew away the cobwebs,' I cackled.

'Cobwebs?' He frowned. 'Where did you see cobwebs?'

'Not *literal* cobwebs,' I laughed. 'I just meant, it's been a while for me, y'know?' Then again, of course he didn't know. This guy probably had a phone full of fuckbuddies ready to spread their legs for him whenever he wanted.

Which was exactly why I needed to stop thinking about yesterday.

We were attracted to each other. We slept together to get it out of our systems and now that we had, that was that. He was just being kind by taking me out today so that I wasn't sitting at the hotel on my own. End of.

'Here we are.' Romeo pulled over in a car park.

Wow. It was a restaurant right by the sea with huge windows giving uninterrupted views.

The waiter showed us to a table and once we'd ordered, I took a sip of the wine that Romeo had recommended.

'You were talking about Biscotti and your mum before,' I said. 'Are you close to all of your family?'

'Most of them. My mother especially. Although she has lived here for over thirty years, I still think she finds it difficult being away from her family and friends in England. It was easier when we were all living at home, but now with me always working at the hotel, my brother in London and my sister in Rome, she gets lonely. I know she misses us a lot.'

'I can imagine,' I said, tearing off a piece of bread then popping it in my mouth.

'Do you have siblings?'

'Yeah – a younger sister. She drives me up the wall, but I love her really,' I said. 'And how about your dad?'

Romeo's face turned to stone.

'We do not get along,' he said bluntly.

'Oh no, why?' I blurted out, then realised I was being too nosy. 'Sorry, it's none of my business.'

'It is okay. I do not like how he treats my mother. He is disrespectful. He has cheated on her many times. Last time she went to London, she came back to find two women in the house with him, so instead of divorcing him, she thinks the solution is never to leave him home alone again.' Romeo shook his head.

'That's terrible.'

'It is. She gave up her career in London to come here and focus on raising the family. He never wanted her to work, but I know that she did. Now that we are all grown, this is her chance to reclaim her life. I have told her so many times that she should divorce him and return to England, but she will not. She is very loyal. *Too* loyal. He does not deserve her.'

'I'm so sorry to hear that. If my dad ever cheated, Mum would chop his cock off.'

'I would not blame her. It is a betrayal of the highest kind.' His face tightened again.

'Yep.' My stomach clenched as I thought about the times it'd happened to me.

'Mamma stays because I know that she will feel embarrassed to leave. From what I heard from her sister, many people told her that leaving to go to live in Italy with him was a mistake. And for so long I think she painted the picture of having a perfect life here, the handsome boyfriend, sunshine, sea... it all must have sounded so glamorous. So if she returned, I think she is afraid to look like a failure and have everyone tell her that they knew it would not work, so it is easier to stay.'

'Yeah. I guess it's harder to leave the older you get and if she's been keeping up appearances for so long, it's probably terrifying to tell everyone she's been living a lie. But if her family and friends love her, they'd understand and welcome her back with open arms.'

'Exactly.'

'And if they haven't been happy for a while and she's wasting her life, it's better to make the break now before she wastes any more of her life, right?'

'This is what I have been telling her. She does not know this but I have set up a bank account for her, so that when she is ready to leave him and return to England she will have money for a fresh start.'

'Wow.' My eyes popped. 'That's so sweet of you.'

'It is nothing compared to all that she has done for me and my siblings. I just want her to be happy and I know she will be happier if she is back in England. She did take us there for a while when we were younger, but my father sweet-talked her. He said if they got divorced it would bring shame and bad luck on the family, so she brought us back. In the end she decided it was easier to stay than leave.'

'Were they ever in love?'

'It is hard to say. From what I could tell, my parents were a terrible match. It was all based on lust. She was flattered that a model was interested in her and loved his accent. And he loved being able to say that he had a beautiful girl from London worshipping him. She boosted his ego and he liked that. That wasn't the basis for a marriage.'

'Your dad was a model?'

'*Sì*. For many years. He met Mamma when he was modelling in London. According to my English aunt, he promised Mamma the world, so she left her teaching job and moved to Italy to be with him which was a mistake because he was always travelling. By the time she realised that he was a ladies' man, she was already pregnant with me and so she committed to staying here to raise me. They got married but he never changed. I still remember the arguments.' Romeo winced.

'I'm sorry.' I rested my hand on his and gave it a squeeze, trying to ignore the electricity shooting through me. Romeo was opening up to me, so now wasn't the time to think about how good it felt.

'And when his work started to dry up, he made me do modelling instead, so he could live the experience through me.'

'I didn't realise you were a model!' My eyes popped. I wasn't surprised, because *hello*, look at him.

Romeo nodded solemnly.

'That was the career path he wanted me to follow. He wanted me to be successful and have the money and women like he did.'

'And you didn't want that?'

'In the beginning, I thought it was cool. Even though I hated the way he treated Mamma, he was still my father and he was kind of famous so I looked up to him for that, not the way he treated Mamma, so it felt good that he was proud of me and that I was following in his footsteps. And I will admit, I liked the attention. I was just a kid at the time and at that age it is good to be popular, no?'

'Yeah,' I said.

'But when my skin started to break out, things changed. Some brands would use make-up and retouching, but because I did not fit that mould of perfection any more they did not want me. And that affected me. A lot.'

'How old were you?'

'Fourteen or fifteen, I think.'

'Shit. Dealing with rejection as an adult is tough, but it must've been extra shitty at that age.'

'It was. When I finally got through it, I knew that I did not want to pursue a career based on my appearance. That is why I get frustrated when people judge others, including me, by the way I look. Of course I enjoyed the benefits in my twenties, so that does make me a hypocrite, but now I am old enough to know it does not matter. I am more interested in the beauty of someone's heart.'

'Really, though?' I cocked my head to the side. 'You're seriously saying that any woman, even someone who let's say was at the back of the queue when God was giving out good looks, has just as much chance of dating you as a supermodel?'

'Why not?' He shrugged his shoulders.

'Bullshit!' I shook my head. 'People say that looks aren't important, but it's the first thing people see. It's what first attracts you to someone, right?'

'That is true, but I can tell you from experience that even if someone who the world considered to be the most beautiful woman in the world was standing in front of me but she had an ugly personality, it would mean nothing.' That made sense. I'd dated loads of hot guys who were horrible people and the attraction fell flat. 'Looks catch your attention, but it is someone's soul that will keep it.'

'So, what did you think when you saw me for the first time?' I said, then wondered if I really wanted to know the answer.

'I thought you were very beautiful,' he said without hesitation.

'Awww, *grazie!*' I blushed. 'But that proves my point. You judged me by my appearance.'

'I had not finished.'

'Uh-oh, that doesn't sound good!'

'You are right. I thought that you were beautiful, but when you started talking about jet lag and drinking...'

'You thought I was a bimbo!'

'*Bimbo* is too harsh. I just thought perhaps you were not someone that I would be interested in. But truthfully, I was not ready to be interested in anyone.'

'So... considering what happened yesterday, I'm guessing something changed?'

We still hadn't discussed what it meant (although I was pretty sure it was nothing), so now was the perfect time.

'I got to know you better. Which is exactly my point. You are beautiful, but that alone was not enough. There always has to be more.'

'I hear you,' I nodded. The waiter put our dishes down on the table and I deliberately stayed silent until he'd left before continuing what I wanted to say. 'Speaking of yesterday...'

Romeo's phone vibrated loudly. He reached into his pocket then pulled it out.

'I have to get this. It's Victoria. *Ciao*,' he answered. '*Sì*, she seems happy. I will keep checking on her. I know.'

Romeo's expression turned serious. Soon afterwards, he ended the call.

'Everything okay?' I asked.

'We...' He paused and dragged his hand down his face. 'What happened yesterday, it cannot happen again. That was Victoria, asking if I had checked on you and reminding me not to cross any lines.'

'Do you think she suspects something?'

'I have no idea, but it is too risky. I cannot make any more mistakes.'

My mouth dropped open.

'So yesterday was a *mistake*?'

'No.' He grabbed my hand. 'I do not regret it. It was incredible. But I cannot sacrifice my dream again.'

'I know,' I added, remembering what he'd told me about what happened with his ex.

'We should eat, while it is hot,' Romeo said, pulling his hand away, and I knew that the conversation was over.

It was fine though. I knew from the start that it was a one-time thing.

And I was fine with that.

Honestly, I was.

We only hooked up to get it out of our systems, so mission accomplished.

Right?

33

SAMMIE

'So, how's it going with Romeo? Have you stood on a balcony yet and called his name?'

'Eh?' I frowned.

'Y'know, *like Romeo, Romeo, where the hell are you Romeo* or however Shakespeare wrote it in *Romeo and Juliet.*' Stella laughed.

'I'm sure he's never heard *that* before,' I scoffed.

'I know! Totally original! But anyway, have you resisted temptation?'

'We fucked yesterday.'

'*Whaaaatttt?*' Stella screamed down the phone. '*Where? How?* Spill the tea, coffee, Aperol Spritz and *everything!*'

'*Spill the Aperol Spritz!*' I cackled. 'I like it!'

'Stop stalling and dish the dirt. I told you all about when Max gave me the first *Beef Injection* as you called it, so make sure you don't miss out a single detail. For starters, where did you do it?'

'On a pottery table.'

'*Noooo!*' she screamed again.

'It was kind of hot. I was attempting to mould a bowl on the pottery wheel thingy and he stood behind me and showed me how to do it. One minute he was pressed against me with his arms around my waist and the next thing I knew we were kissing then bonking on the table.'

'Love it! It's like an X-rated version of the scene from *Ghost*.'

'It totally was. And we got clay *everywhere*! Well, luckily, I didn't get any up my vag, which was a relief! Then again, clay's natural. Remember when we used to do those clay face masks when you stayed over at mine and we had a girly night. It always left our skin so soft, so maybe it would've been fine!' I cackled.

'I know vaginal rejuvenation treatments are a thing, but I've never heard of anyone inserting clay up their fanny before!'

'It could be the next big beauty craze. They could call it a Fanny Facial or Coochie Clay Mask!'

'Oh my God!' Stella snorted. 'Anyway, enough about the clay. How was the sex?'

'Easily the best shag of my life. Two thousand out of ten. And before you say it, I know that's not technically possible, but I don't care. That's how amazing it was.'

Just as Stella had asked, I filled her in on everything.

'I'm happy for you, hon. After all the crap you've been through on this trip, you deserved to have something to put a smile on your face.'

'Yeah. It's been a rollercoaster, but those orgasms definitely helped.' I groaned as I replayed the sensations of him being inside me and how good it felt when his tongue licked my clit.

Such a shame I wouldn't get the chance to experience it again and that I'd missed the chance to have him go down on me properly.

'I don't mean to get serious but what's the plan? Was it just a one-off?'

'Course!' I said. 'I'm not stupid. This isn't like you and Max. We live in two different countries, so it can't go anywhere. And he's massively scarred by his parents' experience.'

'What happened with his parents?'

'They had a holiday fling when his dad was modelling in London and his mum moved to Italy to be with him and it was a disaster. So, there's no way he'd entertain the idea. Anyway, like I said, it was just a one and done thing. Thinking about anything beyond that is crazy.'

'So you're not gonna hang out any more?'

'We had lunch today at his favourite restaurant by the sea and he reminded me that we couldn't do anything again.'

I filled Stella in on the call from Victoria.

'He's right. It's risky. Do you think you'll be able to keep your distance?'

'Totally! It was just sex. I've only got four and a bit days left here. It'd be stupid to start catching feelings. I'll be fine!' My voice shot up higher than I'd meant it to, but what I said was true. As much as I liked Romeo, I knew what this was. It was just a fling. Nothing more, nothing less.

'Okay, well, just be careful.'

'Thanks, but I'll be fine. Tomorrow I'm going to ask my *chauffeur* – still can't believe I've got one of those – to take me to a beach which is supposed to be like the Maldives of Italy, so I'll go swimming there, do a bit of reading on the beach then find somewhere to eat. It'll be fun.'

Although I would've preferred to hang out with Romeo, we'd agreed that we couldn't see each other any more outside of the hotel, so that was that. It was for the best all round.

And anyway, I was a strong, independent woman. I'd survived just fine being single. I didn't need a man to take me around to different places to have a good time.

'Sounds amazing! Keep me posted and send pics!'

'Will do. How's everything with you?'

'All good. I'm loving working on this website design project for the Romance Library. I've got a meeting with the owner tomorrow, so me and Max are gonna stay the night afterwards. Sunshine Bay is supposed to be stunning.'

'I've heard of that place. Sounds lush! You guys are always travelling, here, there and everywhere. I wish I could do more of that.'

'What's stopping you? You spoke about spending time in the US years ago and never did. If I had an American dad and dual citizenship and had the option to go and spend however long I wanted over there like you, I would've jumped at the chance.'

'You trying to get rid of me?' I chuckled.

'No! It's just, ever since I decided to push myself out of my comfort zone, I've been so much happier and I just want the same for you, that's all.'

'I know. But it's different for you and Max. You run your own businesses. My boss wouldn't allow me to go away that much. Especially not if I want to become head receptionist. Coming here was pushing myself out of my comfort zone and look how that turned out.'

I was about to say that it'd been a shitshow. But it hadn't been all bad. I'd visited loads of stunning places and I'd had two mind-blowing orgasms.

Yeah, on reflection, the trip had started off badly, but thanks to Romeo, it was already memorable.

'Like you said, it's only Monday evening, so you've still got four full days left. Anything can happen.'

'True.'

'I'd better get back to work. Not all of us can spend our days lounging by the pool in sunny Italy.'

'Ha! Now you know how I felt when you were in Spain! If I don't speak to you before tomorrow, hope the meeting goes well. Enjoy Sunshine Bay.'

'Thanks. Laters.'

'Laters.' I hung up, then jumped off the bed.

Tonight I'd make the most of the villa's facilities, then tomorrow I'd go on my solo beach trip. Although there would be no more sex to go with the sun and sea, I'd still find a way to enjoy myself.

* * *

It was Tuesday morning and I was in the villa's kitchen making breakfast.

It would've been easier to grab something from the restaurant, but Romeo was doing the morning service. And if I saw him, my traitorous mind would start replaying flashbacks of him fucking me on the pottery table, which was the last thing I needed.

As long as I kept my distance, those memories would fade.

By the time I returned to London on Saturday, I would've forgotten all about how hard he made me come.

Twice.

Yep. Luckily we'd stopped things before we got in too deep.

Today I was going to have a lovely time at the beach and I wasn't going to think about Romeo and the way his lips tasted at all.

Easy peasy.

34

ROMEO

I reached for my phone, then jerked my hand back again.

That was the third time I had attempted to pick it up to message Sammie in the last five minutes before reminding myself that it was not a good idea.

When I had told her at lunch yesterday that it was better we did not see each other again outside of official meetings at the hotel, I meant it.

Things had gotten out of hand.

I should never have invited her to the pottery studio.

I should never have kissed her.

And I *definitely* should not have fucked her.

But although I knew I was supposed to regret it, I did not.

Fucking Sammie was the best thing I had done since... since forever.

I did not even need to think about whether it was the best sex I had ever had. I knew it for a fact.

I loved the way she tasted.

I loved the way she responded to my touch.

I loved the way her body moved beneath mine and how amazing it felt as I buried myself inside her.

I loved the way she screamed my name when I made her come. Twice.

I loved *everything*.

But I hated the fact that I wanted to do it all over again. Because we could not. There was too much at stake.

That was why I had taken her back to her driver's meeting point after lunch yesterday and had not contacted her since.

Despite that, I was sure there was not a minute that had passed when I had not thought about her.

And that was why I could not message to invite her out. Even if I wanted to.

It was a bad idea anyway. Today I was taking Mamma and Biscotti to one of the most beautiful beaches in Salento. Mamma loved it there and I was sure Sammie would like it too. I'd already crossed too many professional lines. I could not start crossing personal boundaries too by introducing her to Mamma.

Mamma would get excited that I was spending time with a woman and start asking questions which would make things more complicated than they already were.

I shook my head, slid my phone into my pocket, picked my keys up off the desk and headed to my car.

As I climbed into the driver's seat, started the engine, then set off, I exhaled. I loved working at the hotel, but it was good to know that I had time off.

During the second week of our guests' stay, things were much more relaxed.

Most of the couples had breakfast in their villas, but I tried to spend at least a few days doing breakfast service at the restaurant just in case. Afterwards I would work in my office for an hour or two, helping the guests organise their couples excursions. Then I would have the rest of the day to myself, before returning for dinner service to catch up with the guests, ask if they'd enjoyed their trips and find out their requirements for the following day.

This evening, though, I would not be working and tomorrow I had the whole day off. After working long hours all last week, I was glad to have a break.

Once I'd pulled up outside of my parents' house, I switched off the engine. I had barely stepped out of the car when Biscotti raced over.

'*Ciao*, Biscotti!' I crouched down and stroked her beautiful chocolate fur. She had made an incredible recovery and seemed more like herself which was great to see.

'Hello, son.' Mamma threw her arms around me and squeezed tight like it had been three years since she had seen me instead of just days.

'*Ciao*, Mamma.' I kissed her on both cheeks. 'Are you ready?'

'Yes, I just have a few things in the hallway. Can you carry them out for me?'

'Sure,' I said, ruffling Biscotti's fur again before striding towards the hallway. I was relieved to see that Papà's shoes were not there. I always preferred it when he was out. I picked up the beach umbrella, two folding chairs, a large bag and cooler box, then carried them to the back of the car. 'What do you have in here?' I asked as I heaved them into the boot. 'Rocks?'

'Just a few essentials for the beach, snacks for Biscotti and of course some things I made for lunch.'

'Feels like there's enough to feed an army!'

'With all of the long hours you work, I have to make sure that you're well fed,' Mamma said, as she strapped in Biscotti with the special dog harness then checked she was comfortable on the back seat, before sliding herself into the passenger seat. 'Are you eating properly?'

'*Sì*,' I said as I set off to the beach. She had asked me the same thing when I visited on Sunday.

'I wouldn't have to worry about you so much if you settled down with a good woman to take care of you.'

'Mamma.' I rolled my eyes. 'I do not need a woman to take care of me and I keep telling you. Times are different now. Women have their own careers. Like Mirabella.'

'Your sister works too hard. You *all* work too hard. When will you have time to find a wife and have a family with all of this *working*?'

'I am happy.'

'I'm not so sure,' she huffed. 'I can't remember the last time you brought a woman to meet me. Not since...'

'Mamma,' I warned. 'I do not want to talk about that.'

'Okay, but I don't understand. You're such a gorgeous man. Any woman would be lucky to have you. Is there really no one special?'

My thoughts immediately turned to Sammie, which was stupid because it was just sex.

Sì, I admit that the connection between us was incredible and Sammie was unlike any other woman I had met, but when Mamma said *special* she meant someone I was dating, *properly*.

'How is Biscotti?' I changed the subject. 'When is her next vet appointment?'

Mamma launched into a long account of how much progress Biscotti had made since my last visit. I was glad about the level of detail because it kept her from asking more questions about my relationship status for the whole journey.

Once I had parked, I took out everything from the boot and we set off with Biscotti.

'It's so beautiful,' Mamma said as she slid off her sandals and sank her feet into the fine, white sand.

'*Sì*,' I said, looking out to the crystal-clear turquoise sea.

Luckily, because it was not high season, the beach was reasonably quiet. There were many other beaches in Salento that were less popular with the tourists, but Mamma liked this one. Probably because she liked being around people from other countries, including England. Hearing their accents made her feel more at home.

After Mamma had chosen a spot, I took out the beach blankets, set up the umbrella and arranged everything whilst she went for a swim.

'When Mamma is back, we will go for a walk,' I said to Biscotti as she curled up beside me under the umbrella which I had angled over her to make sure she stayed cool.

Once Mamma had returned, I removed my T-shirt and led Biscotti down to the sea. We walked along the shoreline and we were only a few minutes away from our chosen spot when I stopped in my tracks.

My eyes popped.

Emerging from the sea like a goddess was Sammie.

What was she doing here?

Sammie was wearing a pink bikini and the sight of her set my blood on fire.

Those curves.

Those perfect breasts.

Those legs.

Her beautiful face.

Everything.

My cock instantly thickened and I wished that I could sprint over to Sammie, scoop her up in my arms, carry her somewhere secluded and fuck her all over again.

My brain was so focused on fantasising about all the different ways I would take her that I did not realise she had seen me until it was too late.

'Hey, you!' Her face broke into a smile, causing my heart to race. That was the other thing I liked about her. When she smiled it was like everything became brighter.

'*Ciao.*' I swallowed hard, warning my body to calm down. 'What are you doing here?'

'You recommended this beach to me, remember? I didn't realise you'd be here today too!'

'I came here with Mamma and...'

'Oh my God! Is this Biscotti?' She crouched down on the sand and started stroking her chocolate-coloured fur. 'She's gorgeous!'

Biscotti, who was normally wary of strangers, wasted no time getting closer to Sammie, before she started licking her face.

'Stop!' I laughed. 'Excuse her. She clearly likes you.'

Biscotti was not the only one. I never thought I would be jealous of our family dog, but the fact that she had got to lick Sammie made a wave of envy wash over me.

Flashbacks of my head between Sammie's thighs as I licked her clit invaded my thoughts and I tried to push them away.

'Can you blame her?' Sammie chuckled.

'Honestly, no.' The corner of my mouth twitched. She always made me smile.

My eyes raked down her body, taking in the sight of her breasts, stomach and between her legs, before sweeping back up again.

Seeing her damp bikini bottoms reminded me of how soaked her thong was when I'd lifted up my T-shirt in the pottery studio. She was so wet for me and I loved it.

As I followed the droplets cascading from her neck down between her breasts, my cock twitched again.

Our eyes locked and we held each other's gaze.

'There you are!' Mamma's voice snapped me out of my trance and I spun around to face her.

'I-I, Biscotti was enjoying the sea,' I said.

'I was worried because this is the first time she's been out properly since her operation and I tried calling you, but there was no answer.'

'I left my phone in my bag. I did not want it to get wet.'

'Aren't you going to introduce me to your friend?' Mamma grinned.

'*Sì.*' My brain was currently being controlled by my dick so I was not thinking straight. At least Mamma's arrival had cured my boner situation. '*Scusi.* This is Sammie. Sammie, this is my mother.'

'Lovely to meet you!' Sammie beamed. 'Actually, no. No, I don't mean it isn't nice to meet you, when I said *no*, I meant I should say it in Italian. *Piacere di conoscerti*,' she said proudly.

'Oh, my goodness! She's English *and* she speaks Italian!' Mamma clapped her hands together excitedly. 'I'm *so* happy to meet you, Sammie! Is this the surprise that you said you had for me, darling?' She turned to face me.

'No,' I replied quickly.

'That's a shame. I was just saying earlier how lovely it would be if Romeo found a new *friend*. So, how do you know my lovely son?'

'I'm one of the guests at the hotel and Romeo's my Love Alchemist.'

'Oh.' Her face fell. 'So where's your match?'

'With any luck he's in hell!' Sammie cackled and a smile

touched my lips. I was glad she was able to laugh about the situation.

'You two didn't get on?' Mamma frowned.

'The arsehole left me at the hotel, no note, no message, nothing. Then I found out he'd gone back to his pregnant ex!'

'No!' Mamma gasped. 'That's terrible. Romeo, how did this happen?' She glared at me like I was responsible. 'You poor love.' Mamma rubbed Sammie's back affectionately and another jolt of jealousy shot through me.

It was like everyone except me got to touch Sammie today.

'Oh, no, don't worry. It felt shitty at first, but your amazing son has been looking after me, so things are much better now.'

Sammie turned to face me and licked her lips.

Those soft, full lips that I wished I could taste again.

Electricity crackled in the air around us and my mind took another unauthorised trip to Sammie fantasy land. This time I was picturing how it would feel if those lips were wrapped around my...

What the hell was I doing?

I could not be thinking about doing those kinds of things with Sammie when my mother was only standing a few feet away.

'Wait. Are you two *together*?' Mamma's hand flew to her mouth.

'No,' I said quickly. 'My boss asked me to make sure Sammie was looked after. Love Alchemists are not allowed to date guests.'

'Yeah,' Sammie jumped in. 'Romeo was just doing his job. He's been the perfect gentleman.'

Mamma glanced at me, then at Sammie, then back at me.

I knew that look.

That was the look she gave when she was not convinced about something.

Like when I used to tell her I was going to a friend's house to do homework when really I was sneaking out to see a girl.

'Hmmm,' she said. 'Sammie, have you eaten?'

'Er...' Sammie's eyes flicked to mine like she was not sure how to respond.

'We were just about to have lunch. You should join us.'

'Oh, no, I couldn't...' Sammie said awkwardly. 'I'm sure there won't be enough. I'm fine. I'll just get a sandwich somewhere.'

'Nonsense. Romeo was just saying that I'd brought enough food to feed an army. Weren't you, Romeo?'

'*Sì*,' I said awkwardly.

'That's settled then!' Mamma's eyes lit up. 'It'll be lovely to speak to another Brit and find out more about you, Sammie.'

'You can tell me all of Romeo's secrets too!' Sammie grinned.

'Don't you worry! I've got *lots* of those. I was going through old albums last week and took a few snaps on my phone, so I can show you old baby pictures too!'

'Perfect!' Sammie grinned and turned to face me.

'*Mamma mia.*' I shook my head, realising there was nothing I could do.

As I watched the two of them link arms when Mamma led Sammie to our blanket, a mixture of emotions flooded my chest.

I was glad that Mamma seemed to like Sammie. And I was happy that she was here. Especially as I had thought about inviting her myself earlier.

But I was supposed to be spending less time with her, not more.

And something told me that having lunch together and allowing Mamma to get to know her better was about to make Sammie even harder to resist...

35

SAMMIE

'Linda.' I wiped a paper napkin across my mouth. 'Your hands are blessed! That was delicious!'

'Thank you.' Linda, Romeo's mum, blushed.

She was an absolute darling and a total stunner. I had no idea how old she was, I guess she had to be in her late fifties or early sixties, but she could easily pass for at least a decade younger.

Linda had tanned skin, long, rich chocolate-brown hair and green eyes. And her tall, toned figure looked incredible in her bright orange swimming costume.

And with his dad being a model, it was easy to see why Romeo was so ridiculously handsome.

'Would you like another sausage roll?' Linda said. 'I made plenty. They make me feel at home.'

'Don't you get homesick?' I asked, then instantly regretted it. From what Romeo had said at lunch yesterday, it seemed like a sore subject.

'All the time,' she sighed. 'But my husband is here and look at this place.' She gestured towards the sea. 'It's like paradise. Brighton beach just doesn't compare.'

'Too right!' I laughed, thinking about the famous beach a couple of hours away from London. It was nice enough, but the rocky beach with greenish, murky water was miles apart from the white sand and crystal-clear waters here.

'Mamma.' Romeo reached into his bag. 'I have the surprise for you that I mentioned on the phone.'

That was probably Romeo's way of changing the subject. He'd already been kind enough to let me gatecrash his special lunch with his mum and adorable Labrador, Biscotti, so I hoped I hadn't put my foot in it, again.

'You didn't have to bring me anything.'

'I wanted to.' Romeo squeezed her hand and my heart melted.

Romeo was already a catch, but seeing how much he adored his mum and how they talked and laughed together made him a million times more attractive.

After pulling out the bowl that was in brown protective paper he handed it to Linda. As she unwrapped it, I gasped. I hadn't seen the finished version but Romeo had painted it orange.

'It's beautiful!' she said, tears filling her eyes. 'I love it so much! And it's my favourite colour. Thank you.'

'It was a team effort. Sammie helped me...' Romeo's voice trailed off like he was embarrassed.

'She did?' Linda looked at me and her face broke into a wide smile. 'Well, thank you, Sammie.' She leant forward and kissed my cheek. 'And thank you, my darling. I shall treasure this. I'm so proud to have raised such a thoughtful son. You'll make a lucky woman very happy one day...'

Linda's eyes flicked to mine and she smiled again.

'Romeo, darling, I'm feeling a little tired. Would you mind taking me and Biscotti home?'

'I thought you wanted to spend the rest of the afternoon on the boat?' He frowned.

'We shouldn't keep Biscotti out for too long and I'm not feeling up to it.' She fanned herself dramatically. 'Perhaps you can take Sammie instead.'

'I am sure that Sammie has other plans,' Romeo said quickly.

'Um.' My brain froze. I knew I was supposed to come up with an excuse to say no, so that we wouldn't be alone together, but I couldn't think of one. 'Actually, I don't have plans.'

'That's perfect!' She winked at me before wiping her forehead which was already bone dry. 'Shall we go?' She jumped up. 'The sooner we leave, the more time you'll get to spend on the boat *together*.'

Never mind the matchmakers at the Love Hotel.

Looked like I'd just been set up by Romeo's own mother.

And considering the filthy thoughts that had been running through my head ever since I spotted a sexy, shirtless Romeo on the beach earlier, and how much my shameless vagina had been begging for a repeat performance of our time together on the pottery table, I wasn't even sorry about it.

36

ROMEO

'*Ciao*, Mamma.' I waved from the car window.

'*Ciao*, Linda,' Sammie added. 'Lovely to meet you and hope you feel better soon.'

I was about to say that I hoped Mamma felt better soon, but when she winked at me, my earlier suspicions were confirmed.

Mamma was not ill. She was pretending to be unwell, so she could push me and Sammie together.

She had set me up.

Maybe I should ask the hotel if they were looking for matchmakers, because Mamma had a natural talent for it.

'I think my mother likes you,' I said as we set off towards the port where the boat was docked.

'You reckon?' Surprise filled Sammie's voice.

'*Sì*. There were moments during lunch that I wondered whether she liked you more than me. I am worried that she wants to adopt you.' I laughed.

When I saw how well they bonded so quickly, it brought a smile to my face.

As much as Mamma wanted to see me settle down, she was

also very protective. She disliked almost every woman I ever took home. Including my last long-term girlfriend. Yet she spent one afternoon with Sammie and adored her.

Not that I could blame her. Sammie was very easy to like.

'I'd gladly let your mum adopt me. She'd have to share me with my own parents, though! Seriously, she's such a sweetheart. Her food is divine and my God, she's a stunner. Now I can see where you get your good looks from.'

'Papà would hate to hear you say that. He is happy when everyone says we look like him, but I prefer to be compared to Mamma. She is beautiful inside and out.'

'I bet all your mates thought she was a MILF when you were growing up.'

'MILF? I do not know this word.'

'*Mum I'd Like to Fuck.*'

'Ohhh.' I nodded, then winced. 'I do not like to think of her in that way, but it is true. Many of my friends had a crush on her. At the time it was embarrassing.'

'It's cool! Your mum would clean up if she put herself back out there. I'd kill to look as hot as her at her age. Must be nice to be so beautiful that you know you're gonna attract loads of attention.'

'I do not think that a woman like you has any trouble attracting attention,' I growled as my eyes raked over her face, slowly travelling downwards before fixating on her thighs.

Sammie had changed out of her bikini into a short dress and I had noticed that it kept riding higher up her thighs, exposing her soft skin.

A few days ago, I would have found it distracting, but now I had tasted what was between those legs, it was even harder to concentrate.

'You'd be surprised!' she said as we stopped at the traffic lights.

'Well, you have *my* attention.' I turned to face her and our eyes locked for a few seconds before my gaze moved to her chest.

When I saw her nipples poking through her dress, my cock thickened. She was not wearing a bra and her dress strap had fallen from one shoulder. All it would take was one little tug and her breast would be exposed. And if that happened, I would beg her to let me take it in my mouth.

I knew I was not supposed to be thinking of her in that way, but I could not stop myself.

Was Sammie thinking the same?

She did not seem too upset when I had said we could not continue seeing each other so perhaps she had already got me out of her system. I wished I could do the same, but she was too tempting.

'Are you checking me out?' she asked.

'*Sì*,' I said, my eyes returning to hers. 'It is hard not to.'

'What happened to keeping our distance?'

'We tried, but somehow we ended up on the same beach at the same time and now thanks to my mother, we are in this car, alone.'

'Anyone would think the universe is trying to force us together,' she said, her eyes still firmly fixed on mine. 'So it's not our fault.'

'Exactly.' I inched closer.

'And if our lips accidentally touched, that wouldn't be our fault either.'

'I agree.'

Our mouths were now only millimetres away from each other.

Just as I was about to close the gap, a car horn tooted, causing us to jump.

When I looked up, the traffic light was green, so I continued driving.

For the rest of the journey, I tried to keep my eyes on the road, but I found my gaze returning to her bare thighs several times.

Eventually, we pulled up at the port. There were a mixture of boats lined up, including small fishing boats and a few larger ones.

'We are here.' I stopped in front of a blue and white boat.

'Wow. It's much bigger than I was expecting,' Sammie said.

'My granddad left it to me, my brother and sister, but I am the only one here, so I use it the most. Come.' I took her hand and led her up the steps. 'There's not much to it. This obviously is the main deck and down here, there's a small living area with a fold-out bed, a bathroom and small kitchen.'

As I took Sammie downstairs she scanned the interior.

'It's so cute!' A wide smile spread across her face. I was glad that she liked it. 'How often do you come here?'

'Maybe once every couple of weeks? It depends on how busy things are at the hotel. We should set off. I want to make sure we get back before it starts to get dark.'

Sammie followed me upstairs and I started the engine.

'It's beautiful out here,' Sammie said once we were further out at sea. 'It's so peaceful and calming.'

'*Sì.*'

'But it's also hot.' She wiped the back of her hand over her forehead. 'I should change into my bikini.'

'Would you like some help?'

I could not lie to myself any more. I wanted Sammie again. And if she felt the same I would let whatever we wanted happen.

We were in the middle of the sea. No one was around. None of my bosses would ever find out.

'If you're offering, it'd be rude to say no.' She cocked her head.

'It would be *very* rude.' I reached forward and stroked her shoulder. 'But to change into your bikini, first you will have to take off this dress.' I ran my fingers over the thin strap, which once again had fallen down.

'That's true. Maybe you could help me get out of it.'

'You are asking a lot, but I suppose I could do this difficult task for you.' A mischievous smile tugged at my lips. I slid one strap down, then reached for the other. As the dress dropped around Sammie's waist, my breath caught in my throat and my Adam's apple bobbed. '*Mamma mia.*' I swallowed hard as I took in the sight of Sammie on the boat, topless.

Her nipples were rock hard and the sight turned my cock to stone.

'Sammie,' I growled. 'I want to feast on you. Will you allow me to give you pleasure?'

She bit her lip, sending another shockwave straight to my dick.

'Seeing as you asked so politely, I suppose I could let you,' she smiled as her hand trailed up my thigh, then shifted between my legs before she ran her hand over my cock.

'*Cazzo.*' I squeezed my eyes shut. 'I will not last if you touch me. First let me make you come.'

I dropped to my knees, then pulled her to the edge of the deck seat.

After leaning forward, I cupped her breasts then caressed them before rolling her nipples between my fingers.

'I love your breasts,' I said.

'Really?' she said through a ragged breath. 'Most men think

they're too small. The last guy I went on a date with asked if I'd ever thought about getting a boob job.'

'You are not serious?' I paused.

'I am.'

'*Testa di cazzo.*' I shook my head as I remembered that Edward had also commented about her breast size.

'What does that mean?'

'It means *dickhead*. Forget about what those other *boys* told you. You are with a real man now.'

I leant forward again, took her nipple in my mouth and as I sucked on it, Sammie cried out and threw her head back.

'Oh, God. Yes,' she panted as I continued sucking one nipple, whilst squeezing the other with my fingers.

After I'd finished lavishing her perfect breasts with attention, my tongue travelled down her stomach until I reached the dress which was still around her waist.

'Lift up your hips,' I commanded and Sammie did what I asked as I rolled down her dress, before tossing it on the deck.

I took a moment to rake my eyes over her body, before my gaze dropped to her pink lace thong.

'Spread your legs so I can fuck you with my tongue,' I growled.

Once she'd done as I asked, I swiped my tongue over the sodden fabric.

'You are so wet for me,' I said, dragging the top of the thong down with my teeth.

'Fuck, that's hot,' Sammie panted, lifting up her hips again to make it easier for me to pull it down her thighs.

After tossing it on the deck to join her dress, my eyes swept over Sammie's now completely naked body.

I could not believe my luck.

I had just unwrapped the most beautiful present.

This amazing woman had given me permission to lick and suck every inch of her, right here on this boat, in the middle of the sea.

To repay her, I was going to make her come so hard that when she screamed my name, everyone back at shore would know who was responsible for her orgasm.

After stretching her legs wider, I dipped my head and licked her slowly from her clit to her opening, then back up again.

'Fuck,' she cried out, lifting her hips up from the seat.

As I lapped at her clit, Sammie gripped the back of my head, pushing it deeper into her.

She tasted so good. How had I survived the past two days without feasting on her?

When I started circling her clit with my tongue, then inserted two fingers inside Sammie, she cried out again.

'Oh, God, Romeo,' she screamed. 'I can't! It's too good.'

Too good?

If only she knew, I was just getting started...

37

SAMMIE

Jesus, Mary and fucking Joseph.

As I looked down and saw Romeo's head between my thighs, shockwaves of pleasure rocketed through me.

I couldn't believe I was on a boat in the middle of the sea, sprawled out butt naked with a hot Italian stallion going down on me.

The fantasy alone would've been enough to get me off, but having it happen to me in real life was mind-blowing.

Romeo wasn't joking when he said he was going to feast on me. The man was eating me out like he hadn't had a meal for weeks.

I had no idea how he knew how to move and angle his fingers inside me like he was doing right now, or how he knew exactly how to suck, lick and circle my clit with his tongue to bring me so close to the edge, but it felt fucking amazing.

'I-I can't,' I panted, bucking my hips into him and pushing his head deeper between my legs. 'I'm gonna come.'

Romeo took that as a signal to circle my clit faster and as he slid a third finger inside me and starting fucking me harder, I knew I was hurtling over the cliff.

'Jesus, fuck, oh God! Romeo!' I screamed as my orgasm ripped through me, shooting from my toes upwards and causing my whole body to shake.

Romeo lifted his head and gave me one long, slow lick, before removing his fingers from inside me and licking each one clean.

'I could eat your pussy all day,' he said and as I looked in his eyes which were the colour of charcoal, I knew he meant every word.

'Play your cards right, and I might just let you do that,' I teased as I struggled to catch my breath.

As I imagined myself spread across a bed with Romeo going down on me over and over again, a fresh wave of tingles erupted within me.

Sign. Me. Up.

'Now it's your turn.' I attempted to haul myself off the seat.

'Later,' he said, easing me back down. 'My cock is jealous of my fingers and tongue right now. It is begging to be inside you.'

'Begging, eh?' I swiped my finger between my legs and started touching my clit which was still sensitive from the attention Romeo had lavished on it.

'Sammie.' Romeo squeezed his eyes shut, then opened them again. 'Seeing you touch yourself. I... Are you deliberately trying to make me come in my pants?'

'No, I'd rather you came inside me.' I reached for his shorts.

Luckily there was no belt or buttons this time, so after I'd gripped the top of his shorts and boxers, I pulled them down his hips slowly.

His cock sprang free and even though I saw it when we first

shagged on Sunday, my breath still hitched. Romeo's dick was huge.

'Hold on,' he said, reaching down to his shorts on the deck, pulling out his wallet and then a condom.

'Allow me.' I plucked it from his hand, ripped open the packet then rolled it down his long, hard length. 'Are you sure we can do this here? We're not gonna get arrested for indecent exposure?'

'I am sure. There is no one around.'

'Well, in that case, sit your arse down. This time, I'm gonna ride your cock.'

Romeo smirked and once he'd sat down, I got up, straddled him then lowered myself onto his dick.

As he filled me up, we both groaned.

'You feel so good,' Romeo said, thrusting beneath me as I started riding him hard and fast.

He leant forward, took my nipple in his mouth and teased it between his teeth, whilst he rolled and flicked the other nipple with his thumb.

'Your breasts are incredible, Sammie,' he growled into my chest. 'They're the perfect size for my mouth.'

A wave of electricity rocketed through me. He really meant it.

For a long time I'd had a complex about the size of my tits. I'd always envied women with bigger boobs like Stella and felt self-conscious about them.

I only ever wore padded bras and always felt nervous before getting undressed in front of a guy for the first time, but I'd noticed that these past few days I hadn't even thought about it.

When I'd changed out of my bikini into the dress earlier, I didn't bother with a bra. Maybe it was because I felt so comfortable around Romeo and as I looked down, I understood why.

Romeo was sucking, licking and worshipping my boobs like they were covered in his favourite gelato.

'Fuck, yeah,' I cried out as I continued bouncing up and down, watching Romeo's dick sliding in and out of me.

I couldn't decide what was better. Having Romeo go down on me on a boat, or getting fucked on one.

Romeo dipped his fingers between my thighs and when he started stroking my clit, my brain scrambled.

How was I supposed to concentrate when he was sucking my nipples and circling my sensitive bud all whilst impaling me on his talented cock?

'I'm so close,' I panted, riding him faster as my hands roamed over his solid abs.

A gust of salty sea air hit my bare skin and the boat rocked beneath us.

'Come for me, Sammie. I want to hear you scream my name again.' Romeo pushed himself deeper, thrusting his hips in perfect sync with mine.

'Oh God, oh God!' I squeezed my eyes shut. 'Romeooooooo!' I screamed so loud I was sure they could hear me back in London.

As my orgasm detonated inside me, a deep guttural growl flew from his mouth.

I collapsed on top of him. Our bodies were slick with sweat and as our chests heaved against one another, my head buzzed in the best way.

When we'd both managed to catch our breath, I lifted my head and looked up at him.

God, he was beautiful and so, so talented.

The pottery table sex was hot, but this was even hotter.

The way we fucked felt so right – like we'd been doing it for years, not days.

'Sammie.' Romeo stroked my cheek. 'That was...' He paused, like he was searching for the right words. 'Incredible.'

'I know, right?' I smiled. 'But maybe it was just beginners' luck.'

'You think we fuck like beginners?'

'Ha! No way. With your skills, you could be a sex professor! No, what I meant is maybe it was beginners' luck that we connected so well. Maybe if we'd done it more times, it wouldn't be so amazing.'

'That is what you think?' He raised an unimpressed brow.

'What I'm trying to say is, surely it couldn't be this amazing *all* the time.'

'It sounds like you are challenging me.'

'No, just being realistic. Of course I'd love it to be, but I don't see how.'

'All this guessing and uncertainty is not good,' Romeo said. 'If you want to know for sure that the sex we have enjoyed so far was not just beginners' luck, there is only one way to find out. We will just have to fuck again...'

38

ROMEO

'*Again*?' My eyes widened as Sammie straddled me on the sofa bed below deck and waved another condom packet in front of me. 'I know I said we should do more "testing", but you are going to break my cock!' I laughed.

'Good! Then I can take it home with me.'

'I knew it!' I shook my head. 'You only want me for my body.'

'Can you blame me?' She ran her hand down my chest, then gripped my dick. 'It's a *very* beautiful body.'

'What about my mind? Or my incredible personality?' I clutched my heart like she'd wounded me.

'And your giant ego!' She giggled and the sweet sound made my heart swell. 'You're probably right. After giving me four orgasms today, you've earned a rest. You can give me more later.'

After we had fucked twice, we had fallen asleep for an hour, then headed below deck in search of food.

Mamma had snuck some leftovers into my bag which we had quickly finished before guzzling down the bottle of water I had left in the fridge.

We had meant to just rest for a little while on the sofa, but before we knew it, I was on top of Sammie and we were fucking again.

The truth was, I would happily continue until my cock really did fall off, but it was starting to get dark.

'Have you got any more of those bread ring snack thingies?'

'You mean the *taralli*?'

'Yeah! You've got me addicted to yet another thing.'

Taralli were little ring-shaped crunchy snacks made with white wine, flour and olive oil that were typical in this region of Italy.

'They are all finished, but now that I know you love them, I will get some for you.'

'You're the best!'

'I try,' I smiled. 'We should head back to shore.'

'Do we have to?' Sammie crossed her arms and pretended to sulk like a teenager.

'It is better. And you must be hungry again by now.'

'Yeah. I've probably burned more calories this afternoon than I have all week. At least I won't have to torture myself at the gym when I get back.'

The mention of her returning to London made my stomach tighten. But I was not going to focus on that. I wanted to enjoy the time that we had together.

'Why would you need to torture yourself at the gym?' My face creased.

'To get rid of this,' she squeezed her stomach, 'and tone up these.' She slapped her thighs.

'Sammie. You do not have to punish your body.' I dipped my head and planted a soft kiss on her stomach, then peppered her thighs with more kisses. 'You are beautiful, exactly as you are.'

Her eyes widened with shock, like it was the first time anyone had ever told her this.

'Really?' She frowned.

'*Sì.*'

'You're such a charmer.' She waved her hand away dismissively.

'No.' I took her hand in mine. 'It is not charm, it is the truth. *Sei bellissima.* You are beautiful.'

I closed the gap between us and pressed my mouth on hers. Sammie melted against me, then snaked her arms around my waist.

There was something different about this kiss. It was not the wild, frenzied, animalistic kisses we had before which were fuelled with the desire to get each other naked as quickly as possible so we could fuck.

This time it was slow, sensual and deep.

As our tongues gently flicked against each other, warmth flooded my body. Earlier I had said that I could eat Sammie's pussy all day, but now I was adding kissing her to that list too.

And talking to her.

And being inside her.

Just *being* with Sammie made me feel alive.

It was like I had been unconscious for years and she brought me back to life.

Sammie was a whirlwind. A firecracker. She lit me up like no other woman ever had.

Her stomach rumbled loudly and we laughed before slowly pulling away.

'Sorry!'

'This was why I needed to take you back to shore earlier to feed you. But I got distracted. You are addictive.' I stroked her cheek.

'I could say the same about you.'

'*Grazie.*' I kissed her gently on the lips, before pulling away and shaking my head. 'It happened again!'

'It's not my fault!' she giggled. 'Go!' Sammie shooed me away. 'Do your boat driving thing before I end up snogging your face off.'

'I am going!' I laughed.

And as I headed towards the steps to restart the boat, I smiled, hoping that it would not be long before I got to kiss her all over again.

39

SAMMIE

Even if a hundred people armed with Brillo pads scrubbed my face they wouldn't be able to wipe away my massive smile.

I was so bloody happy.

As I sat out in the sunshine on the patio of my luxury villa, eating my favourite *pasticciotto* pastry and sipping a freshly prepared cappuccino, whilst gazing up into the clear blue sky, butterflies flooded my stomach.

A week ago, I was feeling like shit and wondering if I'd have to go back to London because my match had disappeared. Now it was a completely different story. Forget being on cloud nine. I was floating on cloud nine billion.

And it was all thanks to Romeo.

Honestly, that man.

When it came to describing how thoroughly amazing he was, I didn't even know where to start.

First there was his kindness.

As soon as we docked the boat last night, he asked me what I wanted to eat. When I said I felt like pizza, he drove miles just to take me to a place that he loved that did *panzarotti* which was a pizza that has been folded over and fried, so all the cheese, tomato and other toppings were inside.

Once our order was ready, Romeo took me to sit on a bench opposite the sea, where we'd watched the stars whilst we devoured the *panzarotti*, which was bloody delicious.

Then he dropped me back at the hotel (away from the entrance so no one would see us) and waited in his car until I'd texted to say I was safely back in the villa.

And if that wasn't enough, this morning he sent me a message asking me to text him when I was awake and he would ask a Cuisine Champion to bring my favourite pastries and a cappuccino to my villa.

Talk about thoughtful.

Don't even get me started on how kind he had been taking me around all of these different places and looking after me after Edward screwed me over.

Or how sweet he was to his mum. And Biscotti.

And when he said that I was beautiful *exactly how I was*, I felt like I was going to dissolve faster than ice cream on a warm chocolate brownie.

No one had ever said that to me before.

Every man I'd ever been with had either criticised the size of my boobs (too small), my arse and belly (too big) or thighs (too wobbly). But not Romeo. He worshipped my body like an evangelist praised the Lord every Sunday.

With him I felt seen, heard, appreciated.

And of course there was the sex.

Holy macaroni.

Romeo had given me more top-tier orgasms in a few days than I'd had in my whole life.

Yep. He was the total package. Romeo had more green flags than a St Patrick's Day parade.

But he lived in Italy.

Life was so unfair.

I'd been telling myself that it was just sex and I wouldn't catch feelings, but it was too late. Feelings had been caught, *big time*.

I had no idea what to do about that, but it was now Wednesday and I wasn't leaving until Saturday so I didn't have to think about that now.

In forty minutes I'd be meeting Romeo again. He had a day off and wanted to take me to another beach.

I popped the last bit of pastry into my mouth, downed my cappuccino then went to shower.

Half an hour later, I was locking up the villa to meet Romeo. I headed out of the hotel grounds, then walked the short distance to where he had dropped me off last night.

As I approached Romeo's car and he spotted me, his face broke into a smile and my stomach flipped. Just like it had when I'd first met him. I should've realised then that he was the one I was supposed to be with, but it didn't matter now.

'Hey, you,' I smiled as I slid into the passenger seat.

Romeo leant forward, wrapped his arms around me and gave me a long, slow kiss.

I'd noticed yesterday when we were kissing on the sofa below deck that something had shifted. And I felt the same today. This wasn't a frantic, 'I need to fuck you immediately' snog like it was the first few times. Somehow the connection felt deeper.

We continued kissing for ages, neither of us wanting to pull away. But then the sound of a fire engine siren snapped us out of our hypnotic snog sesh.

When I looked into his eyes, Romeo was staring at me like I'd just told him I could give him a lifetime supply of his favourite pizza.

He looked at me with awe and amazement. If I could bottle this feeling and commit his expression to my memory forever, I'd be the happiest woman alive.

'We should go,' Romeo said. 'Otherwise I will end up kissing you for hours.'

'Yeah, or someone will drive by from the hotel and see us.'

Romeo started the engine and then set off.

'How was your breakfast?' he asked.

'Delicious as always. Honestly, I don't know how I'm going to go back to eating toast or muesli after the food I've had at this place. I've been totally spoilt.' Thinking about going home made my stomach twist, so I quickly changed the subject. 'Will it take long to get to the beach?'

'Not too long,' Romeo said solemnly and I wondered if he was thinking the same about me going back.

Then again, maybe he didn't care. I could be just another guest with benefits.

No.

I refused to believe that. Romeo was different. I felt it in my soul.

I'd always rolled my eyes at the quotes on Instagram that said you'd know when you'd met the right man because he'd let you know you were special through his actions. But Romeo had done all of that and more.

This wasn't just another fling to him. I was sure of it.

Romeo pulled into a car park, we collected our things and headed to the beach.

'Wow!' I said, taking in the sight of the pure white sand and turquoise water. 'I can't believe that there are so many beautiful beaches here. You're so lucky to have this all on your doorstep. What's the water like?'

'It is amazing.' Romeo spread out a blanket on the sand, then loaded our bags on top. 'But do not take my word for it. The best way to know is to try it for yourself.'

'Last one in the water has to buy lunch!' I said, whipping off my kaftan, then racing down to the sea.

I thought I was easily going to beat Romeo, but seconds later he shot past me and raced straight into the water.

'Looks like I am the winner and you are taking me out for a steak dinner at the fanciest restaurant in town.' He punched his fist in the air triumphantly.

'Sure! There's an amazing restaurant at this place called the Love Hotel that does a nice steak. I'll take you there, shall I?'

Romeo grinned, swam towards me, lifted me out of the water and spun me around before lowering me back into the sea and cupping my face.

'You can take me anywhere you want.' He kissed me softly. 'But not today. Today, I will be taking you for lunch at another one of my favourite restaurants.'

'Oooh!' I said, feeling honoured that he'd shared these special places with me.

'Until then, let us enjoy the water together.'

* * *

I'd had another amazing day with Romeo.

We'd spent hours swimming side by side in the sea, kissing and cuddling in the water, then drying off in the sun on our beach blanket whilst enjoying more kisses and taking selfies together, before going back into the sea for more swimming and snogging.

It was a good thing the beach was pretty deserted so other people didn't have to keep witnessing our intense public displays of affection. But something told me that even if the beach was packed, I wouldn't have cared. Whenever Romeo's lips were on mine it was like the rest of the world didn't exist.

There were a few times that things got very hot and heavy and in all honesty, if Romeo hadn't raced back down to the sea to cool off, we could've ended up banging on the beach.

As much as I wanted to shag his brains out, part of me also liked that today it hadn't all been about the sex. It was more about just enjoying each other and our shared love for swimming.

Romeo took me to an amazing restaurant for lunch where I had the most delicious seafood and now we'd returned to the beach for a walk.

'I am glad that you liked the restaurant,' he said as he took my hand and led me further down so we could walk in the sea.

'I bloody loved it! It's crazy how much better everything tastes in Italy. Coming here has really opened my eyes.'

'To what?'

'To everything. I didn't realise until I came on this trip that I've been stuck in a major rut. I've been in the same job for years, dated the same types of guys and made the same mistakes, but coming to the Love Hotel, visiting all of these different places, trying new things and meeting you has shown me what's possible. How enjoyable life can be. How much I'm missing out on.'

And what it's like to be with an amazing man.

'It is easy to get stuck. Do you think you will change your job?'

'No. Even though I've been doing the same job, I'm hoping to get promoted soon, so I couldn't leave now. I wouldn't be able to change my career anyway.'

'If you could do any job, what would it be?'

'I don't know,' I said, inhaling the salty sea air.

'What do you like most about your current job?'

'I enjoy the social part of it. Like chatting to people who come in for meetings or speaking to them on the phone. I like the organisational bits too, like if my boss is travelling and asks me to research places for her to go for lunch or organising the work parties and events. But I don't get to do that as often as I'd like. If I'm promoted though, I'll get to do more of the events stuff, so that's why it's worth staying.'

'Maybe you could go into event planning or work at a reception for an events company?'

'I'd love that. But you need proper experience. That's the problem. I know I could probably do a job like that, but it's convincing someone to give me a chance, y'know? Which is why it's important for me to stay where I am because at least I'll get the opportunity to get some experience, so if I want to move on in a few years, my CV will be stronger. Did you have a lot of experience when you got your job?'

'Sì. I had worked in hospitality and different hotels. But I did not have experience with the matchmaking side of things. But I was able to learn.'

'Your job must be so much fun! I know you work hard, but it also must be pretty rewarding too.'

'It is. When a couple comes together and you get messages to say they are happy and in love, it is very satisfying.'

'Bet you were over the moon when you saw the shitshow with me and Edward unfolding. Sorry to tarnish your perfect record!' I let out a weak laugh.

'You have nothing to be sorry for. I knew he was wrong for you as soon as I met him.'

'Really?' My eyes popped. 'Wish you'd given me the heads up!'

'I told Victoria my concerns, but sometimes it takes time for couples to bond so we needed to be sure. Of course we had no idea that he would do what he did, but as much as I hated to see that you were hurt, I am glad that he left, because it meant that I got to spend more time with you.'

'Same! When we get married, we can raise a toast to Edward. The devious little fucker who pissed off back to his ex, leaving the path clear for me to get with my amazing Love Alchemist who's a billion times better.'

Romeo's mouth lifted into a cheeky grin and I realised what I'd just said: *when we get married.*

Gah!

I thought I was over my putting my foot in my mouth crap.

'I didn't mean... I was just joking.'

'I know.' Romeo stroked my cheek.

'Actually.' I paused and turned to face him. 'Seeing as I've already put my foot in it, maybe now's a good time for us to address the elephant in the room...' My voice trailed off.

'Wait,' he frowned. 'I know that saying. That means to have a difficult conversation, right?'

'Yep. I don't want to sound like a needy bitch, but what are we doing?'

I felt bad for asking, seeing as he'd told me before we got together that he wanted to work at the Love Hotel in the US, but I really liked him and I needed to shoot my shot. I wanted to at least know if he felt the same way I did.

'We are walking on the beach.' He grinned.

'You know what I mean.' I rolled my eyes.

'Honestly?' He paused and my heart stuttered as I braced myself for his response. 'I do not know. I did not plan for this. This situation is complicated. I know I need to keep my job and pursue my dream. But I also know that I cannot stay away from you. I have tried. But you are too hard to resist. How do *you* feel about everything?'

'Pretty much the same. I need to keep my job, otherwise the last almost five years will have been for nothing and I'm so close to getting promoted. And I have a whole life set up in London, but I like spending time with you.' That was the understatement of the year. I was grateful that I hadn't blurted out that I thought about him all the time. Or that I was falling for him.

'I also love spending time with you. You make me happy.'

'You definitely do that too. I swear, your cock has ruined me for life!' I laughed.

'So this is all about sex for you?' His face fell.

'It isn't for you?' I said, trying to play it cool.

'No.' His expression hardened. 'The connection is deeper and you know it. If it was just sex, it would be much easier.'

'Okay,' I sighed. 'You got me. It *is* more than sex, but you're here and I'm going back to London. I just don't know how it can work long-term.'

We both stared at each other in silence for what felt like hours but was only seconds.

'I wish I had an answer,' Romeo said. 'The sensible thing to do would be to stop things now, before we get any deeper.'

'Been there, done that, worn the T-shirt. Last time we said we'd keep our distance we ended up fucking on your boat.'

'So we continue?' he asked.

'Yeah.' I shrugged. 'I've only got a few days left here, so we might as well. And after that, well. I guess we have to cross that bridge when we come to it.'

'*Sì*. So until then, we just enjoy every moment of our time together. Agreed?'

'Agreed.'

I knew it wasn't the best solution, but right now, it was all that we had.

Romeo had said that we should live in the moment, and as he leant down to kiss me and I melted into him, I knew that was exactly what I intended to do.

40

ROMEO

As the last guest left the restaurant, I exhaled. I loved my job, but today felt longer than usual.

After spending my time off with Sammie, it had been hard to go back to a normal routine.

Somehow things did not feel right without her.

Yesterday I had dropped Sammie off outside the hotel again and I saw her briefly at breakfast today. But I had spent most of the day in my office and attending meetings to make sure that everything was organised for the guests' final night tomorrow.

The couples were responsible for choosing how they wanted to spend their last evening, but it was my job to make their dream night a reality. If they wanted a romantic dinner on the beach, I had to liaise with the Cuisine King and his team to create the menu and organise the setting.

Every guest's requests were different, so there was a lot of preparation involved. I was only able to spend an hour at the restaurant for dinner service because after two days off there was a lot to catch up on. That meant that I had not had time to chat to Sammie for long when she came for dinner either.

But I had messaged to ask if she wanted to meet after my shift ended. Perhaps we could go for a drive. I did not care what we did as long as we spent time together.

Once I had collected my things from my office, I texted Sammie to check that she still felt comfortable walking outside of the hotel where I would meet her.

When her message popped up on the screen, a wide grin spread across my face.

SAMMIE

Yep! See you in ten xx

A jolt of excitement shot through me. I quickly drove to the agreed meeting place and parked up.

Right on time, I saw Sammie walking towards me. Even though the road was only lit by streetlights, I could already see that she looked beautiful. But she would still look amazing even if she wore a rubbish bag.

Sammie was wearing a long summer dress with a scarf wrapped around her shoulders and had her hair tied up.

'Hi!' She opened the car door then slid onto the passenger seat.

'*Ciao, bella.*' I leant forward and kissed her.

As our mouths connected, my whole body sprang to life. It felt like it had been much longer than twenty-four hours since we last kissed.

'Mmm,' she groaned with pleasure. 'That's my kind of welcome! So, where do you wanna go tonight?'

'We can go for a drive, if you like?'

'Shall I tell you what I'd really love to do?'

'What?'

'Sounds kinda crazy, but ever since I got here, I've wanted to go skinny dipping!' A mischievous grin spread across her lips.

'I love that you want to try that,' I chuckled. It was so Sammie.

'*Grazie!*' she beamed. 'I'm supposed to be creating memories and it seems like it'd be fun. What do you reckon. You up for it?'

'Of course!'

'I'm guessing it's too risky to do it at the hotel, so is there somewhere else we could go?'

'*Si!*' I started the engine. 'I know just the place.'

It did not take long to get there. Once we had parked up, I went to the boot and took out the towel and torch I kept in the car, then we headed to the beach.

'Sounds silly, but I guess I never expected it to be so dark,' Sammie said. Although a couple of lights in the car park illuminated the area so it was not pitch black, it did not stretch all across the beach. 'There won't be sharks in the water, will there?'

'No!' I laughed. 'I will keep the torch on, so we can see better. But perhaps it is good that it is dark.'

'True. In case someone comes. We don't want to flash them!'

I started taking off my clothes and Sammie's eyes raked over my body, scanning me from my chest, down to my cock and back again.

'Are you just going to watch me or are you taking off your clothes too?' My eyebrow lifted.

'Oops! I got distracted!' She laughed.

When she slid down her straps then stepped out of the dress, so she was just in her underwear, I understood what Sammie meant about being distracted.

And when she peeled off her bra, exposing those beautiful breasts, my breath caught in my throat. The urge to lean down and suck on her nipples was strong, but tonight Sammie wanted to go skinny dipping, so that was what we would do.

As soon as Sammie removed her knickers, I knew I had to get in the water to cool myself off.

'Ready?' I held her hand.

'Yep! Let's go!'

We ran into the sea, our bodies sinking into the cool water.

'This is amazing!' Sammie said as she swam around me. 'I feel so free!'

'It is a good feeling.'

'You've done it before?'

'*Sì*, a few times.'

'You dirty dog!' She cackled.

'You are calling me a dog? And how can I be dirty when I am literally swimming in the sea?' I smirked.

'It's an English saying.'

'I know!' I laughed. 'I am pulling your leg and taking a piss.'

'You mean taking *the* piss!' she snorted.

'Oops!' I slapped my forehead. 'I always get those mixed up.'

'I'm sure lots of people do take a piss in the sea though.' Sammie wrinkled her nose. 'Although probably not as often as I see people doing it in my local pool.'

'You cannot be serious?' My mouth dropped open.

'I'm not joking! I used to think it was just kids, but I saw a guy pissing in the pool once too.'

'Nice,' I grimaced. 'Well, you are not at your filthy pool now, you are in this beautiful water so you should enjoy it. Shall we swim together?'

'Love to!'

We swam and chatted in the sea for what felt like ten minutes but actually turned out to be forty-five and like every time I had been with Sammie, it was a lot of fun.

'That was brilliant!' Sammie said as we walked hand in hand from the sea to where the towel was resting on the sand. 'At first I wanted to do it just because it's a bit naughty, but I'm surprised what a difference not wearing a bikini makes. It felt kind of sensual. Like I was gliding through the water. And because I didn't have anything clinging to me, somehow it made swimming easier.'

'I am glad you enjoyed it.' I squeezed her hand. 'I hope this does not mean that you will be swimming in your local pool naked.' I laughed.

'Could you imagine!' Sammie cackled. 'I'd be banned!'

'I do not think they would ban you. They would be too busy admiring your body. Just like I am.' I stood in front of her and swiped some droplets of water off her cheek with my thumb.

Sammie bit her lip and stepped forward.

We were now so close that our wet bodies were touching. I swallowed hard and my dick thickened, poking her belly.

'Mmm.' She squeezed her eyes shut. 'Maybe we should continue the fun here.' She gestured to the towel. 'I've never had sex on the beach before.'

My eyes darted from left to right, looking to see if there was any sign of anyone else.

'You are a bad influence,' I growled, before trailing soft kisses down her neck, across her collarbone, then dipping my mouth to her breast and taking a long hard suck on her nipple.

'Fuck,' she groaned, throwing her head back.

Just as I slid my hand between her thighs and was about to touch her clit, the beach lit up and I saw car headlights approaching in the distance.

'There is someone coming!' I bent down, picked up the towel and thrust it in front of Sammie to shield her.

Once Sammie had grabbed it, I quickly picked up my boxer shorts, stepped into them and then pulled my T-shirt over my head.

Sammie wriggled into her dress, whilst holding up the towel.

Thankfully, by the time the couple from the car stepped onto the beach, we were both fully dressed.

I picked up the towel and torch, then took Sammie's hand. We nodded our heads in acknowledgement to the couple, who gave us a knowing smirk, and we headed back to the car.

'Phew!' Sammie blew out a breath. 'That was close!'

'It was.'

'I wished they'd come a bit later so we'd had time to dry off. Wearing clothes when you're dripping wet is super uncomfortable. Especially after experiencing the pleasure of swimming in the buff!'

'If they arrived a few minutes later and I was doing my job, you would still be very wet...' My mouth lifted into a cheeky smile.

'See! Told you that you were a dirty dog! You're not wrong though. You have a habit of doing that...'

'That is good to hear.'

As we slid our damp bodies onto the car seat, a wave of disappointment hit me. I was not ready for the evening to end, but I had an early start in the morning. I wished that we could spend the night together. It did not have to involve sex. I would be happy to just hold Sammie.

'I wish we could spend the night together,' Sammie said and my eyes widened.

'I was just thinking the same.'

'I spotted a baseball cap in your boot. Could you not just wear that and sneak into the villa? I mean will they even check if I have guests? I would've thought the cameras are just for surveillance – to make sure that no unauthorised people are on the resort. But say if I was to leave via the back of the villa and return with someone, would they really question it? Especially given that I don't have a match.'

'Hmmm.' I rested my finger on my chin. 'Maybe. That could work.'

'It's worth a try. Then we'd get to spend the whole night together.'

It was risky, but I knew where the cameras were, so I could keep my head low when I passed them.

'Okay,' I smiled, excitement rushing through my veins.

'Great! Let's do it!'

41

SAMMIE

'We did it!' I squealed as Romeo slid through the door, removed his cap, then leant forward and kissed me, causing goosebumps to erupt over my skin.

'*Si*. It was good that we came in together so that security would not think I was a stranger coming to your villa to attack you.'

'Yep.'

Once we'd both showered, Romeo went to get some water, whilst I climbed into bed.

I let out a loud yawn. All the swimming tonight and over the past few days, combined with the heat and the marathon sex sessions, had caught up with me.

When Romeo stepped into the bedroom with his towel still wrapped around his waist, I swallowed hard. I didn't think I'd ever get tired of looking at his body.

After dropping the towel, he climbed into the bed beside me.

'Come here.' He patted his chest.

I shuffled over and rested my head on him, inhaling his scent.

'This is heaven,' I sighed with happiness, as he wrapped his arms around me. Another yawn shot from my mouth. 'I wanted to have some sexy time, but...'

'I am tired too.' He stroked my hair. 'And when I said I wanted to spend the night together, I did not mean I wanted sex. I just wanted to be with you.'

'Awww.' My heart melted. This man was adorable. 'Thanks for understanding.'

'You do not need to thank me,' he chuckled and I loved feeling the vibration from his chest. He was right, but I was so used to men only being interested in one thing, that somehow I felt I needed to apologise for not giving up the goods.

But then I remembered that this was Romeo. And like he'd repeatedly shown me, he wasn't like other men.

If only he lived in London, I thought for the millionth time today.

'*Buonanotte*, Sammie,' Romeo said as he switched off the light.

'Goodnight,' I replied, before slipping into a deep sleep.

* * *

I rolled over on the bed and as I felt the empty space beside me, I sighed.

Romeo had only been gone for a few hours, but I missed him.

Last night was amazing. I felt so safe and happy being wrapped up his arms and feeling his heartbeat and warm, soft skin under me.

If only I'd suggested sneaking him into the villa sooner, we could've enjoyed more nights like that. It'd been fine with him wearing the cap and dipping his head when he saw the cameras. We'd worried over nothing.

I wished Romeo was here right now.

Bloody hell. I had it *bad*.

If I had withdrawal symptoms after such a short space of time, how the hell was I going to cope after tomorrow when I went home for good?

My stomach clenched. I couldn't believe that today was my last full day at the Love Hotel. I really didn't want to go home.

I really didn't want to leave Romeo.

My phone pinged and as I saw his name on the screen, butterflies erupted in my belly.

ROMEO

Buongiorno, bella.

Are you awake?

Let me know and I will send over something from the kitchen.

ME

Hey! Yeah, just woke up and the bed feels empty without you...

Normally I'd be worried about coming on too strong, but I felt comfortable expressing myself around Romeo.

ROMEO

I wish I could be there with you and deliver your breakfast personally, but I must go to the office now.

ME

> Awww. Me too. No worries. I know you have to work. Maybe you could stop by later? I'll go for a swim in the sea this morning, but this afternoon I'll be chilling at the villa.

ROMEO

> Va bene. I will come and see you this afternoon after I have finished preparing for the evening dates and done lunch service.

ME

> Okey dokey. I'll be ready and waiting…

ROMEO

> I look forward to it.

> Enjoy your day.

Romeo went offline and I held the phone to my chest. I had fallen so hard for this guy it was ridiculous.

Still, I couldn't spend the last day in bed, pining. I had to make the most of the sea, the beach and the amazing facilities.

Time to get up.

* * *

I stretched out on the daybed by the pool in my villa. I must've dozed off. I wasn't surprised. I spent hours going in and out of the sea this morning. Then, after grabbing a quick bite to eat at the pool bar, I'd headed back to the villa, showered, then told myself I'd read on the daybed for a while, but I must've fallen asleep.

A flashback of the dream I'd just had invaded my brain.

Oooh. I blushed. It was very X-rated. I wasn't surprised,

considering I'd read a sex scene on my Kindle before I drifted off.

In the spicy romance I was reading, the male main character had just gone down on the female main character in a limo.

But in my dream, it was Romeo who'd gone down on me whilst I sat at the edge of the pool.

It was funny how the mind took what had happened in my book and my surroundings whilst I was reading it and came up with a fantasy like that.

Maybe when Romeo came over, we could recreate it? He seemed like he was up for trying anything, which was one of the things I loved, I mean *liked* about him.

Seconds later, my phone pinged.

Wow. I was just thinking about Romeo and then he messaged. Telepathy or what?

ROMEO

I can come over in ten minutes, va bene?

ME

Perfect!

I jumped up off the daybed and raced towards the door.

ME

I'll leave the main villa door open so you don't have to ring the buzzer, you can just slip straight in.

The quicker he got inside, the better.

ROMEO

Perfetto.

I quickly went to the bathroom to freshen up and change

into a new bikini. I was just about to walk out to the daybed when I saw Romeo slip through the door.

Without even giving him a chance to close it behind him, I pulled him into me and gave him a long, slow kiss.

'Mmm,' he groaned. 'That is a good welcome.'

I laughed as I remembered I'd said something similar when he'd greeted me in the car last night.

After leading him to the sofa, we started kissing again and desire raced through me. Another flashback of my steamy dream popped into my head.

Actually, now was the perfect time to ask if Romeo would want to help make it a reality.

'Remember when you said you could happily eat my pussy all day?' I asked.

'*Si.*'

'I had a sexy dream earlier and I was wondering if you'd help me bring it to life.'

'What is it?' A mischievous smile touched Romeo's lips.

'So, I'm sitting on the edge of the pool minding my own business when a hot Italian guy who looks a lot like you swims over, pulls off my bikini bottoms and goes down on me right there.'

'Such a naughty girl.' Romeo's smile widened.

'Yep!' I beamed. 'That's me! You have no idea about the filthy thoughts that go through this.' I tapped the side of my head.

'I can only imagine...'

'So? What do you think? It's my last day here and I'm trying to create a few more memories. For my future wank bank though – not for the Love Hotel memory book!' I cackled.

'I think that I would *very* much like to help you. But I have some conditions.'

'What are they?'

'First, and I do not like to say this because normally I love it, but you cannot scream my name. No one can know it is me that is making you come.'

'Aye, aye, captain!' I saluted. 'What else?'

'Second, once I have recreated your fantasy, you will let me fuck you.'

'*Oh, no*, please don't torture me with more of your life-shattering orgasms expertly delivered by your award-winning penis!' I doubled over with laughter. 'You've got yourself a deal!'

Romeo grinned and began peeling off his clothes, starting with his branded T-shirt, swiftly followed by his shorts.

'I do not have my swimming trunks, so I will have to go in your pool naked.'

'Yeah, yeah, I believe you! I reckon after skinning dipping last night you just don't want to wear clothes any more. I suppose I can find a way to cope with ogling your perfect body again!' I joked as my eyes dipped between his legs.

Romeo dropped his boxers on the floor then strode naked to the pool, giving me a delicious view of his boner and toned arse.

Once he was inside, I raced out to the patio, then perched on the edge of the pool, just like I had in my fantasy.

Let the fun begin.

As I watched Romeo swim multiple laps, my body ached with desire, wondering when the hell he'd come to feast on me.

Finally, he swam over, sank to his knees in front of me then fixed his gaze on mine.

'Open your legs,' he growled and the gravelly command combined with the anticipation of what was about to happen almost made me come on the spot.

I did as I was told then lifted my hips as he placed his hands at the top of my bikini bottoms, then rolled them down *oh, so, slowly.*

God. I was so wet for him right now.

Once he'd finished, Romeo tossed the sodden bikini bottoms on the ground, spread my legs wider, then buried his face between them.

'Oh, God!' I cried out as he gave me a long, luxurious lick.

Romeo's head snapped up and I instantly missed the heat from his warm breath between my thighs.

'Remember, no names,' he whispered. 'I am not supposed to be here.'

'I'll do my best, but y'know, it's kind of difficult to control myself when your tongue is so talented.'

Romeo smirked, then returned to worshipping my pussy, licking and sucking on my clit like it was the best thing he'd eaten all week.

I threw my head back and covered my mouth to muffle another loud moan. The pleasure was almost too much.

I'd done so many wild sexual things this week. And now I could add being eaten out on the edge of a swimming pool to my fantasy list. This was so fucking hot.

I squeezed my eyes shut, desperately fighting the urge to come. I didn't want this to end.

I felt the wave building inside me. I was seconds away from exploding but then a scream jolted me out of my thoughts.

'Romeo?' a woman's voice boomed. 'What the hell?'

My eyes flicked open, Romeo lifted his head from between my legs and spun around.

As I saw Victoria standing by the front door, my mouth crashed to the floor.

Fuck.

I was supposed to close the main villa door when Romeo came in but got so distracted that I forgot.

'Victoria!' Romeo jumped up, then remembered he was stark naked and grabbed his dick to try and shield his crown jewels.

I admired his optimism, but although he had big hands, his cock and balls were even bigger, so there was no way they'd be able to cover up those bad boys.

Then I remembered, *I* was sitting on the edge of the pool with my legs spread, flashing my pussy to his boss too.

I quickly crossed my legs, but I already knew it was too late.

She'd seen everything.

We were screwed.

'For God's sake, Romeo!' Victoria barked, covering her eyes. 'My office! Now!'

42

ROMEO

'What the actual fuck, Romeo!' Victoria slammed her hand on her desk as I stepped into the office.

Unsurprisingly, she had not waited for me to get dressed. After she'd stormed off, I'd climbed out of the pool, dragged my clothes on then raced to see her.

'I know how it looks,' I sighed as I sat in the chair. 'I am sorry for what you saw, but this is not... I have feelings for Sammie. And she has feelings for me too. I would not do this with any other guest.'

'Forgive me if I don't believe you, Romeo, but you also told me you'd never get involved with a guest, full stop. Then I walk in and see you going down on one! I know I told you to look after Samantha and make her happy, but I didn't mean you should do that by giving her oral! That's taking the Love Hotel's commitment to going the extra mile to satisfy our guests *way* too far.'

'I understand why you are upset, but I cannot apologise for falling for her. I have not felt this way about anyone for... I want to say years, but that would not be true. This is the first time I have ever felt this way.'

Victoria's mouth opened, then closed again and her eyes bulged.

'Oh my God!' she shouted. 'You're actually in *love* with her!' She laughed in disbelief.

'No.' I shook my head. 'I have strong feelings. But it is not *love*. It is too soon for that. I...' My voice trailed off as I started to question my denial.

I thought that Sammie was incredible. Confident, funny, easy to talk to, beautiful and our connection was off the scale. But *love*?

'Romeo.' Victoria's voice softened. 'You of all people should know that love doesn't have a set timeline. Some people swear they fell in love at first sight. For others it takes months. Some people are head over heels in days or weeks. How many of our guests have told you before they've left that they've fallen for their match? One? Two?'

'No. The majority develop strong feelings within the first week and usually by the end of the trip...'

As reality hit me, I swallowed the lump in my throat.

Of course people fell in love quickly here.

That was the whole point of the hotel and why it had been so successful.

Shit.

I loved her.

I had fallen in love with Sammie.

I blinked, then blinked again as I tried to process the realisation.

'Here's what I'm going to do about what I just saw.' Victoria narrowed her eyes then leant forward.

My chest tightened. I was so close to getting the opportunity to go to the US, but now I had blown it.

I did not even know why I was thinking about a transfer when Victoria was going to fire or at best suspend me. She was clear from the start that I should not cross the line. She had given me dozens of warnings and I had not listened.

'I understand.' I got up from my seat.

'Where are you going?' She frowned.

'I am leaving.'

'Sit down!' she commanded. 'You didn't even wait to hear what I intend to do.'

'Tell me,' I said, bracing myself for the punishment.

'I'm going to do absolutely nothing.' Her mouth twitched. 'When some guests were asking for you and you weren't answering your phone, something told me to check Samantha's villa. When I walked up the path and saw the front door was cracked open, I thought it was weird. Then I heard her scream and I was worried, so I knocked and when Samantha still didn't answer, I pushed it open. I wasn't expecting to see your head between her thighs. And at first, I was furious.'

'I apologise again that you saw us.'

'But now that I'm thinking more calmly and I can see you're clearly smitten, maybe I can show some leniency.' She rested her finger on her chin, like she was considering her next move.

'I would really appreciate that.' My pulse quickened. Maybe there was a chance that I was not going to get fired after all.

'Samantha's going back to London tomorrow. And frankly, thanks to that dickhead Edward, the start of her experience here was a shitshow. So the way I see it, if you helped her to *enjoy herself*, which judging by the screams that I now know were because of pleasure rather than pain, you did, then what's the harm? Plus, Samantha's friends with Jasmine, right?'

'Correct.'

'Good. So Samantha will be aware of the importance of not blabbing to the world about how well she was *serviced* by her Love Alchemist because she got matched with a guy who left after a few days to go back to his pregnant ex. *Yes.*' A wide smile spread across her face. 'As long as you both show the utmost discretion about Samantha's stay here, I'm confident that this doesn't have to be a problem. But if it does, we'll have to have another more serious conversation. Understood?'

'*Sì.*'

My shoulders relaxed and I exhaled. I was not going to lose my job.

That was great news.

Keeping my career was one thing.

Now I had to work out how not to lose Sammie forever.

43

SAMMIE

I paced up and down the living room for the hundredth time, my heart thundering against my chest.

Romeo was going to lose his job and it was all my fault.

If I hadn't asked him to recreate my bloody fantasy, he'd still have his career.

Or I could've at least remembered to close the front door. Victoria wouldn't have opened it if it wasn't already cracked.

Romeo shouldn't have come to my villa. We'd said from the start that it was too risky to do anything on the grounds. But instead of being grateful that we hadn't been caught, we got complacent.

And now Romeo had paid the ultimate price.

I checked my phone again. Romeo hadn't replied to the dozens of texts I'd sent. He must still be with Victoria. I was desperate to find out what had happened. Then again, you didn't need to be a genius to know that it wouldn't be good.

Stella would know what to say to calm me down. I dialled her number.

'Hey! How's it going?' she answered. 'Enjoying your last full day?'

'I was until me and Romeo got caught.'

'Er, Sammie… sorry, I should've mentioned, Jasmine's here – she and Alejandro came to London for the weekend and, er, you're kind of on loudspeaker.'

'Shit.' My stomach bottomed out. Although I now considered Jasmine a friend, she was still part of the Love Hotel's management and she'd warned me off getting involved with Romeo, so the last thing I wanted was for her to find out.

Then again, now that Victoria knew, it wouldn't be long until the news travelled.

'You and Romeo are involved?' Jasmine said. I tried to read her tone, but I couldn't. 'Is it a fling or something more?'

'More!' I replied quickly.

'And he feels the same?'

'I'm pretty sure that he does. But we don't know how to move things forward and it's a shitstorm because Victoria walked in on us and'

'Were you kissing?' Stella asked.

'He was eating me out whilst I sat on the edge of the pool…' I said sheepishly. A flashback popped into my mind, sending a wave of desire zipping through my bloodstream.

'Oh my God!' Stella shouted. '*Brilliant*! That's so much worse than what Jasmine saw when she walked in on me and Max.'

'I shouldn't laugh, but…' Jasmine giggled.

'You two!' I scolded. 'Now isn't the time to joke about it. It's too soon! Romeo could lose his job over this.'

'Shit, sorry,' Stella said. 'Is there anything you can do, Jasmine?'

'I'm not sure…' Jasmine said. 'Like I said from the start,

they've relaxed the rules on employees, but with guests... I can speak to Victoria though.'

'Thanks. I just hope that...' There was a knock at the door. 'Hold on a sec.' I raced to the door, flung it open and when I saw Romeo, my heart bloomed. 'Ladies, I better go. Romeo's here.'

'Good luck,' Stella said. 'Update us as soon as you can, okay?'

'Will do.' I hung up. 'What happened? Did you get fired? I'm so sorry! I should never have'

'It is okay.' He wrapped his arms around me. 'I did not get fired.'

'You *didn't*?' My eyebrows shot up to the ceiling. 'What did Victoria say?'

Romeo led me to the sofa and as he explained their conversation, relief washed over me.

'Thank God you didn't get the sack!' I threw my arms around him. 'I was so worried.'

'I knew you would be, that is why I came here straightaway. I wish that I could stay, but I must go. The couples' final dates will start soon.'

'Okay.' My shoulders slumped again. I was sad that I'd be alone this evening, but the important thing was Romeo's job was safe. And it wasn't like I was in a hell hole. I could have dinner at the beach bar or something. Although I'd prefer to be with Romeo, watching the sun set with a cocktail in my hand wasn't a bad way to spend my last night here.

'The dates should finish by about eleven. I know it will be late, but perhaps we can do something together afterwards. It is your last night here, so I would really like us to spend time together.'

'I'd love that!' I brightened instantly.

'*Perfetto*. I will message when I am on my way.' Romeo kissed me, then left.

I leant back on the sofa and exhaled.

Looked like my last night was going to be great after all.

* * *

Romeo had just messaged to say that he was ten minutes away.

Although Victoria had given us her blessing, it was still on the condition that we were discreet, so after locking up the villa, I walked to our normal meeting place outside of the hotel. Just as I arrived Romeo pulled up, jumped out of the car and opened the door for me.

'*Buonasera, tesoro.*' He leant down and kissed me softly on the lips.

'*Tesoro?*'

'It is a term of affection – like darling or baby. Technically it means treasure, which is also accurate.' He grinned as I slid onto the passenger seat.

'Treasure. Yep, I could get used to that!' I smiled, then my face dropped as I realised there wouldn't be time for me to *get used to it*, seeing as this time tomorrow I'd be back in London. 'So where are we going?' I said quickly.

'It is a surprise.'

About half an hour later Romeo drove us down a beautiful cobbled street, then parked up.

'What is this place?' I said, admiring the pretty stone buildings.

'I am taking you to my home.'

After stopping outside of a dark wooden door, Romeo opened it and I followed him inside. He switched on the light, led me up one staircase then another before opening a door. When I stepped through it, I gasped.

It was a rooftop with views of the town.

The midnight-blue sky was illuminated with beautiful stars and as my eyes scanned my surroundings, I spotted there was a small table set up with battery-powered candles in the centre, along with a bottle of my favourite prosecco resting in a silver ice bucket beside it.

'Wow,' I said. 'You're so lucky to live here. This rooftop is beautiful! Look at the views. You can even see the sea from here!'

Although it was dark, I could still make out the gentle ripple of the waves in the distance.

'*Grazie, Tesoro.*' He smiled, then pulled out a chair for me.

Once I sat down, he opened the prosecco, poured a full glass for me and half a glass for himself, sat opposite me, then lifted his glass in the air.

'What are we toasting?'

'To you: the most incredible woman I have met.'

'*Grazie,*' I smiled, thinking how bittersweet it was that I'd found a man that thought I was amazing, but couldn't be with him. I pushed the thought out of my head. I didn't want to ruin the moment.

'I am sure that you ate earlier, but I am hungry, so I will cook. Would you like something?' He walked towards a small barbecue.

'It'd be rude not to!'

Once the charcoal was ready, Romeo gave me a quick tour of his house, then brought a tray of seafood back up to the rooftop. There were huge prawns, plus different types of fish on a skewer that looked like salmon, tuna and something else. Then he brought out another tray.

'Is that...?' I grimaced as I looked at the suckered brown tentacles. '*Octopus?*'

'*Si.*'

'Ugh,' I winced.

'Have you ever tried it?' he asked.

'No, but...'

'It is delicious.'

'I doubt it.' My face crumpled.

When everything was cooked, Romeo piled it onto our plates. I devoured the fish and prawns, which tasted so fresh I could've sworn Romeo just plucked them from the sea, but I gave the octopus a wide berth.

'Here.' He lifted a forkful to my mouth. 'Just try.'

I opened reluctantly as he slid it inside. And as I chewed, my eyes bulged.

'Oh... It's actually not bad!'

'Told you!'

'Let me try another bit. Just in case...' I grinned.

For the next hour, Romeo told me all about the dates he'd set up for the couples and I filled him in on how I'd spent the rest of my day, which mostly involved packing, having dinner at the pool bar before a beach walk, then returning to the villa.

After we'd finished eating, he moved our chairs to the edge of the rooftop so that we could take in the views, then wrapped his arms around me.

I rested my head on his shoulder. Everything was so pretty. Romeo was lucky that he could come and watch the stars whenever he wanted.

'Thank you for bringing me here,' I said, as Romeo stroked my hair. 'It really means a lot.'

'*Piacere*,' he said, then leant forward and kissed me slowly.

The kiss lasted for what must've been minutes but still didn't seem long enough. I swear I could kiss this man for days.

'Are you still hungry?' Romeo asked as he gently pulled away.

'I'm sure I have room for whatever you want me to eat...' I smirked.

'Get your mind out of the gutter, young lady!' he grinned, stood up then held out his hand. 'Come. I will take you for dessert.'

'At this time?' I looked at my watch. Bloody hell. I knew it was late but I didn't realise it was after two in the morning. 'What restaurant will be open at this time?'

'You will see.'

Romeo led me out of his house and down the narrow cobbled streets. We stopped at a building with its hatch open. Wow. It was a bakery kitchen.

Trays of pastries lined the large metal worktops and as the scent of freshly baked goods flooded my nostrils, my mouth watered.

'What would you like?'

'We can actually *buy* this stuff, *now*?'

'*Sì*. It is fresh from the oven. They bake early to give time for everything to be delivered to different bakeries.'

When I spotted my favourite pastries, my eyes brightened and I nodded my head towards them.

'I think you already know what I'd like.'

'*Va bene*.' Romeo grinned.

Ten minutes later, we were sitting on a bench near the sea eating freshly baked *pasticciotto*.

'*Grazie mille*,' I said, wiping some pastry crumbs from the corner of my mouth. 'I didn't think it was possible, but these are even tastier straight out of the oven.'

'I am glad you like it. I am sorry I could not organise a special romantic dinner like the other matches had, but I hope that this fresh *pasticciotto* will make up for it.'

'Are you joking?' I raised my voice. 'Tonight's been bloody

brilliant! You organised a late dinner on a rooftop. No, not just *any* rooftop. On *your* rooftop. You showed me your home, views of this beautiful town, you cooked a delicious barbecue feast under the stars, then took me to get my favourite pastry which I'm now eating by the sea with the most incredible man created. If that isn't romantic, I don't know what is!'

'Oh.' Romeo blushed. '*Grazie,*' he said before stifling a yawn. '*Scusi.* I am tired.'

'I'm not surprised. You've been working all day, then we had that emotional rollercoaster this afternoon and now it's almost three in the morning and we're still out. Come, on, Mr. It's time to get you to bed. Are you staying at the hotel tonight?'

'*Sì.*'

'Great! Let's go.'

When we arrived at the hotel, this time Romeo insisted that he drop me off within the grounds because it was too late for me to walk alone. I'd hidden under a blanket in the back seat so the security guard at the gate wouldn't see me with him.

I expected Romeo to say goodbye in the car, but he insisted that although the grounds were safe, he'd walk me to my room. Because Victoria had asked us to be discreet, he put on a jacket to cover his uniform and wore the cap again.

'Thanks for walking me home and for an amazing night,' I whispered when we got to my door. 'Have a good sleep.'

'I am not ready to leave you yet,' he said. 'So, unless you have any objections, I would like to stay the night with you.'

'Course! I'd love that!' We stepped inside, this time closing the door behind us.

Romeo then flipped his baseball cap backwards, gently nudged my body back, then leant against the doorframe and kissed me *oh, so slowly.*

As our tongues gently flicked against one another's, a moan slipped from my mouth. This was heaven.

Then, without saying a word, Romeo scooped me up in his arms, carried me to the bedroom, kicked open the door, then laid me down on the bed.

He straddled me, then gently peeled my clothes off before removing his.

Romeo's dark eyes bored into me like lasers and I couldn't tear my gaze away.

I didn't move. I didn't talk. I wasn't sure I could, even if I wanted to.

'Sammie,' he growled, 'I would like to make love to you now. *Va bene?*'

'*Si*,' I panted, struggling for breath, before nodding enthusiastically.

He rolled on a condom, then slid inside me. As our bodies rocked together in perfect harmony, I realised that what he'd just said was true.

Romeo had said he wanted to make love to me and that was exactly how it felt.

In the beginning it was just sex, but now it was clear from the way he looked at me and the way I knew I was looking at him that there were real feelings involved.

Deep feelings.

And as Romeo peppered soft kisses over my breasts and brought me to orgasm, I knew that something had shifted.

What I'd said earlier to Stella and Jasmine was true. This wasn't just a fling.

This was *more*.

So. Much. More.

This was *real*.

We hadn't discussed how we'd make it work beyond tomorrow, but I knew one thing for sure: Romeo was the best thing that had ever happened to me.

And there was no way that I could lose him.

44

ROMEO

As I stood at the bedroom doorway and watched Sammie sleeping, my heart swelled, then sank.

I could not believe that in just a few hours she would be gone.

When we were on my rooftop last night, staring at the stars with her head resting on my shoulder, I realised again that what Victoria said was really true.

I loved Sammie. So much.

When I said that I wanted to make love to her, I meant every word.

She was the one. I was sure of it.

I had finally found my perfect match.

And she was leaving.

Sammie stirred and I strode back over to the bed. I did not want to wake her up, but at the same time, I could not leave without giving her a proper kiss goodbye.

The final morning when guests were leaving was always hectic because I saw each one off personally. That meant that the only chance I would get to see her would be when her car came to take her to the airport. And in light of Victoria's conditions, I could not express myself in front of my colleagues.

It was now or never.

'Sammie,' I whispered. 'I must go now.'

Her eyes opened slowly.

'What's the time?'

'Six-thirty.'

I had only had about two hours' sleep, but spending the night with Sammie was worth it.

'Will I see you later?' she croaked.

'Only when the chauffeur arrives, so I want to say goodbye to you properly, now. Here.' I handed her a red book. 'This is for you.'

'What is it?' She frowned.

'It is *our* memory book. Just because we were not matched by the hotel, it does not mean that we do not still have important memories.'

In the album I had included a selection of the selfies we had taken together this week. And unlike when I tried to prepare a shortlist of photos for Sammie and Edward, I had many wonderful photos to choose from.

'This is beautiful!' she said as she flicked through the pages, then laughed at a selfie of us pulling silly faces on the beach.

'*You* are beautiful.' I took her head in my hands and kissed her like it was the first time, whilst still hoping that it would not be the last.

Sammie pushed her mouth against mine, our lips crashed hungrily.

The kiss evolved into something softer and deeper. As her fingers raked through my hair, I felt something wet on my cheek and pulled back.

'*Merda*,' I said. 'Do not cry, Sammie. This is not the end. I promise.' I wiped her cheeks with my thumb. 'We will speak every day. And we will be together again. *Va bene?*'

'*Va bene*,' she croaked, her eyes still watering.

Sammie had always shown such a confident, hard exterior, so I knew that being vulnerable around me was a big deal and something that I did not take lightly.

'I must go, but I will see you later. Do not forget to eat the rest of the *pasticciotto* for breakfast.'

I kissed her forehead softly, then headed towards the door. Just before I stepped through it, I turned to look at Sammie again.

She was still crying and my heart shattered.

I had told her I would find a way for us to be together again.

I did not know how, but I had promised.

And I would not let her down.

45

SAMMIE

So this was it.

As I locked the villa door for the last time and wheeled my case to reception, my stomach churned. I felt sick. And I'd cried more this morning than a hungry newborn baby.

I wasn't normally a crier. Especially not over a guy.

But as I'd told myself many times, Romeo was no ordinary man. He was out of this world. And in less than five minutes, he'd be out of my world, for good.

My thoughts turned to his kindness this morning. When I went in the kitchen, he'd left me a bag of the *taralli* snacks we'd eaten on the boat that I'd loved with a note to say he'd got them for me in case I got hungry on the plane. So sweet.

Then there was the amazing memory book. It was so unexpected and I hadn't realised just how many beautiful photos we'd taken together. Definitely a million times better than those awful ones of me with shithead Edward. And that was because Romeo was my perfect match. We were meant to be.

I wanted to believe what he'd said earlier: that we'd find a way to be together again. I really did, but wanting something wasn't enough to make it happen.

My heart was breaking now, but the pain that would come when we realised in weeks or months that we couldn't make it work would be even worse.

I was gonna need a whole cupboard full of chocolate to get me through this.

'Sammie?' Aldo called out as I approached his Mercedes. 'Are you ready?'

'Er...' I scanned the reception area looking for Romeo. He wasn't here. I looked at my watch. It was a few minutes past the agreed meeting time. Had he already come and left?

The churning in my stomach intensified. I knew we'd already said goodbye, but I was really hoping to see him one last time.

He said we'd see each other later. Had he changed his mind?

'Could we wait a few more minutes, *per favore*?'

'*Va bene*,' he nodded, putting my suitcase into the boot.

I scanned the hotel grounds again but there was no sign of him and when I checked, there were no messages on my phone.

'Samantha, sorry to rush you, but we must leave if we want to make it on time,' Aldo said. My chest tightened. I looked at my watch again. He was now ten minutes late.

He said he'd be here. And I believed him.

Was I wrong to?

'One more minute. Please.'

Just as I was about to call him, Romeo came sprinting through reception.

'*Grazie a dio!*' he shouted, as he raced towards me. 'Thank God you are still here! I am sorry. One of the guests fainted and I had to wait until the nurse came.'

'Oh my God, is the guest okay?'

'He is fine. He is just sad to say goodbye to his match.' He smiled. 'I feel his pain.' Romeo's eyes locked with mine. He opened his mouth, then closed it again and I wondered what he'd wanted to say.

Aldo hovered, which was his polite way of reminding me I had a plane to catch. Although right now I wasn't feeling very motivated to get to the airport on time.

If I missed my flight, I'd have to stay and me and Romeo could be together.

But sooner or later, I'd have to go back to London.

I had a decent job there. I was about to get promoted. I'd worked my arse off for years to get that opportunity. I couldn't blow it. Staying would just delay the inevitable and fuck up my career prospects. I had bills to pay. Responsibilities.

As heartbreaking as this was, I had to rip off the plaster.

'I should go before Aldo has kittens.'

'Kittens?' Romeo's brows knitted together.

'To have kittens means basically to shit yourself with worry.'

'Mamma did not teach me that phrase.' A small smile touched his lips.

'There are loads of phrases for you to learn. Not as many as I need to learn in Italian though! You never did teach me all the swear words.'

'I will save that for our next lesson. If I taught you everything all at once, you would have no reason to come back.'

'I have more than enough of those, trust me.' Our eyes locked again. God, this was so hard. I hated goodbyes at the best of times, but this felt impossible. The tears started building and I was determined not to start blubbing in front of Romeo again. 'Anyway,' I straightened my shoulders, 'I better make tracks. Say bye to your mum and Biscotti from me and thanks for everything.'

I leant forward and gave him a soft peck on the cheek before quickly climbing onto the back seat and closing the car door.

Aldo got into the driver's seat and after I put on my seatbelt, I heard a knock on the window. I put on my sunglasses so that Romeo wouldn't see my tears, then pressed the button to lower the window.

'*Ciao*, Sammie,' Romeo said and then mouthed something to me.

'Huh?' I said, struggling to follow his words.

Romeo did it again, but slower this time as he waved me off.

I waved back and it was only when Aldo pulled away that I worked out what he'd said.

My heart bloomed and a massive grin spread over my face.

Romeo had mouthed two words.

Ti amo.

My Italian vocab might be limited, but I knew exactly what that meant in English: I love you.

46

SAMMIE

To say that the last three weeks back in London had been shitty was putting it mildly.

Before I left for Italy, I was content enough with my job and was excited about the promotion that my boss had hinted several times was pretty much mine, but despite that amazing news, I'd started hating it.

At first I thought it was because I was still upset about leaving Romeo.

When I'd realised that he'd said he loved me, I cried happy and sad tears all the way to the airport.

I was happy because, *hello*, the man that I adored had just said he loved me.

For once, my feelings weren't one-sided.

But I was also sad because I'd finally found a man that I loved who loved me back and I had to leave him.

Yes. I loved him.

Even though I'd only known him for two weeks, somehow it felt like I'd known and loved him for years.

And who could blame me? Romeo had done so many things to show me that I mattered. That I was special.

That he didn't just accept me for who I was, he loved me because of it.

I'd wanted to tell him how I felt so many times, but I was scared.

Even now that we were still messaging multiple times a day, I still hadn't found the courage to tell him. I would though, when he came over in three weeks.

Yep! Romeo was coming over in twenty days and sixteen hours and I couldn't bloody wait.

Anyway, back to my job. As I was saying, at first I thought that I hated being at work because I was missing Romeo and of course because I'd just come back from the best two weeks of my life. Having the holiday blues was normal for everyone, right?

But a week later, I still had the same feeling of dread when I woke up every morning.

In the end I figured out that it was because after going to Italy and seeing how life could be and what was possible, I didn't want to do the same job any more. Suddenly everything seemed so mundane and repetitive. I wanted more from life.

So just like Romeo had recommended when I was with him in Italy, I'd started applying for jobs that I knew I'd enjoy more, like event organisation and planning and roles that involved more interaction with customers. But so far, I'd had no interest.

When I spoke to a woman at a specialist events employment agency she said it'd be difficult for me to find work in the industry because I had no experience. But how the hell was I supposed to get experience if no one gave me a chance?

Internships weren't an option because I had bills to pay, so that was that. I had no choice. I'd accept the promotion when it was confirmed, get some more event organisation experience and then in a few years hopefully I could work towards pursuing my dream career.

My phone chimed and when I saw it was from Romeo, a smile that was wider than a jumbo jet spread across my face.

ROMEO

Ciao, bella. Thank you for my mug and the card.
I love them!

I laughed as I read his message. I'd sent him a Mr Bean mug I spotted online along with a personalised thank you card with a selfie of us on the beach printed on the front.

ME

Glad it reached you safely. Now every time you drink coffee you can think of your twin brother!

ROMEO

Grazie. But if I need to think of him, I just look in the mirror!

I snorted then replied with a row of laughing emojis.

ROMEO

I loved the playlist too.

ME

Did you like the first track?

I'd also created him a playlist. I hadn't kept up with doing the five songs a day thing for obvious reasons but it was easy to think of how Romeo made me feel.

The first track was 'I'm Too Sexy' by Right Said Fred which I thought was perfect.

ROMEO

I liked it very much. It was kind of you to send a song that was all about you.

SAMMIE

Such a charmer!

ROMEO

How is your day going?

ME

I still can't stand my job, but my day just got much better, thanks to you! How about yours?

ROMEO

I am sorry you are still not enjoying it. Hopefully when you are promoted you will like it more.

I am good. We have just arrived back from Alberobello.

ME

Ooh. I remember going there. That was the first time we got to spend proper time together.

ROMEO

Sì. And it was when I started to realise that you were not the person I thought you were.

ME

You mean a drunk bimbo?

ROMEO

I would never think such a thing!

ME

Haha, yeah, sure!

ROMEO

Says the woman who compared me to Mr Bean.

ME

Oi! Don't diss Mr Bean or I'll take back your new mug! He's a national treasure.

ROMEO

I know. I am not worthy of such a comparison.

ME

You are just as sexy as Mr Bean.

ROMEO

Grazie. Now my head will not fit through the door after that compliment.

ME

I'm sure you'll manage!

ROMEO

I must go. I have a meeting with Victoria, but we will video call later, sì?

ME

Definitely! Ciao.

As I closed WhatsApp, my heart fluttered. Being away from Romeo had been hard, but I was so grateful for his messages and video calls. They were the highlight of my day.

Once I'd finished another painfully long stint at work, I went home, showered, cooked dinner then got ready to speak to Romeo.

We video called every night once he'd finished dinner service and was back in his office or in bed.

When it was his day off or he was sleeping at home, sometimes we'd have phone sex. I'd never been into that before, but not only did I miss him, I missed his talented cock and touching myself whilst watching Romeo on screen made me feel closer to him.

I was so glad there wasn't long until we'd be back together again.

For the moment we planned to do the long-distance thing. Romeo would be over in less than three weeks, then in a couple of months, I'd use some of the few days' holiday I had left to go and see him in Italy for a long weekend.

After that I didn't know what would happen, but we'd work something out.

We had to.

My phone lit up and as Romeo's name flashed on the screen, I let out an excited squeal, before jumping on the bed and accepting the call.

'Hey!' I said excitedly. 'How are you?'

But as I saw Romeo's solemn face, my smile slid from my lips.

'What's wrong?' My face creased with concern.

'I had a meeting earlier with Victoria.' Romeo blew out a frustrated breath.

'Yeah, I know, you said. How'd it go? Did she give you bad news?'

'No. It was good news, but...'

'But if it was good news, why do you look so sad?'

'Because...' He paused and my heart thundered against my chest. 'She told me that... they want to send me to the new Love Hotel. In California.'

'Oh my God!' I screamed. 'That's amazing! That's what you've always wanted! Congrats! I'm so happy for you, darling!'

'*Grazie.*'

'When do they want you to go?'

'In two weeks...' His voice trailed off.

And then it dawned on me.

I was so wrapped up in celebrating his happy news that I didn't even think about what this move would mean.

If Romeo was going to California in two weeks, that meant he wouldn't be able to come to London.

And if he was working there, what would happen to us?

Travelling to Italy for a long weekend was feasible. But California was over five thousand miles away.

Maintaining a long-distance relationship from Italy would be difficult. Trying to do it from the US would be virtually impossible.

'Oh,' I said, my stomach plummeting a billion miles beneath the earth. 'So that means... so that's it then. For us.'

Even though I'd known from the start that this was on the cards, I'd pushed it out of my mind. But that denial had come back to bite me in the arse.

'No. This does not have to be the end. I want this to work. We will find a way.'

'How?'

'I do not know, but...'

'We have to be realistic, Romeo. We've done well keeping in touch for the past three weeks, but now you're going to California, it'll be impossible. You'll be busy settling in and working and flights there are expensive and... it won't work.'

'We have to try.'

'I'm not sure if I can, Romeo.' My stomach twisted. 'If we make a clean break now, it'll be easier, for both of us. I don't want you worrying about me when you're over there. This is your dream. I can't get in the way of that. Especially after what happened the last time you made plans to travel to the States. No.' I shook my head defiantly. 'You'll need to be focused. I don't want you to feel guilty for not having time to call me, especially with the time difference.'

I was sure California was about eight hours behind us so it'd be even harder to keep in touch.

And once he was surrounded by beautiful women over there, he'd soon forget about me.

Plus, when I got this promotion, I'd be working longer hours and have more responsibilities. If I ever wanted to get the chance to pursue a career that involved event organisation, I couldn't mess up this opportunity by spending my days pining over Romeo and wondering when we'd speak or be together.

No. We'd had a good run, but it'd be less painful if we drew a line under things now.

I'd never forget my time with Romeo for as long as I lived, but I'd been in this situation before with holiday romances. They always fizzled out and ended up hurting ten times more than if we'd called it quits sooner.

'Congrats again,' I said, tears welling in my eyes. 'I'm tired. I'd better go.'

'We will speak tomorrow?' Romeo asked, concern etched across his face.

'I... I'm not sure.'

'*Please*, Sammie. Do not do this.'

'I have to go.' I ended the call, collapsed back on the mattress then started bawling into my pillow.

I hated ending the call so abruptly, but I had to set Romeo free.

I wanted him to go to California without having the pressure of trying to maintain a relationship and with me holding him back.

Ending things would crush me, but in the long run, he'd be better off without me.

It was for the best.

I was sure of it.

47

ROMEO

I stared at my phone screen in a daze.

I could not believe what had happened.

Sammie had just ended things.

When Victoria had told me the news, it was bittersweet. I had worked so hard for so long to secure the opportunity to move to the new resort in California and now it had happened, I was sad because of the extra distance it would put between me and Sammie.

I understood her concerns. But I believed in that famous saying: *Omnia vincit amor*: love conquers all. Although right now we did not know how we could be together, I was sure that we would find a way.

I tried calling Sammie back but the phone rang out, so I sent a text to tell her I would call again in the morning.

The news was clearly a shock. She needed time for it to sink in. She had not told me that she loved me yet, but I felt it. And when you love someone, you will do whatever it takes to be together.

Tomorrow was a new day. And I hoped that somehow, it

would be the day where I came up with a plan that would enable us to be together.

* * *

I knocked on Victoria's office door.

'Come in!'

'Do you have a moment?' I asked as I stepped inside.

'Yes. Coincidentally, I've just got off the phone with the Californian Love Empress. She'd emailed to ask for couples bonding activities ideas so I told her what we did here and I shared the suggestions your girlfriend made about the beach games nights and the other ideas you passed on. Management liked her recommendations for having open days and video interviews too.'

'Great!' I said, my chest filling with pride. 'I have many more suggestions that she made typed up on my phone which I have been meaning to send to you.'

'Perfect! They have a lot to do before they open. They're still firming up the activities and hiring new staff.'

'I thought they planned to bring in experienced Romance Rockstars from the Spanish, Jamaican and Italian resorts?'

'That's the main focus of the recruitment drive. The hotel always likes to promote from within the Love Hotel family, but the Californian resort will be the largest so far, so they need a lot of them. And they can't just hire anyone. They need people that have first-class customer service skills, but who are also resourceful, well organised, enjoy arranging events and of course believe in the power of romance. Finding people with those qualities who are also going to be well-liked by our guests is a lot harder than you think.'

'*Si.*'

As I processed Victoria's words, a hundred light bulbs went off in my head.

Victoria just said that the Californian management were looking for Romance Rockstars with great customer service skills who believed in romance and were likeable. And who enjoyed organising events.

Those were all qualities that Sammie had.

She was no longer enjoying her job, an event organisation role was her dream, plus she would not have a problem working in the US.

But most importantly, if Sammie worked at the Californian resort, we could be together.

Excitement and hope exploded in my chest.

'Sorry,' Victoria said. 'I went off on a tangent. What did you come to see me about?'

'I wanted to ask if I could take some time off as soon as possible before going to California, but now I have another idea that I would like to discuss with you...'

Before I had said that I believed I would find a way for me and Sammie to be together and miraculously, I was sure I had found the perfect solution that would help us *and* benefit the Love Hotel.

I hoped that Victoria and the management team agreed...

48

SAMMIE

'Thanks so much, Aunty Jeanette. I really appreciate it. Speak soon.'

I ended the call then headed back to the office with a spring in my step. It was the first time I'd felt happy all week.

My boss had confirmed that if I wanted the head receptionist role, it was mine. HR were preparing the new contract and my new salary and responsibilities would be officially confirmed in a matter of days.

I should be over the moon, but ever since I'd ended the video call with Romeo abruptly eight days ago, I'd felt like shit.

He'd been messaging to ask if we could talk but I'd said I needed time and would be in touch soon.

The truth was, I'd been working on something and I didn't want to talk to him until I knew whether or not it'd work.

What I'd said during our video call was wrong.

I shouldn't have suggested that we cut our losses without first trying to see if it could work.

Romeo wasn't like the other holiday romances I'd had.

He was special.

I loved him. And I wasn't going to give up on what we had without a fight.

So I'd spent days racking my brain, trying to think of how we could be together.

And then the idea came to me.

Yes, I'd just been given a promotion I'd worked my sweet arse off for and had dreamed about getting for years, but was it really what I wanted?

The truth was, it wasn't.

Like Romeo, I'd always wanted to travel around the US but I'd never got around to it because I was scared and I didn't have the right motivation.

But now I did.

That was when it hit me. I could try and get a job out there.

I know, it wasn't my smartest idea. It was batshit crazy.

The chances of finding work were slim. There were probably thousands of people with the same idea who'd already travelled to California looking for work.

But even if there was a 99 per cent chance that I'd fail, that meant that there was still a 1 per cent chance that I'd succeed, right?

I had to try.

I had to know that I'd done everything I could to make this work.

If the world ended tomorrow, what would I regret more: not accepting a promotion or losing the only man I'd ever truly loved?

Exactly.

As irresponsible as it sounded, there was no contest.

That was why I'd asked Dad if we had any relatives in California who could help. He reminded me that Aunty Jeanette lived in San Francisco, so I'd just called to ask if she could put the feelers out and see if anyone knew of any jobs that might be available in the next couple of months. I didn't care what the work was. I'd happily work in a bar, restaurant or clean toilets if it meant I could earn money and be closer to Romeo.

It was a long shot, especially because I didn't even know where in California the new hotel would be and even Jasmine wasn't allowed to reveal the location. But living and working in the same state as Romeo would be better than being five thousand miles away in London.

I'd give it a few more days, then I'd call Romeo and tell him my plan. I didn't want to get his hopes up if it wasn't going to work.

Just as I was about to check my emails to see if I'd received any responses back for the jobs I'd applied for in two restaurants in San Diego, my phone started ringing. It was Stella.

'Hey!' she said. 'You still on your lunch break?'

'Yeah. I've got ten minutes left, so I'm heading back to the office now.'

'Cool. So, how's it going? Any leads?'

'Nothing concrete yet, but I just spoke to my Aunt Jeanette and she's going to ask around in San Fran and I've applied for jobs in San Diego.'

'Great! Max has some contacts at different factories in the US too, so he said he can ask around there.'

'That'd be amazing.'

'I'm proud of you, Sammie.'

'What?' My eyebrows knitted together. 'Why?'

'Because you're not giving up. When we spoke after you'd just hung up on Romeo, you were a mess and sounded so defeated.'

After I'd spent half an hour crying and still didn't feel better, I'd called Stella.

'Yeah, it was just a big shock and I wasn't thinking clearly.'

Stella had tried to calm me down and I thought she was going to offer some words of wisdom, but instead she asked me what turned out to be a powerful question. She'd said, if the roles were reversed and it was her crying down the phone, what would I recommend that she do?

I'd paused then said I'd tell her not to give up. I'd say that if Max really was the one, she needed to fight for him and exhaust every option so she didn't wake up one day with regrets and wishing she'd done more.

'Exactly,' she'd said casually.

And just like that, my tears had stopped.

By the next morning, there was fire and determination in my belly and I committed to finding another way.

'I'm glad you saw sense in the end. Have you told Romeo your plans?'

'Not yet, but I've kept in touch.' I knew how shitty being ghosted felt, so I made sure I always replied. 'In my last message a couple of days ago, I said that I needed more time and would call him by the weekend.'

That only gave me a few more days, but I was confident that I'd hear back from my aunt by then, so it'd be fine.

'Okay, good. I just wanted to check you're okay. Keep me posted and maybe we can meet on Sunday for brunch and you can tell me how the call went?'

'Perfect. Cross your fingers, toes, elbows and legs for me.'

'Will do. Although I can't promise I'll be keeping my legs crossed! Me and Max are going back to Sunshine Bay because I have another meeting at the Romance Library tomorrow and there's just something about the sea air that makes us horny!'

'It's got nothing to do with the sea air. You two are *always* bloody horny!' I cackled.

'Wait until you and Romeo are living in the same country. You'll be at it like rabbits too!'

'Yep! We've been apart for almost a month, so I wouldn't let him or his cock out of my sight!'

'*Soon, hon. Soon.* It's gonna happen. I can just feel it.'

'Fingers crossed. Good luck with the meeting and happy bonking!'

'Thanks!'

I hung up feeling even more positive.

Stella believed that I'd be reunited soon with Romeo and I hoped so too.

Time would tell...

49

ROMEO

As I wheeled my suitcase through the airport, my heart pounded.

It was Sunday morning and I was on my way to London: to surprise Sammie.

The past week had been a rollercoaster.

When I first suggested to Victoria that the hotel hire Sammie, after being silent for what felt like hours, she finally agreed that it was a good idea.

She said she could not promise anything, but she would speak to the management and get back to me.

It took five agonising days before Victoria told me that they were interested, especially because Jasmine had also vouched for her, but they said that Sammie would have to go through the same interview process as other applicants and only then could they make a decision.

That was good enough for now. We had a chance, which was a big deal.

This kind of news was too important to share over a video call and it had been a month since I had seen Sammie and I missed her like crazy. Which was why I had decided to fly to London to surprise her face to face and hopefully convince her not to give up on us.

Although we had still been messaging, it was not as frequent as before and I was worried that I needed to do something to prove that I was still as committed and determined as ever for us to be together.

It was a risky move. Particularly because she had messaged yesterday to ask if we could video call and I had said I would prefer to speak today instead.

I hoped she did not feel rejected, but I knew that if I saw her face I would blurt out the news and I wanted to do it in person.

My phone chimed.

It was Stella.

After I explained that I wanted to surprise Sammie and needed Stella's help to make it happen, Jasmine had passed on her number.

Stella screamed when I first called her. And when she told me that she'd already arranged to meet Sammie today so thought it would be easy to set up the surprise, I was so relieved.

STELLA

All set. I'm going to Sammie's in a couple of hours then I'll take her to the meeting point.

ME

Grazie. I will board the plane shortly. Ciao.

My chest bloomed.

In just a few hours, I would be in England.

And hopefully I'd also be back with the woman I loved.

50

SAMMIE

'What made you want to come here again?' I asked as Stella and I walked from Brighton station towards the beach.

'I thought it'd be nice!' Stella replied. 'And I know you've been missing the sea since you got back from Italy, so I reckoned this would help.'

'Hon, I love Brighton beach as much as the next person, but it's nothing like the ones in Italy.'

I sighed as I remembered the conversation I'd had with Romeo's mum, Linda, when I'd said the crystal-clear waters couldn't compare to the murky greenish-blue sea here.

It wasn't just the beaches I missed about Italy. It was Romeo.

I was so looking forward to video calling him yesterday like we'd planned earlier in the week. But when I'd messaged to ask when would be a good time and he'd asked if we could speak today instead, my heart sank.

At least spending time with Stella would take my mind off it and by the time we got the train back to London tonight there wouldn't be long to wait until we could chat.

Sadly, Aunty Jeanette hadn't had any luck finding any job

leads, but I wasn't gonna give up. I'd find something and that was what I planned to tell Romeo tonight. I needed him to know that I was trying.

I was also finally going to tell him I loved him.

Butterflies fluttered in my stomach. I couldn't wait to speak to him again.

When we got to the seafront, Stella and I went down the steps and walked along the pebbled beach.

Although it was cloudy and windy, I supposed she was right. It was nice to get out of London and smell the sea air.

'I'm dying for the loo.' Stella winced. 'I'm just going across the road to find a toilet.'

'I'll come with you.'

'No,' she said quickly. 'Just wait there, close your eyes, breath in the sea air and imagine you're back in Italy. I won't be long.'

'Okay,' I sighed.

I took a few steps towards the sea, closed my eyes and inhaled deeply.

As a reel of memories showcasing the fun I'd had by the sea with Romeo flashed through my mind, I smiled.

I pictured the time I bumped into him on the beach then ended up having lunch with Linda and Biscotti.

Then I remembered our time on the boat.

Next, my mind replayed the memory of us chatting as we walked along the other gorgeous beach he took me to. Then I chuckled as I thought about our fun skinny-dipping session.

Oh, sweet memories.

I'd give anything to be with Romeo right now. To hug him. To inhale his gorgeous scent. To kiss him.

Just to be with him.

'Enjoying the views?' a deep voice sounded from behind me.

A deep voice with a sexy Italian accent that I instantly recognised.

No.

It couldn't be.

I spun around and when I saw Romeo standing there my jaw dropped.

I blinked quickly, blinked again, then prodded his bicep, my eyes wide with disbelief.

'We have not seen each other for more than a month and you greet me by poking my arm?' He raised an eyebrow. 'I was hoping for a better welcome than that!' The corner of his mouth turned up into a smile.

'Are you...?' I rubbed my eyes, then prodded his other bicep. 'Are you *real*?'

I must be dreaming. There was no way Romeo was here.

'The last time that I checked, I was very real. Perhaps if you allowed me to kiss you, that would prove it?'

'Yes, please,' I nodded, my eyes still the size of saucers.

Romeo stepped forward, dipped his head, wrapped his arms around me, then pressed his lips against mine.

At first, I was rooted to the spot, still questioning whether this was a vivid version of one of the millions of fantasies I'd had since I left.

But when he deepened the kiss and slid his tongue inside my mouth, a bolt of electricity rocketed through me.

And then I knew.

This was real.

Oh my God!

I snaked my arms around his back and pulled him into me.

The kiss grew frantic and emotional, like it'd been decades since we'd last locked lips.

As I melted into him, the rest of the world disappeared.

Romeo had come to me. We were together again.

This was a billion times better than all of my dreams put together.

When we eventually pulled away, we looked at each other in a daze.

'You're *here*,' I repeated.

'*Sì.*'

'When did you arrive? How did you know I'd be here? How long are you staying?'

'So many questions!' He laughed, before giving me another soft kiss.

'The plane landed a couple of hours ago. And as for knowing you'd be here, I had a little help.'

Romeo looked over his shoulder and I spotted Stella about fifty metres away, grinning like an idiot.

'You two!' I shook my head. 'I'm worried about how good Stella was about lying to get me here. But I'm glad she did, because it's great to see you and because there's something I need to tell you that's long overdue.'

'Let me guess. You have found another celebrity to compare me to,' he smiled.

'No! You're an original. No one could ever compare to you.' I took his hands in mine. 'What I've been wanting to tell you, is that I... I love you.'

Romeo's eyes lit up and his face brightened.

'*Grazie, Tesoro. Ti amo anch'io.*' Romeo leant forward and kissed me again.

'That means you love me too, right?'

'*Sì.*'

'Phew!' I wiped imaginary sweat from my brow.

'But you already know this.' He rolled his eyes and laughed. 'I told you when you left for the airport.'

'I thought that was what you said, but for all I knew you could've been saying *don't forget your passport!*'

'Maybe it would have been better if you did!'

'I was tempted!' I smiled. 'You didn't answer my last question. How long are you here?'

'I have to return to the hotel in two days. And I am hoping to bring you back with me.'

'What?' I frowned.

'How would you feel about having the opportunity to become a Love Alchemist in California?' A grin that was bigger than the *Titanic* spread across Romeo's face.

'Wait, *what*?' My eyes popped.

'The management want to interview you. If it goes well, once you have been trained, you could work at the new resort, which means that we would be together.'

'No fucking way!' I screamed, before jumping up and down, throwing my arms around him then squeezing Romeo so tight I was scared I'd break him. Then again, with his rock-hard body, that wasn't likely.

'So you think it is a terrible idea,' he laughed.

'It's the best idea in the history of brilliant ideas! How did this even happen?'

As Romeo explained how he thought of it and everything that he, Victoria and Jasmine had done to present it to the management team, my heart bloomed.

'So what do you think?' Romeo said. 'Would you like to come back to Italy then come on an adventure to California with me?'

'I haven't even had the interview or got the job yet!'

'You will get it. They would be lucky to have you. *I* am lucky to have you.'

'And I'm lucky to have you,' I said, thinking how amazing it was to have found a man who truly believed in me. 'And hell yeah, I'll come to Italy, California and wherever with you!'

Romeo cupped my face then gave me another long, slow kiss.

And as our lips locked and I melted against him, pure joy washed over me.

I'd gone to the Love Hotel to find my perfect match, but I'd left with so much more.

Not only had I found the love of my life, I'd found a new direction.

Now I had the opportunity to secure a new job, plus work and travel abroad.

I was the happiest I'd ever been.

All because I'd fallen in love.

Yep.

Love was powerful.

Love was brilliant.

Love had changed my life.

And my romantic adventures with Romeo were only just beginning.

EPILOGUE
SAMMIE

Five days later

'Oh my God!' I glanced down at the phone screen, my heart almost leaping from my chest. 'It's ringing!'

'Answer it.' Romeo squeezed my hand. 'It will be fine.'

'You've got this, Sammie.' Linda gave me a reassuring smile.

I was at a gorgeous beach in Salento having a picnic with Romeo, Linda and Biscotti and was about to find out whether I'd got a position on the Love Alchemist trainee programme and a job in California.

After spending two blissful days with Romeo in London (okay, a lot of that time was spent in my bedroom) and begging my boss for some last-minute unpaid leave, we flew to Puglia and the next day I had a series of interviews, which I think went well. But now, forty-eight hours later, it was the moment of truth.

I was about to find out whether I'd be able to start a new adventure with Romeo or whether we'd be kept apart.

Here goes...

'Hello,' I answered.

'Hi, Samantha, it's Victoria. Thanks for attending the interviews. We were really keen to speak to you, particularly because of your ties to the hotel, both from your own unique experience of being a guest there and your connections with Jasmine and Romeo. We felt that gave you a special insight into how important and powerful the work we do is.'

'Great!' I said, wishing she'd just cut to the chase and put me out of my misery.

'So, unfortunately, you won't be going to California with Romeo next week...'

'Oh.' My heart plummeted. At least I'd tried. Even though I didn't get the job, I was still going there anyway.

When I'd begged my boss for the unpaid leave, I'd also told her I was handing in my resignation. It was a risky move, but I knew I couldn't be away from Romeo. I'd waited so long to find a man like him, so I couldn't let love slip through my fingers.

'That's because we'd like Romeo to go to Spain with you first, where you'll be personally trained by Jasmine before all four of you head off to California.'

'Wait, what?' I shouted, then put the phone on loudspeaker because I wasn't sure she'd said what I thought she had and I needed two extra pairs of ears to confirm it.

'I said we'd love you to join the Love Hotel team and train to become a Love Alchemist. Congratulations!'

'Oh my God!' I jumped around on the sand and Romeo did the same before lifting me up and spinning me around. 'Thank you so much! This is amazing!'

'So I take it you're happy?' Victoria laughed.

'Soooo happy!'

'Excellent! Like I said in the interview, the initial role in California for you and Romeo will be for three months. The main objective is to help get the resort set up and off to a flying start. After that, we'll reassess because in Romeo's case and several other Romance Rockstars, we have to look at work visas and other boring paperwork stuff. But we have several new resorts opening around the world, so there's the possibility of more travel and we know you're a couple, so we'll look for opportunities where you can be together.'

'That sounds perfect!'

'*Grazie*, Victoria!' Romeo called out.

'*Prego*, Romeo. I appreciate you putting Samantha forward. I know she'll be a real asset to our team.'

'Awww, thanks!' I beamed. 'Actually, Victoria, what did you mean when you said the four of us would be going to California?'

'Oh, sorry, yes. Jasmine and Alejandro will also be moving there temporarily to help get things set up.'

'That's brilliant!'

'It is indeed. This resort will be our biggest and most ambitious yet. We already have some high-profile singletons who will be joining us as guests to find their perfect match.'

'What, like celebrities?' My brows shot up to my hairline.

'Yes,' she said. 'A certain singer who you'll almost certainly know will be visiting us to find the one at the Californian resort, so I'm sure the world will be watching.'

'Oooh!' I said, dying to know who it was.

Although Victoria still hadn't revealed the exact location, something told me it would be somewhere glam like Beverly Hills. So although they probably invited guests from all over the US, I reckoned that there was strong possibility that the guests would include the rich and famous too.

Imagine you're a normal person who got accepted to go to the Love Hotel and then all of a sudden when you rocked up, you got matched with Harry Styles or Michael B. Jordan? That'd be crazy!

I could already tell that working at the new resort was going to be loads of fun and doing that with the love of my life and my new friends, Jasmine and Alejandro, was gonna be a blast.

'I'll email the paperwork shortly. Everything still okay with your current employer?'

'Yep.'

Normally I had to give a month's notice, but when I told my boss what had happened and promised that I'd help find a replacement, she took pity on me and reduced it (I think the fact that she'd got married four months ago and was still in the honeymoon cloud of happiness helped). So I'd fly back to London, work a full week next week, then I'd be free to start my new life.

Everything had worked out perfectly.

'Excellent. Well, I'll leave you to celebrate. Congrats again!'

'Thank you.'

I ended the call and Romeo picked me up and spun me around before kissing me softly. Then we remembered Linda was there, so we needed to behave ourselves.

'Look at you two,' Linda beamed. Biscotti barked then rushed over before licking my leg excitedly. 'I knew from the moment I saw you two together that you were meant to be. You've shown me that true love can conquer all and I'd like another shot at that whilst I'm still young enough to enjoy life.'

Romeo and I both froze and our gazes shot to Linda.

'Do you mean...?' His voice trailed off.

'Yes, son. I'm going to leave your father. I'm going back to England. It's time. You've got Sammie now, Mirabella is settled in Rome and if I'm in England I'll get to see more of Giorgio and my family. Yes, I'll miss the beach, but I can always come and visit. Plus, it sounds like I'll be coming to visit you both in California soon,' she smiled.

'Mamma.' Romeo raced over to Linda and pulled her in for a hug. 'I am so happy for you.'

'Thank you. It's going to be tough financially but—'

'You do not have to worry about money, Mamma,' Romeo cut in. 'I have been saving. I have an account for you with enough money for you to rent your own place for the first few months.'

Linda's eyes widened and tears rolled down her cheeks.

'Thank you, son. I love you so much.' Linda threw her arms around Romeo. 'Time for a fresh start for all of us,' she said as she gently pulled away.

'We should toast this.' Romeo pulled out a bottle of my favourite prosecco and poured it into three plastic champagne flutes. I hadn't even seen that he'd packed them, but clearly what he'd said before was true. Romeo believed in me so much that he'd come prepared to celebrate my success.

What an amazing man.

'To Mamma and her new life. And to my soulmate, Sammie.' Romeo raised his glass and my heart fluttered. 'Here's to love.'

'To love!' I said, clinking glasses with them both. 'And our long and very happy future together.'

* * *

MORE FROM OLIVIA SPRING

Another book from Olivia Spring, *What Happens in Paradise*, is available to order now here:

www.mybook.to/WhatParadiseBackAd

ACKNOWLEDGEMENTS

Hello! Thanks so much for reading *Too Hard to Resist*. I hope you enjoyed Sammie and Romeo's romantic adventures in Italy.

There's lots of people I'd like to thank for helping me to get this book out into the world.

Grazie mille to my brilliant husband for your continued support and for supplying me with lots of food and hugs when I was locked away in my writing cave working hard to finish this book.

Big thanks to my amazing beta readers, Emma Grocott, Mum and Loz for your first-class feedback.

Huge thanks to my editor Megan Haslam and the entire Boldwood team for bringing my books to a wider audience.

Shout-out to Rachel Lawston for creating yet another gorgeous book cover.

Thanks to copyeditor Cecily Blench and proofreader Rachel Sargeant for helping my words shine.

Sending big appreciative hugs to the lovely Camilla Isley for checking over the Italian.

I'm so grateful for all of the brilliant book bloggers, Bookstagrammers, ARC readers and BookTokers who have written amazing reviews and shared gorgeous posts to help spread the word about this book. I appreciate you so much!

And last, but not least, a giant-sized thank-you with a cherry on top, to *you*, dear reader for choosing to buy and read this novel. Your support means the world!

Can't wait to share more books with you very soon!
Until next time...
Lots of love,
Olivia x

ABOUT THE AUTHOR

Olivia Spring is a bestselling author of contemporary women's fiction and romantic comedies, now writing spicy romance for Boldwood.

Sign up to Olivia's mailing list for news, competitions and updates on future books.

Visit Olivia's website: www.oliviaspring.com

Follow Olivia on social media here:

facebook.com/ospringauthor

x.com/ospringauthor

instagram.com/ospringauthor

bookbub.com/authors/olivia-spring

ALSO BY OLIVIA SPRING

The Love Hotel Series

The One That Got Away

What Happens in Paradise

Too Hard to Resist

Boldwood
EVER AFTER

x♡x♡

JOIN BOLDWOOD'S
**ROMANCE
COMMUNITY**
FOR SWEET AND
SPICY BOOK RECS
WITH ALL YOUR
FAVOURITE
TROPES!

SIGN UP TO OUR
NEWSLETTER

HTTPS://BIT.LY/BOLDWOODEVERAFTER

Boldw**oo**d

Boldwood Books is an award-winning fiction publishing company seeking out the best stories from around the world.

Find out more at www.boldwoodbooks.com

Join our reader community for brilliant books, competitions and offers!

Follow us
@BoldwoodBooks
@TheBoldBookClub

Sign up to our weekly deals newsletter

https://bit.ly/BoldwoodBNewsletter

Printed in Dunstable, United Kingdom